Vegas Goodbye

Kirk House Publishers

Content Warning

This book contains themes and depictions related to suicide, suicidal ideation, drug abuse, overdose, grief, and loss.

Reader discretion is advised. If you are in crisis or thinking about harming yourself, please reach out for help immediately.

- You can contact the **Suicide and Crisis Lifeline** in the United States by calling or texting **988** or visit 988lifeline.org.
- For help with drug abuse, addiction, or overdose, call the **Substance Abuse and Mental Health Services Administration (SAMHSA) National Helpline** at **1-800-662-HELP (4357)**. This free, confidential, 24/7 helpline can connect you with treatment resources and support.
- If you or someone you know is experiencing a drug overdose, call **911** right away.

Take care of yourself and consider whether this content is right for you at this time.

VEGAS GOODBYE

DONNA M. CRAMER

First Edition

Paperback ISBN: 978-1-959681-97-7
eBook ISBN: 978-1-959681-98-4
Hardcover ISBN: 978-1-959681-99-1
LCCN: 2025915840

Cover design and interior design by Ann Aubitz

Published by
    Kirk House Publishers
    1250 E 115th Street
    Burnsville, MN 55337
    612-781-2815
    Kirkhousepublishers.com
    Bulk pricing available through publisher

CHAPTER 1

DEBRA FELT A PRICKLY FEELING run up and down her arms. She could not believe it. She was here in Las Vegas. She had made it! Debra dug the reservation confirmation and credit card out of her purse. The hotel lobby was crowded with people checking in and checking out. Groups shuffled by, heading onto the casino floor or out to the pool, judging by how some of them were dressed. With her paperwork in her hand, she dragged her wheeled suitcase into the lengthy line. There were at least twenty people ahead of her. *This might take a while,* she thought glumly. Like you have somewhere else to be, the voice in her head snarled. You've got nothing but time, Debra. No one is waiting or even looking for you. She looked down, nodding slightly to herself. She heard a commotion at the very front of the line. She noticed a man waving his arms and gesticulating madly at the desk clerk. She craned her neck to see the man causing the disturbance, but the people in front of her partially hid him. It did not help that Debra's stature was so short. She often could not see past people who towered over her by several inches.

"Damn it," she heard the man snarl as he raised his voice. "They said I was all set and could check in online. I prepaid the entire bill, but now you tell me I don't have a room. What is wrong with you? This is incompetence!"

Debra closed her eyes, attempting to block out his harsh words. She hated listening to people argue and hearing people talk to others using such a demeaning, demanding tone. She shivered. His words reminded her too much of Gary, her first husband. He had always been so demanding of service workers and restaurant employees. One small mistake, and he had been ready to jump all over them. The man's use of the word "incompetence" had triggered Debra. Gary always used to call others incompetent.

"Incompetent," he would sneer, placing extra emphasis on the final syllable.

Even though Debra could not see this man, she could hear him slam his hand on the counter as he demanded to see a supervisor at once. People in the line were shifting and sighing. This man and his demands were causing the already slow line to stop. Now, another worker rushed over to the woman who was attempting to help the rude man.

"What seems to be the problem, sir?" she heard the woman say politely.

"I want my room, and I want it now." The man snapped.

She smiled as she envisioned the man suddenly throwing his body on the ground and flailing his arms and legs as a toddler might.

"Look, Dawn, there's his room right there," the other woman said, pointing at the computer screen.

"Oh, sorry, my error," the first woman said, looking more than frazzled. "Your room is right here and has been paid in full. I overlooked it. I am so sorry."

"Just give me my key card," the man said in a clipped voice.

"Here you are, sir. Enjoy your stay."

"Humph," the man said by way of reply.

Debra craned her neck to get a better view of this unpleasant person who had caused all this trouble for nothing. He appeared to be alone and seemed to be around her age. As he walked quickly from the counter, he did not turn around; he only headed toward the elevators as if in a great hurry. *Hope I don't run into him again,* Debra thought. His unpleasantness and aggression had been so overt that it had seemed to permeate the entire line. Everyone sighed in relief now that he and his unpleasantness were gone.

CHAPTER 2

JIM SLAMMED THE HOTEL ROOM DOOR so hard he could hear it echo down the hallway. There had been a mix-up with his room reservation, which infuriated him. The desk clerk could not have cared less until he got loud and irate. He viciously kicked his suitcase into the room. He opened the door back up and, using all his strength, slammed it closed once again. He opened it again—slam, open, slam, open. He realized he was enjoying the loud crack and boom that the door made as it slammed closed. There was something so satisfying about the loud, harsh noise. He enjoyed the violence of slamming with every ounce of his strength. It was a needed relief after being cooped up on the plane for all those hours with those miserable, insipid losers who had been his fellow passengers. He had gotten stuck in the middle seat of a packed flight. He had protested, but the flight attendant, who seemed to have an I.Q. of 50—55 if he was generous—had informed him that no other seats were available. He had slammed his bag into the overhead compartment, almost hitting the muscular man in the aisle seat directly in his fat head. Who did this guy think he was, Arnold Schwarzenegger? Buff asshole with his overdeveloped muscles! It would serve him right if that fat head exploded like a watermelon dropped on the sidewalk.

"Watch it, buddy," the man had said severely.

Jim had looked at him with a withering glance as he stowed his bag.

"I'm certainly not your buddy," Jim had sneered.

The man had shrugged, looking down, apparently not wanting to engage in further confrontation. *Too bad,* Jim thought, *it might be fun to punch him in the mouth.* See if he was as strong and tough as he looked. The man continued staring at his phone and did not make further eye contact with Jim, simply moving his legs aside so Jim could slide into his seat. The woman nestled against the window, leaning on a purple pillow, made an intake of breath. Jim realized that he had elbowed her as he sat down. Jim made no attempt to apologize and contemplated crashing his arm into her again, but she quickly curled her body away from him and leaned further into the window. Jim shifted in his seat, grabbing the ends of the seat belt and glaring at his seatmates first, and then at the stragglers still walking down the aisle.

A group of men passed, all relatively young, with happy grins as one said, "can't wait to get there, this is going to be one fun weekend."

Jim glared at them. Fun? Weekend? What the hell did those words even mean, and how could these men be so happy when they had an over-5-hour flight ahead of them? Here they were crammed in next to each other with less room than sardines have in a can, and they were happy about it? How stupid could they possibly be! Plus, the plane could crash, killing them all. They were all silly people with stupid desires, wants, and needs. A plane crash wouldn't be the worst thing that could happen; it might be the best.

CHAPTER 3

DEBRA LET OUT A LONG SIGH as she quietly closed the hotel room door. Now that she was in Las Vegas, she felt strange, buzzy, restless. She was unsure of what to do next. She had booked the room for one week. This would give her plenty of time. She thought she might not stay here the whole week, but having too much time would be better than not enough. She was more than committed to her plan. She didn't want to feel rushed. After being so out of control during Ron's illness, she wanted to be in control. Never knowing what would transpire each morning, each night, and each minute with him. Maybe Ron would feel better and be somewhat coherent, but then it was all too possible for her to get coffee and come back and see his labored breathing, his eyes glazed over and distant, and the pain, always the pain, so much pain. No, she wanted control, and reserving an entire week would let her decide when and exactly how. She had dreaded the plane ride as she had driven to the airport. She had never traveled solo by plane. She didn't know if anyone would try to talk to her or if she would be ignored entirely. She found it relatively easy once she had arrived at the airport. She pretended that she was with Ron, that he was in the restroom, and that he would join her soon. While waiting for the plane in the waiting area, she even looked up from the book she had several times, sending her gaze down the corridor as if waiting for someone's return. Once in her seat and with her book firmly glued in front of her face, no one bothered or even tried to speak with her. She declined the refreshments offered by the flight attendant and found that the 6-hour flight seemed mercifully shorter than she thought it would. Standing in the taxi line, she found herself pretending that she would be meeting Ron at the hotel. When the taxi driver, who you could tell wanted to be chatty, inquired about what she was doing, she said without hesitation, "I'm meeting my husband at the hotel."

She was beginning to feel odd and adrift in the quiet hotel room. She looked around the small room, the smallest and most economical choice. *No need to pay for luxury*, she thought grimly. Suddenly, she felt her mind flash back to her last trip to Las Vegas with Ron. He had ordered champagne, and it was waiting for them in the room with a large pink bow attached when they entered. Ron had always wanted a view, and he had opened the drapes with a flourish to reveal an expansive view of the strip.

"It will be beautiful at night," he had said, smiling.

Debra crossed to the closed drapes and opened them, looking out onto the back of the hotel, any view obstructed by large mechanical objects that must be part of the heating or air-conditioning system. *No beautiful view here, not anymore, not ever*, Debra thought, and pulled the drapes closed. Should she do it right away, right here, right now? Get it over with? She considered the prospect but then decided no, not yet, it wasn't time yet. She would know when. Her stomach rumbled. She looked down at her midsection with surprise. She hadn't been eating much at all lately, well, basically ever since Ron had passed. She smiled. It was somewhat humorous that she was hungry now. She could grab something from the vending machine or go downstairs, explore a little bit, and maybe find something to eat. There had to be fast food in the hotel. She and Ron had never actually stayed in this hotel. They had been to the one next door twice. *Why not?* She thought. She wouldn't do anything tonight, maybe tomorrow or in a few days. She looked at the sad, washed-out older woman without makeup in the mirror. She ran her fingers through her hair, not caring to make the effort to take a comb from her bag. She pocketed the key card and headed downstairs to find something to eat.

CHAPTER 4

THE LINE AT THE FAST-FOOD PIZZA PLACE and the burger bar had been out of control and noisy. Debra was still hungry, though, and had opted for the small Mexican cantina. It was in the hotel but opened up onto the strip. It had been busy as well, but the harried hostess had seated Debra at the corner of the bar, assuring her that she could get anything from the menu while sitting at the bar. Ron had loved Mexican food. Maybe she could order his favorite food in his honor, she thought, smiling to herself. As she looked up, she noticed a man about her age at the other end of the bar. It seemed he was alone, just as she was. He nodded and smiled broadly at her. *Oh, no,* Debra thought. The last thing she was interested in was making friends, and if he thought that she wanted to have sex with him, well, that was the last thing on her mind. She stared at the menu assiduously. She would not look up at the man again. *Been here for five minutes and already attracted a creeper, great,* she thought glumly.

"Is this seat taken?" she heard someone say quietly and politely in her left ear.

She looked up.

"It is," she said, clipping her words and doing her best to look annoyed. "My friend will be joining me any minute now."

The man smiled kindly and said, "So sorry, I didn't mean to bother you. I shouldn't have even asked. It's just that those frat boys or whoever they are at the end of the bar are about to break my eardrums. I just thought… I shouldn't have even asked. Please enjoy your night."

Debra noticed how incredibly sad the man looked. As she looked into his piercing blue eyes, she saw they were very much the same color as Ron's eyes had been. The man turned to move away through the crowd. Right before the crowd swallowed him up, Debra raised her voice.

"Wait," she called.

The man turned back toward her but did not move back in her direction.

CHAPTER 5

DEBRA HOPED SHE WOULD NOT REGRET inviting the man to sit on the empty stool beside her, just to her left. She wasn't sure if she knew how to have a substantive conversation anymore. She certainly wasn't used to speaking at length to any man. She stared into her drink and only then realized how antisocial and odd she must seem. She glanced over at the man, noticing that he was looking down and then staring at his drink, too.

Just then, the bartender rushed over. "Menus?" he inquired pleasantly.

"Are you having something to eat tonight?"

Debra glanced once again at the man next to her and nodded subtly. He reached out his hand to take a menu, shrugging. Now they both stared at their menus as if deciphering a foreign language.

Finally, the man took in a breath and said,

"I'm John, by the way."

"Nice to meet you," Debra said quietly. "Debra," she all but whispered her name.

The bartender was already back. John ordered the taco appetizers, and Debra ordered a chimichanga, which had always been Ron's favorite menu item.

"Chimichangas always make me think of chihuahuas because that's what my son always used to call them when he was small," the man said.

Debra smiled. "Are you here with your son?" she inquired gently.

"No, no," he said, shaking his head but changing his answer and saying, "yes, yes, I am."

"Ok," Debra said, feeling she was probably being lied to.

"Who are you here with? Oh, I don't mean to pry, I mean it's not exactly my business, I was making conversation," he said, looking down again.

"My friend, Kathy," Debra said without hesitation. She was not about to let a stranger know she was alone, especially one who seemed a little weird.

"She's out there, somewhere gambling."

"My son as well," the man said.

"My son, he's meeting some friends his age tonight."

Debra nodded. Silence enveloped them once again. People were laughing and talking all around them, and the two of them sat there, quietly engaging in stilted conversation with long pauses. Finally, John laughed.

"Look at the two of us, you would think we didn't even know how to socialize. I'm sorry, it's been a while since I've been out; I've had some things happen in my life."

"Me, too," Debra said, looking down.

"How about we start over? Forget the past. Just be here, right now, tonight. Hi, I'm John," he said in a more upbeat voice and held out his hand to shake.

Debra noticed his striking blue eyes again, the same dark blue as Ron's. She held out her hand.

"Debra, nice to meet you, John."

"Well, that's better. See, we do both know how to act in public."

Debra giggled quietly. Their attention was directed to the other end of the bar, where a large party of young men was holding court. They were all whooping and yelling while one man balanced a shot glass on his forehead. John and Debra exchanged a glance and laughed at the improbable scene.

"Hey, say what you want about us, but at least we're not with that group."

"You're right about that," Debra agreed.

"I mean, I've seen more maturity from my kids when they were preschoolers."

Debra nodded.

"I wonder what they'll do next. Maybe do acrobatics across the bar like a Cirque show?"

"Possible," John agreed, "or they could make a pyramid like high school cheerleaders."

"How about break dancing across the floor, if they even know what break dancing is," Debra suggested.

"No, no, I have it for their next party trick. They will break out in song with 'The 12 Days of Christmas,' but instead the song will be entitled 'The 12 Fools of Vegas.'"

"Good one," Debra said, laughing. They continued to try to top each other with increasingly ridiculous suggestions for the young men until their food arrived. Debra found she was enjoying the man's company. He was easy to be with and asked no more personal questions.

"This food is good," John stated.

Debra agreed.

Debra told John the story of how she had seen the rock star Neal Vaughn on the strip on an earlier visit and how he had been so very drunk but had still attracted quite a crowd—until he had begun projectile vomiting on the fans closest to him. Debra had, of course, been with Ron, which she did not mention. John mentioned his son again and how they saw David Norris, the famous singer, at a restaurant. John mentioned his wife—my ex-wife, he added—had loved him and they had decided to send their son over for an autograph, which his wife desperately wanted, thinking they would have a better chance if a kid were asking, since the man seemed like he didn't want to be bothered. When his son approached the singer with a pen and paper, the singer took the paper and started to write until John's son said, "Who are you again?"

"Needless to say, we didn't get the autograph."

Debra laughed at the story. She looked up, realizing that the bar was much quieter now, the boys at the other end had left long ago, and only a few couples were seated at the surrounding tables.

John looked at his watch. "Wow, it's been two hours. Time jetted by."

Debra nodded.

"Won't your friend be looking for you?"

"Probably, eventually," Debra said.

"How about your son?"

"Probably, eventually," John repeated and smiled, crinkling up his eyes.

The bartender approached with the check. "You folks want anything else?"

"No," they both said. John grabbed the bill. Debra reached into her purse to remove her wallet.

"No, no, I've got it," John said.

"No," Debra protested, "it's not fair for you to pay the whole bill. I can't let you do that."

"Debra, I hope this doesn't sound weird, but I have had a better time with you here tonight than in months, maybe longer. It would be my pleasure to pay for an exceptionally well-spent evening."

A lump formed in Debra's throat as she realized that she had enjoyed her time here, too, probably the first time she had enjoyed anything since Ron had passed.

"I, I enjoyed myself too," she stuttered. "Still, I just can't let you pay for everything."

"Ok, then, tell you what. Meet me tomorrow for coffee or lunch, and you can pay then. If you have time and want to, no pressure."

Debra hesitated for just a minute, then she stuck out her hand.

"Deal," she said, nodding as they shook hands.

CHAPTER 6

JIM GLARED AND TAPPED HIS FOOT IMPATIENTLY. He stared at the large watch that he kept on his wrist constantly. It was 10:15 a.m. Why was this bank so crowded? Didn't these people work? It was a weekday! He glanced around the lobby and over to the side where glass-enclosed offices stood, only one in use. The others were all empty. There appeared to be no security guard, he mused. Why was the teller behind the counter taking so long? What? She didn't know how to count or do basic math. He wished he had just used the ATM to get the money he needed for his purchase, but since this was one of many options, he had wanted to look around. However, now that he was here, he wanted to go. He wanted to get on with his task. Finally, only one more person in front of him, an older lady who was fumbling with her check, and now she dropped the pen she was using to sign the check on the floor right at Jim's feet. He sighed and bent to pick it up.

"Whoops," the lady said breezily, "butterfingers." She started to laugh, but then, noticing Jim's glare, she hastily grabbed the pen.

She muttered "thanks," returning to face the teller again.

Jim slapped his card on the counter.

"Withdrawal," he snarled.

"How are you today, sir?" the young girl replied chirpily.

"Having a good day, I hope."

Does it look like I'm having a good day, stupid? Jim thought to himself without saying the words out loud.

The teller continued to smile at him insipidly.

"You know, sir, you don't have to come into the bank for a simple withdrawal; it can be done at any ATM. You don't even have to leave the casino floor."

"I know that," Jim said, his tone clipped and angry.

The teller stared at him; he stared back, imagining her head exploding in a puff of smoke. He envisioned the shiny floor covered in metallic-smelling blood. Maybe she was reacting to the look on his face or hearing his thoughts, Jim wondered. He found he did not care if this was the case. Either way, she stopped smiling. She turned away to get his money. She counted it out for him. He snatched it out of her hand. She opened her mouth as if to say something, but since he thought he might punch her or someone else if he heard one more "Have a nice day," he turned on his heel and fled, pushing past a man with a walker just entering the bank. He let the door shut on the lady directly behind him, and she made a startled sound. Like he gave a damn about any of them—they could all go to hell.

♦ ♦ ♦

Jim wandered down the street aimlessly. He had walked from the crisp, clean streets of the newer tourist area of Vegas down to the older area, which still boasted tourist attractions, but the further he walked off the beaten path, the seedier the area became. He knew what he had come to purchase. He wandered between two pawn shops before deciding on the best one. The guy behind the counter seemed disinterested at best, stoned, drunk, or high at worst. He was taking little interest in his customers. Jim peered into the locked display case. There was little, if any, need to be picky at this point; probably, any of the items he was looking at would get the job done. And that was all that mattered—getting the job done. He got the clerk's attention and gestured to him.

"That one," he said, pointing to the handgun lying innocuously on a piece of felt behind the glass.

"I want to purchase that one."

CHAPTER 7

JIM HAD COME DIRECTLY BACK TO HIS ROOM with his purchase. He sat down in the not-quite-comfortable chair facing the window. He had paid extra to get a room with a view of the strip. He looked down, watching cars come and go from the hotel's main entrance and watching microscopic people walking back and forth, back and forth. What was he waiting for? He had the gun ensconced securely in the safe. He could take it out right now. Why the hold-up, why the wait? He would have to re-up his reservation if he stayed one more night. "Right now, do it right damn now," an insistent and none too pleasant voice repeated in his head. He lowered his head between his knees. He was tired of the sadness and the guilt. And there was anger, oh yes, there was plenty of anger too. "Now!" he heard the voice repeat in his head. He cast his gaze out the window again. There were plenty of cars and people down there. He rose from the chair with a jerk. He headed toward the safe.

Jim held the gun in his hand until his fingers cramped. He practiced aiming it repeatedly. He moved throughout the room, deciding on the best location. Tonight, I'll do it, he finally decided. In the end, he put the gun down on the floor.

"Do it fucking now!" he yelled at himself.

He shook his head, picked up the gun, unlocked the safe, and secured it back inside. He stood at the door for five minutes but finally

went downstairs. Maybe he would gamble or get a drink. He felt
hungry.

CHAPTER 8

JIM STOMPED AROUND THE CASINO FLOOR with a disagreeable look on his face. Why had he even come down here? So many people, so much noise. He glared at a woman smiling kindly at him until she averted her gaze and looked away. He glanced at the crowded bar filled with young people, laughing, drinking, and dancing. He snorted audibly. He hated them. He hated them all. He turned away so that he no longer had to look at the young people at the bar. He attempted to walk away so quickly that he walked right between a couple, brushing into the woman and half pushing her out of the way.

"Hey, buddy, watch yourself," her companion remonstrated loudly.

Jim glared at them so sullenly that they both looked away. Jim stood on the edge of a group of people, watching the poker players gathered around the tables. He felt someone standing next to him, but he did not look, even as the person nudged gently into his body. When he felt a slight push of human contact against him once again, he turned his head to look at who was so close to him. He stared at a young woman dressed provocatively in tight clothes with a very low-cut shirt that emphasized her breasts.

"Hey, baby," the woman whispered to him.

Jim said nothing and took half a step to move his body away from her. He looked at her again. Disgusting, she was little more than a kid! She had to be in her early twenties, if not her teens. She had no interest in him. A man over twice her age. What was she doing here? Where were her parents? He glowered at her.

"Hey, baby," the woman repeated.

"You look like you could use some company. Are you lonely? How about a little date?"

Jim felt his stomach turn. Being approached by someone this young was like a knife in the heart.

"No," Jim said, "I am not looking for anyone. I don't want a date or anything else. Please leave!"

"You just look so sad and angry, baby. I could help relieve some of that tension."

Jim resisted an urge to grab her and fling her body away from his.

"I said no. Are you deaf? Can't you hear? I want nothing from no one. Go away or you'll be sorry!" he growled.

The girl raised her eyebrows as she began to move away.

"Okay, baby, okay, don't get all irate. I was only asking."

He looked down, already regretting his angry response. He looked back up, thinking maybe he should apologize, but the crowd had already swallowed her.

CHAPTER 9

JOHN GLANCED BACK AT HIS HOTEL ROOM door as he prepared to go downstairs. It was almost time to meet Debra for the coffee they had planned last night. He smiled in anticipation as he exited the room. He noticed the number on the hotel room door, 1113. 1113 was his son's birthday. Looking at the door was a constant reminder of his son. It was crowded downstairs, more crowded than John anticipated on a weekday. He wandered around, peering into restaurant windows, watching the gamblers at the tables, and the young people already at the boisterous bar pulsating with songs they all seemed to know but with lyrics he couldn't understand. He drifted away from the bar and watched the poker players at the edge of the table games. When he felt a hand on his shoulder, he drew back, startled, but as he turned, he saw that the person who had touched him was Debra. He felt a smile cross his face and watched as she smiled back at him. He was feeling calmer already, just seeing her face.

"Didn't you hear me calling your name?" she inquired.

"It's so noisy in here," he replied.

CHAPTER 10

JIM STALKED BACK AND FORTH OUTSIDE THE ARENA. This had to be the most stupid idea ever. He was going to a concert for a band that was now old and washed up. They hadn't played together since the nineties. Sure, they had been hot then, and that one album, Stay and Play, had multiple hit singles on it, but they hadn't done anything in years. Why had he thought this was a good idea? He glared at the people standing next to him. What was that smell? He realized he was half standing in a long drink line stretched so far back that it was almost out to the lobby. The large man next to him, dressed all in black, clearly hadn't had time to shower before coming here. Jim wrinkled his nose, not caring whether he was being obvious or not. Why in hell would you go out and not shower before? The man had no self-respect! And the woman with him, how could she stand the stench? She hadn't found it in her repertoire to say, "Hey, honey, you stink like a barnyard animal." Clearly, this was ok with her! *People*, he thought, derisively curling his lip. He stepped away and found himself surrounded by a group of people who were, loudly and off-key, singing hit after hit of the band's old songs with great gusto and glee.

"And, baby, when I say stay, you say why when it's all just play."

How insipid! Could the lyrics be any worse? He pushed away from this group and brushed past a woman holding a cup of wine.

"Watch out!" she said severely.

He glared, and she looked down. He stepped toward the bathroom line, removing himself from the direct crush of people entering the arena. He looked around. He should leave. Why was he even here? He should go back to the room. He had a critical mission to accomplish. He looked down at his boots, contemplating leaving even stronger now. He looked up and found himself mesmerized, staring at two men directly across from him, one younger and one older. The two men, oblivious to his presence, enraged him. Leaning against the wall, he slapped his hand hard on the wall, causing a man next to him to look up.

"You ok, buddy?" the man slurred.

"Fine," Jim growled and stepped away.

This was it. He was going back to the room. He had had enough!

CHAPTER 11

DEBRA LOOKED AROUND at the crush of people. Why had she said she would meet John inside the arena? They should have met somewhere else and entered together. *Or just not come at all,* she thought ruefully. This was the worst idea ever. Their morning coffee yesterday had gone so well that they had decided to meet for dinner at a cute Italian restaurant adjacent to their coffee shop. Food was already being prepared for lunch at the restaurant, and the smell of garlic was so sweet and pungent that they had both remarked they would like to try the restaurant. This idea had seemed to have promise at dinner last night, but this was after a carafe of wine, she thought grimly.

John had said to her at dinner, "What are you doing tomorrow?"

Debra immediately thought of the free tickets she had been given on arrival. When she checked in, the clerk handed her the tickets and room card as if he were giving her a special gift.

"What are these?" she had said, turning them over in her hand.

"Oh, they're free tickets for you. You and Mr. Myers are part of our preferred members club, and this month's free gift is tickets to Nevermore. The band—you must remember them—were really big in the nineties, I guess," the young clerk trilled.

"They were," Debra affirmed.

"They are playing their hit album in the arena on Thursday. People are desperate for tickets, and they're all sold out. Aren't you lucky to get them as part of your package?"

"Lucky, Debra repeated, I'm lucky."

She told John about the tickets.

He said, "Wow, what are you? Are you some high roller or something?"

"No," Debra had demurred, laughing.

"Look, if you aren't interested, or maybe you could go with your son instead of me," Debra said, realizing this might be the better option.

"I'm sure he wouldn't even know who they were," John said, shaking his head. He then looked up at Debra.

"Why not?" he said, smiling, and that sparkle she was coming to like became present in his eyes again.

"I would like to go. I want to go with you, Debra."

"Ok," she said, holding his eye contact. She opened her purse.

"I have them right here," she said, handing him one of the tickets.

"I'll meet you there tomorrow night."

"Deal," John said, smiling once again. He raised his hand to brush the hair off his face.

She noticed his watch once again. "That is a beautiful watch," she said, admiring it.

He looked down at it, and she wondered what she had said to cause such a look of sadness to cross his face.

"Thanks," John said, looking down at the watch like he had never seen it before.

"It was a Father's Day present for me three years ago. It was my son's idea. He had seen me admiring it in a store once and convinced my ex-wife that I just had to have it. They shouldn't have bought it. It's the most expensive piece of jewelry I've ever owned. I think they paid more for it than I paid for my engagement ring."

He shook his head and looked down, looking so sad once again.

"My son-in-law, David, spent a lot of money on my daughter's engagement ring. He still refuses to tell us how much."

John continued to stare at the watch. They were beginning to share some personal information with each other for the first time tonight. Debra was unsure why it made her feel so nervous to say anything about her personal life, maybe because she would no longer have a personal life soon, or perhaps because she did not want to think about Devon. It did hurt her to think about leaving Devon, and the last thing she wanted to do was make her daughter hurt or feel sad, but it would be so much better for Devon with Debra out of the way.

"What's her name?" John asked.

Debra realized that she had been staring into her glass of wine and had even lost awareness that John was across the table from her.

"Devon," Debra smiled, "her name is Devon. You know, I don't even know your son's name."

It was John's turn to stare into his glass of wine and do so for such a prolonged moment that Debra thought he might not answer.

Instead, he said, "Devon, that's a pretty name. What about your ex? He's not a D name, too, is he? Because that would just be too weird, wouldn't it?"

Debra snickered and was relieved to see that they were smiling at each other again. Inexplicably, the mood seemed to have lightened. But then, just like that, his question brought an image of Ron back into Debra's mind, and she closed her eyes as if that would drive the image away.

"My husband—my ex-husband—was, I mean, is not Devon's father."

"Oh, ok," John said, nodding at her.

"You know, John, not to be rude, but I don't want to talk about families anymore. Devon's father—well, I was young, and that is a long, unpleasant story." Debra shivered and stared at the white linen tablecloth, which she realized was now spotted with a drop of wine that she had not even realized she had spilled. Debra felt tears well up in her eyes and tried to blink them away quickly.

John grabbed her hand gently from across the table.

"Hey, it's ok. You know, I don't want to talk about family, either. So, don't worry about it."

"Anyway," Debra said, looking up, "that is one very handsome watch."

John looked down at it, smiling now. "Yes, Debra, it is. And it's expensive, too. Did I tell you that?" he teased.

"Hey, who's luckier than me?" he said, but she heard sarcasm and something else enter his voice.

"What time is that concert tomorrow, 8 p.m.?"

Debra nodded her assent.

♦　♦　♦

"John, John over here."

He turned at the last minute and saw a hand frantically waving at him. The crowd was so large, and Debra was not that tall, so at first, all he saw was a waving hand. He pushed his way toward the hand. It was Debra. He was happy to see her, and a warmth entered his body; he could tell a smile was broadening across his face.

"Hey," he said and touched her shoulder gently.

"I thought I would never find you in this mob scene," Debra said.

He nodded. "It's crazy, that's for sure. I've never seen so many 40- and 50-year-olds regressing and acting like 19-year-olds simultaneously."

Debra nodded. Any conversation was made impossible by a large group passing by jubilantly singing "Stay and Play" at the very top of their lungs. Both Debra and John shook their heads. John rolled his eyes.

"I'm so glad I found you."

"When I saw you, it looked at first like you were leaving. I was afraid you had given up and were heading out," Debra said.

"No," John said, "I was walking around trying to find you. I figured you would turn up eventually. However, I was almost ready to start bursting out in song at any moment. Hey, want to buy a t-shirt before we go in? It's what I would have done years ago."

"Well, we can at least look," Debra said, grinning. "Let's go."

"Ok," John said, suddenly bursting into song, "and I say stay and..."

Debra joined in, "and you say why, when it's all just play."

They both laughed.

CHAPTER 12

JIM FOUND HIMSELF FEELING ANGRIER and angrier a little more each day. Nothing was right. Every single person around him was an irritant, an annoyance. Either the damn cleaning person showed up way too early or not at all. Yesterday, he had come back to the room, and it was still a mess with his dirty, wet towels still piled in the corner of the bathroom. When he had called about the room not being cleaned and had snarled, "Bring clean towels," before hanging up, so he did not have to endure the smarmy apologies of the employee on the other end of the phone line, it had taken them hours to make it to his room. How hard was it to carry a few towels to a room, and why would it take hours? Incompetent! All people were lazy, incompetent, and stupid. He wished they would all go away, die, and have it over with. Then this morning, he had barely been out of the shower, his hair still wet, and there had been a knock on the door, and a pleasant voice trilled, "Housekeeping."

Great, he wasn't ready to go downstairs yet, and now here they were, so eager to clean his toilet that he would have to leave the room early. What in hell did this woman have to be so happy about? She had a shit job. They probably paid her peanuts, and she had to clean up God knows what day after day after day. He threw the door open with a scowl on his face.

"Good morning, sir," the young lady with her hair in a bun said, speaking in accented English.

"May I clean your room now?" she said, smiling, but he watched her pleasant demeanor slowly vanish as she was confronted with Jim's surly glare. "One minute," he said, slamming the door in her face. Had he returned the gun to the safe? Or was it still lying on the coffee table? He had been pointing it again last night, practicing. He couldn't remember putting it away. He hurried over to the small brown table between the chairs facing the window. No gun. He ran back to the safe in the closet. It was securely locked. He flung the door back open. The woman was bent over her cart, collecting towels or something.

"Yeah," Jim thundered, causing the woman to jump. He glared and did not apologize for startling her.

"Go ahead," he sighed, "clean the room now."

"Thank you, sir," she said, placing her cart in front of her as if she wanted to give him a wide berth.

He patted his pocket to ensure that he had his wallet.

"Have a good day, sir," she trilled once again.

He snorted and noticed that she was shaking her head at him as he began to walk away.

Once downstairs, Jim felt more agitated than ever. He thought a coffee might calm him down and make him feel better, but the line was out the door when he attempted to enter the coffee shop. These people, so many of them! He wished he could stomp them all like the ants he had stomped as a kid. Relishing the destruction of the anthill the worthless creatures had made and stomping on them all. The best part was stepping on and killing the foolish ones trying to run away. So silly that they thought they were escaping just as his foot thundered down. "Soon," a voice whispered in a low, sinister tone in his head. "Soon, you will do it!"

CHAPTER 13

JOHN WHISTLED AS HE HELD the key card to the hotel door, waiting for the small green light and acknowledging the gentle beep. Another fun time with Debra. This time, they walked outside, down the strip, and back across the bridge between their hotels. She was a pleasure to be with, simply a pleasure. She kept their conversations light and noncommittal, but had kind eyes and seemed to listen attentively when he spoke. They hadn't shared much personal information, but she shared that she had a daughter at dinner. He had come so close to saying, Me too. I have a daughter, too! Luckily, he had stopped himself at the very last second. Did he have a daughter? Could you say you had a daughter if you never saw that daughter? If that daughter wanted nothing to do with you and would never speak to you again? Of course, why should she talk to him after what he had done? It wasn't as if he didn't deserve her estrangement. Debra, of course, knew that he had a son. He had mentioned him many times in conversation, and, of course, they were here together.

"You have a son, and I have a daughter," Debra had said as if there was some congruence.

He had nodded, smiling, but had silently thought, *Oh, Debra, if you only knew what I have and what I have lost*. He crossed the room, staring out the window and looking down yet again at the people milling around the hotel below him, moving in front of the hotel and crossing the street in large clots. He stared down at the people, looking to see if he could see his son returning to the hotel from where? From somewhere, from wherever. He did not see him. He turned from the window. He heard a voice saying, "You can have whatever you want."

His ex-wife had said that! He snorted.

Debra had not yet seen this side of him, the doubting, cynical side. He was keeping that hidden. He was pretty much a good-time Charlie with Debra, always appearing happy, quick with a smile, and even quicker with a silly, moronic joke. Sometimes, he thought he saw a momentary sadness pass through her eyes; he had seen something when she mentioned her daughter, but whatever it was had just as quickly passed. *Don't go deep*, he thought. *No good can come from going deep or letting yourself get close to someone. You know that, you, of all people, know that.* The voice said again, just as clearly as before, 'You can have whatever you want.' Oh, yeah, you can have whatever you want, huh? What if you have no idea what you want? What if there are some things, some people, you will never get back, no matter how much you want them? What if you have no fricking idea, as his son would say! He needed to go back to the bridge. He would look for his son from there.

CHAPTER 14

"JOHN, JOHN," DEBRA CALLED, waving at him across the crowded casino floor. Several people looked up at her, but not John. She moved through the crowd, now just a few feet away from him.

"John," she called again in a firm, loud voice. Two strangers turned to stare at her, but still John did not turn around. How could he not hear her calling his name? She and John had spent part of the last three days together. They both shared a similar sense of humor and could make each other laugh with just a look. They had agreed to meet on the casino floor for a drink or a snack at 8 p.m. Debra had pretended that she had to meet her friend, the nonexistent Kathy, for dinner. She was far from ready to tell John the truth that she had come to Las Vegas alone. She was beginning to feel safe with him, but still didn't know him well. It would be better to keep the fact that she was alone here to herself for now. John had said he needed to spend some time with his son. Neither was pushing the other for more details about their lives, and Debra was happy for this. She would have to walk away if he began to want to know more about her. Debra found she was looking forward to meeting John each day, no matter how brief their meetings were. She was beginning to wonder if she needed to talk to him tonight. Last night, just before they had parted, she felt he had kept eye contact with her a little longer than necessary. Was he looking for a girlfriend, a love interest? Even a one-night stand? She didn't want to lead him on and knew she would soon have to break off all contact. Her one-week stay would soon come to an end; it would be time to complete her plan. She didn't want John to feel attached to her. She would speak to him tonight. "John!" she shouted behind him, but still he did not turn. *What is wrong? Doesn't he know his name?* Debra thought, exasperated. Maybe he has some hearing loss. This was the second time she had walked up to him, calling his name, and he had not answered! She touched him gently on the shoulder. He jumped as if frightened, with a look of fear.

When he saw her standing there, the fear abated, and a broad smile spread across his face, spreading up even into his blue eyes, causing them to twinkle brightly. "Hey," he said warmly, "I didn't see you."

"I was calling you. I can't believe you couldn't hear me."

"It is a little noisy here."

Debra nodded. "It is."

"How was your dinner with Kathy?"

"With who?" Debra said, then quickly remembered who she was supposed to be with.

"Oh, Kathy, good, great, we had a great meal. Steaks were delicious. How's your son?"

John hesitated and looked incredibly sad for just a micro-moment before saying, "He's fine, just fine."

John hesitated but said, "I just noticed that pastry place has some great-looking cinnamon buns. Do you have any room for dessert? It will certainly be quieter there than out here on the floor."

"That sounds like a great idea, and I love cinnamon rolls."

"Sounds good. Let's go," John said.

Once seated at the Le Bon Ami Pastry Shoppe, with an extra-large bun in front of both of them, Debra felt a wave of discomfort. She thought she should say something to John so he didn't get the wrong idea, didn't think she wanted more than a casual friendship. She didn't know him well, but she had a deep sense that he was a kind and gentle man, and she did not want to hurt him when she suddenly disappeared as she would do now in just a few days. She hadn't realized that she had been staring at him while she thought, but now realized that she was.

He smiled at her and said, "What? Something on your mind? I hope nothing is wrong."

"Oh, no, nothing is wrong. I want you to know I have enjoyed our time together."

He smiled broadly, looking pleased, and reached out for her hand.

"Me, too. I have enjoyed our time together more than anything in an exceptionally long time."

Oh, my, this wasn't going well; she was making it sound like she was interested in him instead of trying to back off.

"No, John," and she watched his smile fade quickly. "I am sorry, but what I was trying to say—I don't want you to get the wrong idea. I like you. You are fun to be with as a friend, but I don't, I can't…"

"Oh, Debra, do you think I want a relationship? Did I send out signals? I don't…" but then he hesitated mid-sentence and sat back against the booth.

"Oh, I know what you are trying to say. I'm sorry, I should have realized sooner. All the talk about you and Kathy: you two are together. You're a couple. And here I am bumbling into the middle of your relationship."

Debra stopped for a minute to process his words.

"A couple?" she said questioningly. Then, she realized what he was thinking.

"Oh, a couple, Kathy, and me?"

"Yes, as much as you talk about her, I should have realized it."

"Oh, John," and Debra started to laugh.

"No, no, Kathy and I are not a couple. We are just friends and have been for a very long time. I'm not gay."

"It's ok if you are," John interjected.

"But I'm not."

"I am trying to say… I don't want you to think I am interested in any relationship between us. I don't want to lead you on. I enjoy our time together very much, but I am far from wanting or being able to be with anyone else, if you know what I mean," she finished awkwardly. She hoped she had not hurt him.

"Debra," he said, suddenly serious, "I know exactly what you mean. I enjoy our time together very much, but I am so far from being able to have any type of relationship. I am enjoying our companionship; I won't lie, but I don't even think I can be a friend to anyone now. I have no expectations. I do not want more from you than you are willing to give. I don't want to have a relationship with anyone right now. Our time together has been a great, albeit welcome, surprise, but I am expecting nothing."

Debra relaxed her body against the back of the booth.

"Well, John, guess what, it looks like we are on the same page again. I just wanted to make it very clear. I'm not here for much longer."

"Neither am I, Debra, neither am I."

They both smiled and both noticed a slight glimmer of sadness in the other's eyes. Debra brushed a hand over her face, surprised to find a tear on her cheek.

CHAPTER 15

JIM STEPPED OFF the elevator onto his floor. He walked down the hall. It was quiet. It was still early; most guests were downstairs gambling, drinking, and eating. He was glad to be away from all of them. He felt a strange sense of peace and satisfaction, knowing that a decision had finally been made. He only had a brief time left. It felt good to feel something. It had been a while since he had felt much of anything. What would Justin think? he wondered. He would ask him soon, Jim thought. He entered 1113 silently, brushing his hands on the numbers of Justin's birthday on the door as he entered the silent, dark room.

CHAPTER 16

DEBRA COULDN'T BELIEVE that she had called downstairs and requested the room for two more nights. Last night was supposed to be it. She was supposed to do it last night, but she had not. Another dinner with John had been fantastic. She had talked more about Devon, and he had mentioned that his son was younger than Devon, and it seemed like he was leaving his father on his own in Vegas a lot. John became happy and animated, talking about his son. They had stayed in the restaurant long after the meal, ordering one drink and another until the server looked anxious, as if she wanted them to leave. Debra was slightly tipsy as she had taken the elevator up to the room. She had not realized until she was on her floor that she had not purchased the bottle of liquor that she had intended to wash all the pills down with. She looked in the mirror at herself and found herself smiling as she thought of her time with John. Why did she have to do it tonight? He had said they should get coffee and go for another walk on the strip tomorrow morning. Maybe she would.

CHAPTER 17

JIM FINALLY HAD HIS COFFEE after a 45-minute wait and standing, standing as the young baristas yelled out insipid names after insipid names: "Paul, Suzy, John, Barbara, Debra."

Would it never end! He finally grabbed his coffee. He wasn't sure the order was correct, but he didn't even care. He took it over and added extra sugar. Someone had spilled cream all over the counter. Pigs, people were such pigs. A lady about his age smiled at him. He rolled his eyes and walked away. Jim began to traverse the casino floor. There were fewer people here this early in the morning, but the lights were still bright, and the beeping and honking of the machines were as incessant as ever. He noticed a group gathered around one of the blackjack tables. Several of the men were yelling and whooping with glee. Jim crossed toward them to see what they were so delighted about. One man had just won, and his buddies clapped him on the back. Jim lingered to watch, taking a sip of his coffee. A tall, younger man sidled up next to Jim.

"What happened?" the young man inquired.

Jim shrugged. "Don't know, just got here."

"I could hear them all the way across the casino," the young man said, seemingly amused.

Jim nodded. "They're loud, no doubt about that."

The young man whistled, "Look at that guy, he's betting a lot of money."

Jim nodded once again.

CHAPTER 18

DEBRA DIDN'T USUALLY come down from her room this early, but she had slept terribly. There were so many dreams and visions of Ron all night without stopping, and when she thought she might drift off to sleep, she would see her ex-husband Gary's face in front of her. He was yelling at her as he used to do so often all those years ago. *No wonder I can't sleep with all those people in bed with me*, Debra thought, seeing the first light peek through her drapes. Debra had wanted to leave the room more than anything, and now she was wandering somewhat aimlessly around the casino floor. *Few people are down here at this time of the morning*, she thought. Just then, she heard a roar from one of the card tables near the back of the casino, near the bar. She followed the noise to see what the commotion was about. Some young men were howling in approval. *One of them must have just won*, she thought, smiling to herself. Debra did a double-take. Wait, was that John standing near the back of the crowd with a coffee in his hand? He stood next to a tall young man with dark hair, similar to John's. *That must be his son*, Debra thought. It appeared that the two men were deep in conversation. Debra thought of crossing over to them and saying hi to John, but just as she was about to do so, she stopped. He had not introduced her to his son yet, and he could have if he had wanted to. He seemed as reluctant as she was to talk about family and share his life. *Probably better to keep it that way*, Debra thought. She turned and walked quickly away.

CHAPTER 19

"OK," JOHN SAID with a smile as the waiter walked away after taking their order.

"I told you a story about my ex-wife, a good one, not a bad one. Let me hear one about your ex-husband. Tell me something good about him."

Last night, John and Debra shared a few personal stories and didn't just fill their time with innocuous chitchat. Debra was not entirely sure that John's stories were based wholly on the truth. While he created visions of a happy family when he talked about his son, sometimes a look of sadness would envelop his face, even when the story was meant to be humorous. *Maybe the divorce had been rough,* Debra thought. But, of course, Debra was lying to John as well, telling him that she was divorced from her husband. She did not want him to know that Ron had died, did not want to see the pity that would contort his face or hear the platitudes that he would be bound to express. She had told him that they had divorced recently instead. Debra attempted to gather her thoughts and scanned her memory for something she could tell him without veering too closely to the truth. "Oh, I know, I'll tell you how we met."

"Tell me," John said, settling back against the plush restaurant booth. The steak house was quiet this early in the evening. John poured them both more wine from the carafe on the table.

"Ok," Debra began. "After I left Devon's father, I was a single mother for over ten years. It was a struggle, but I returned to school and finished my accounting degree."

"Good for you," John nodded.

"It took me over five years, but I did it: no more waitressing jobs or erratic hours. I sent out numerous resumes, but I finally landed an interview with one of the most prestigious accounting firms in the city. I was so nervous, but I must have done all right in the interview because they offered me the job on the spot. I started two days later; they told me my boss would be Ron Myers, a tax attorney. They said I would like him. Everyone liked Ron. Still, I was nervous that first day; the three other people in our group were warm and welcoming, and so was Ron. He was older than I was, fifteen years older, but tall and handsome, with hair just beginning to gray at the temples. He dressed in sophisticated suits and was just so handsome and urbane. Very polite. You should also know that I had not dated since I left Devon's dad. I just hadn't been interested and had been so busy with first a baby and then a young child, plus going to school."

"Wait, I think I know how this story ends." John interrupted, his eyes twinkling. "You are going to fall in love with your boss. I picked that up with my finely tuned deductive skills because you already mentioned that your ex-husband's name was Ron."

Debra smiled. "You got it, but there is more to the story that makes it interesting."

"Go on."

"Anyway, I did find him attractive. I was surprised I felt that way and would never have acted on it. That would have been inappropriate. Ron was so lovely, and everyone in our unit loved him. Six months after I had started working there, we had just finished a big project, and the company owner had told Ron that we had all done a fantastic job. That Friday, Ron announced that he was taking us all out for lunch, and it was on him. He took us to one of the city's best restaurants, telling us to order whatever we wanted. We all had a wonderful time, talking and laughing. Everyone agreed that it had been a great deal of fun. It eventually became a weekly occurrence. We would go to lunch or dinner every Friday as a group. Ron always paid, and I got to experience many fine restaurants that were far out of my price range. After a few months, the others started to tease me about how Ron always jockeyed for position so he would be seated next to me. They said he always followed my every word when I was talking. I genuinely enjoyed his company, but I told them they were crazy; he wasn't paying any more attention to me than he was to anyone else. He had asked me for restaurant recommendations a few times, but I was sure that was because he was running out of ideas for where to take us. Their teasing did not stop. They said that we were vicariously dating and that they were just along for the ride.

"'Look at how he looks and smiles at you. It's so obvious,' my two coworkers would say. Even Steve, the other guy in the department, said Ron was smitten. I would say 'Please' and roll my eyes. I had trouble believing he could be interested in me. Then, one day, I asked for Friday off. I tried never to take any time off and never called in sick. The job meant way too much to me. Devon needed braces, and before I finished college and got this job, we couldn't even get regular dental care. My health plan included dental and orthodontic care, and Devon needed braces badly. I scheduled all her appointments outside working hours, but she had trouble with the molds that needed to be taken before the braces could be applied. The plaster made her sick, and we needed to come back for another appointment. I requested the whole day. Ron said it was not a problem. He seemed more concerned that Devon would be all right. When I returned to work on Monday, I asked my coworkers what restaurant they had visited on Friday. They sniffed, and Steve snorted. 'We didn't go anywhere. Ron canceled. He said he had too much work to do. He wants to go out with you, not us, Debra.' I shook my head, but it was strange. We went out every Friday. The group hadn't missed a Friday in months. The following week, Ron seemed a little more distant than usual. I even asked him if he was feeling OK, but he said he was fine and thanked me for caring. That Thursday, I came in, and my desk was gone. It was so weird, and I got so scared. I thought, My God, am I being fired for taking just that one day off, and Ron knew that it wasn't for some silly reason—that it had been for my daughter. Other people had taken days off to buy clothes for a concert they attended or because their dog needed grooming. Ron wasn't in the office when I arrived, and since it was early, my coworkers weren't there either. I was so scared. This young guy, Kelly, from Receivables, saw me standing there looking at where my desk had been and said, 'Are you Debra? Follow me.' I swear to God, I thought I was being escorted out, and I thought they must have thought I had committed a crime or something. Anyway, we got to Receivables, my desk and all my things were there, and the boss of that department, Maeve, came out of her office to greet me, saying, 'Welcome, we are so glad to have you. We need you here. You're replacing Kathleen. She resigned for medical reasons, and we need you now.'

"I was so confused, but she called me into her office to get me up to speed immediately. She said Kathleen had been struggling due to medical issues and was way behind, but Ron had assured her that I was so good that I would get them caught up immediately. I relaxed for the first time. 'This is temporary, and I will return to my old department?'

"Maeve frowned. 'Wow, I guess Ron didn't have time to talk to you. No, it is a permanent transfer.'

"I was stunned and spent the morning pondering and trying to figure out what had happened. I finally decided that Ron had hated me the entire time and had finally found a subtle way to get rid of me. Asking for Friday off for Devon must have been the last thing he could tolerate. I was so busy getting acclimated that I didn't even look up when I felt someone standing over my desk. When I looked up, I yelled, 'Oh,' and pushed my chair back. It was Ron, of course, and he looked at me so upset and sad.

"He whispered, 'Please, Debra, have lunch with me today.'

"I nodded, and he was gone."

John sat staring at Debra, paying rapt attention to her story.

"At lunch, it was just the two of us. Ron was quiet at first, so much quieter than usual. Finally, I spoke up and told him I was sorry if I overstepped by asking for time off for Devon, but it had been necessary.

"'Oh, Debra,' he said, 'please do not think that. I had been planning to transfer you for a while. It happened so quickly, much faster than I anticipated, due to the medical leave issue. I apologize for not giving you any notice.'

"I thought that maybe he wasn't mad at me, but he didn't like me and just needed to get rid of me. 'I thought I was doing decent work. I thought we were getting along well,' I stammered.

"'Oh, Debra,' he said. 'You don't understand. I had to transfer you out of my department because I am falling in love with you. I'd like to date you, but it would be inappropriate for me to be your boss. I don't know if you have any feelings for me or are interested in me, but...' and he looked away.

"I realized then, only then, how very attracted I was to him, too. That maybe I was falling in love too, even though I was scared thinking about being with another man after... well, that's another story, and that's probably more than enough for tonight!"

John smiled. "That's a great story. So, were you happy together at first?"

"We were happy together for an exceptionally long time." Debra looked down, feeling tears rush into her eyes.

"Hey, don't be sad," John said kindly.

Debra looked up at him, again noticing how much his blue eyes reminded her of Ron's. Once again, she missed Ron more than anything. What was the point of being here without him? All her happiness and comfort had vanished just like that with his absence, and she would never forget the end or get over what had happened.

CHAPTER 20

Next evening

JOHN FOUND HIMSELF STARING off into the middle distance once again. He and Debra were meeting for dinner every evening now. They had visited a great art museum that afternoon and realized they were both hungry upon leaving. They decided to stop for an early dinner.

"Won't your son miss you?" Debra questioned. "You could call him, and he could meet us here."

"Nah," John said, shrugging. "What about Kathy? Does she mind that you are leaving her alone so much?"

Debra shook her head.

"She's working in the room. She had a conference on Zoom this afternoon; it's probably still going."

For a fleeting moment, Debra thought of blurting out that she was here alone and didn't have to worry about Kathy because she wasn't here and never had been. She couldn't do that! What was she thinking? They were seated outside, and a gentle, slightly warm breeze was blowing.

John looked over at Debra, noticing that she was silently, solemnly observing him. "Hey, I'm sorry," he said, smiling.

"Sometimes you seem like you are a million miles away, and sometimes you look so sad. John, is something bothering you?"

He shook his head slowly and wearily. "No, no, of course not. I'm tired, I guess."

"Late nights with your son?" Debra questioned, smiling.

John hesitated, taking a breath for just a minute before saying, "Man, that kid, he wants to keep going and going. To be young again and never get tired."

Debra nodded. "I know what you mean. You should tell me a story about your family or your son. A good story like the one I told you about Ron the other night." Debra hoped that eliciting a story from John might alleviate the sadness that was permeating his face and eyes.

"I guess there's not much to say," John said quietly.

"You don't like to talk about your family or the past, do you?" Debra said quietly.

John grew solemn. "No, Debra, I don't," he said. "However, I could say the same about you. I know you are divorced from Ron, but besides the story of how you met, you have told me little about your life."

"I know," Debra said, looking down. Now it was her turn to look sad, so sad that he reached his hand out across the table.

"Hey, it doesn't matter. We are here now, about to enjoy a nice Italian meal. We have some good wine on the way. Let's party, or at least that is what my son would say," he said, laughing.

Debra studied him because she thought his smile and jocular manner were not reaching his eyes. Debra sighed, "I'm sorry. I guess I'm just getting introspective tonight. Kathy always says I overthink way too much."

"I think I like you," Debra said, looking down and blushing, "and I just wanted to know more about you." What was she doing? Why was she saying these things to this man, this virtual stranger, when she was planning to leave for good, to end it all in only a few short days? As she continued studying the table, John squeezed her hand, which was still entwined with his larger one. It seemed neither wanted to break the connection.

"Hey, I like you, too. Debra, I like you a little bit more each day. Maybe I shouldn't be saying that, but it's true, I do."

Debra looked up at him and smiled. "John, who are you?" she said quietly. "I want to know."

He looked stricken and moved his hand off the table and away from hers. "I can't answer that question, Debra, I really can't because who am I? Well, I don't know who I am anymore."

"John, I don't know who I am anymore either. A great deal has changed for me in the last few years. I understand what you are saying. Oh, I am so sorry. I don't even know what I am saying tonight. I don't know why I am being so serious."

"It's ok," John said, smiling. "I should tell you, I mean…" as he opened his mouth to say something, the waiter appeared out of nowhere.

"Well, here we are. So sorry about the wait, folks. Here's your wine. It is one of our best brands, and I am sure you will enjoy it."

He deftly poured both glasses. "And here is our lovely Linda right behind me with your salads—fresh pepper, anyone?"

Debra pasted a smile on her face and looked at John, but she knew the moment had passed; whatever he was going to tell her in all seriousness was gone.

"Fresh pepper, by all means," he said heartily. "Bring it on!"

Jim picked up the phone. He couldn't stand sitting alone in a restaurant. Why had he even come here? And now that he was seated and had a glass of wine in front of him, he couldn't just up and leave without looking strange, could he? He didn't care if he looked weird, but still, he should be polite, at least make an attempt. He stared around the restaurant, feeling himself begin to glower at the other diners. His anxiety was ramping up; he needed to do something to dispel these feelings. He looked around desperately. He looked behind him, where he knew the restrooms were. As he swiveled his head and shifted his body, he felt his phone shift in his pocket. Justin, he would call him, and that would make him feel better! He swiped to the familiar number, immediately putting the phone up to his ear. He felt his body relax as he heard the familiar voice: "Hey, it's Justin, I'm not in. Leave a message."

And Jim began to talk, leaving a message as he had now done for years over and over again. He didn't expect an answer at this point, but still, one never knows.

Debra returned to the table and slid into the booth quietly as she noticed that John was again on the phone. She had seen him on the phone as she had made her way back from the restroom. She noticed that he seemed to be listening instead of talking. He looked at her as she sat down and said, "Yes, right, I agree. Ok, love you too. We'll talk later, son."

John looked at her and smiled warmly.

"He's checking in again?" Debra inquired, smiling.

"I called him, actually," John said. "Hearing his voice always makes me feel better."

Debra nodded. "He's young. You need to make sure he's safe. It's so easy to get in trouble, to fall in with the wrong people without even realizing it. I get it. I always worry about Devon, too."

John nodded.

"You seem like such a good dad."

She was surprised when John closed his eyes instead of smiling back at her. She could feel a quizzical look beginning to form on her face. She tried to defuse the moment.

"Ron, I mean my ex-husband, was great with Devon. I was so glad because she had zero guidance from her birth father, not that she ever saw him, and I am fairly sure he would have had no advice to provide her unless she used him as a negative example of what not to do, how not to act."

She shuddered.

"A really bad dude, huh?" John asked.

Debra nodded, saying no more.

"You know I love my son with all my heart, but Debra, you should know I'm not a good dad because I couldn't, I couldn't stop..." His voice broke.

Debra reached out and touched his hand, which was lying on the white linen tablecloth.

"John, it's ok. You can tell me. I think something is very wrong."

John nodded almost imperceptibly. He opened his mouth as if to continue, then shook his head.

"Oh, look, here comes our food. I can't talk about it now, I can't. I want to make the most of the time we have left. It will be over soon, before we know it."

Debra nodded. "It's ok, John, that's fine with me. Yes, all over before we know it."

The meal had gone quickly and had been so delicious. John looked up, raising one eyebrow.

"The waiter is returning with the dessert tray," he said.

"I don't know if I need more food," Debra noted.

"I agree," John said, "but my son always says you only live once."

"Ok, he's convinced me," Debra said, laughing. "That wasn't hard. John, maybe I could meet your son before we leave?" she inquired.

He looked down at the tablecloth, and she saw his eyes glaze over and look past her as if she weren't even there. What was she doing tonight? These dinners, these conversations meant nothing. Why did she need or want to meet his son? How much wine had she drunk tonight? She was so stupid. Before John could answer, Debra jumped back in.

"John, I'm sorry, I don't need to meet your son. I am sure he would have questions if you introduced him to a strange lady. Plus, for all I know, he is hoping that you and your ex-wife get back together. I know Devon fantasized about me getting back with her father for years before Ron came along, and she didn't even know her birth father. If you two had been together since college, it would have been hard for him when you split up. I'm sorry, I wasn't thinking, I was way out of line."

"No, Debra, you weren't. It's a reasonable request. I have been talking about him, and you've seen me on the phone with him. It's just, I think I mean I can't.."

He ran his hand through his hair.

"Well, mademoiselle, sir, you two look ready for some of our delicious desserts," the waiter said heartily, pushing a large dessert cart in front of him.

This guy, Debra thought, perturbed. This was the second time during this dinner that the waiter had interrupted when it seemed that John was about to say something meaningful! John, however, did not look perturbed but more relieved, as if the distraction had just saved him from something unpleasant.

"Please show us what you got," John said heartily, "and the more chocolate you have, the better."

Debra smiled tightly.

CHAPTER 21

JOHN HESITATED AS HE SWIPED the key card to open his hotel room door. He looked up at the number on the door, 1113, and smiled. He reached up and stroked the number again. He had pointed it out to his son when they had checked in.

"Hey, 1113," he had said. "Is that karma or what?"

After the long, somewhat stressful plane ride, it was the first time he had felt good that day. "Your birthday," he had said happily, almost giddily. "Proves that this whole trip was meant to be."

As he touched the room number now, his thoughts immediately went to Debra. Who would have thought that on this trip, of all trips, he would meet someone? Thinking of Debra brought a smile to his lips, almost unbidden. He had so much he would like to tell her, and so much he kept quiet about. He had nearly admitted some things in the restaurant. Thankfully, the waiter interrupted. *Karma, once again*, he thought ruefully. He entered the hotel room, hoping to see his son propped up on the bed, perhaps watching TV or even eating room service that he had ordered, but no, the room was tidy, both beds made, and the silence was complete, stultifying even. Why would he be in the room? John questioned. It was silly even to believe he would spend time in the room. They were in Vegas! John crossed to the large window, pulling back the drapes to stare down at the strip and the front of the hotel. So many people were moving around down there, and he was so high that they looked like scurrying ants from a distance.

But each one has a story, he thought, *just like me, just like my son*. He wondered what Debra's story was. He knew without a doubt she had one. She was divorced but could look so sad when she mentioned her husband. There was something there. Was she still in love with the guy? Had he left her? He thought of his situation, his ex-wife, and his daughter. It all could have been so different for all of them. It was the little micro-choices that you made each day that made up your life. You could turn down a path and not even realize you were on it until it was too late. Something that seemed inconsequential at the time could later take on an increasingly large and looming presence. One seemingly innocuous choice and you were down the path farther than you thought, with no way back. His family would probably still be together if he had made different choices. His daughter would not hate him. He would be here right now in this room with his wife instead of alone with only his son for company. Not that he wasn't grateful for his presence. He loved him so much. He didn't want him ever to leave him, even though he knew that was impossible. A child couldn't follow his father around for the rest of his life. He touched the window, which was slightly cool to the touch. He heard a noise in the hallway. He looked back toward the door. He waited for the door to open and for his son to enter yelling 'Dad' with that omnipresent grin on his face. If only he could have the relationship with his daughter that he had with his son! Maybe he should tell Debra some of what was going on; he somehow felt that he could, that she might listen and understand, if not all of it, at least some of it. He closed his eyes; that was way too much to ask. Again, he was expecting too much from someone and would surely be disappointed. It's better to keep it casual and light. Their time together was to be so brief; the less she knows, the better. Don't be a fool, a voice whispered in his head. He nodded as if concluding a conversation, casting his eyes toward the door again. He heard a noise in the hallway. He thought his son must be having trouble making the key card work. He crossed the room to open the door for him.

CHAPTER 22

JIM WAS EXHAUSTED from all the noise and commotion downstairs. He was lying in his pitch-dark hotel room. It was late, after 2 a.m., yet all he could hear was the sound of doors slamming one after another, and between the slams, he heard the running feet, laughter, and giggling. What were all these assholes doing? Were they all drunk? Why didn't they just go to bed and shut the fuck up? It was Vegas, he sighed. Guess you were expected to be wild and stay up all night. He had a slamming, thundering headache that would not allow him to sleep. He had been so stupid as to think he was feeling better earlier this evening. When he first came up to the room, he felt happy. But the longer he had been in the room and the more glimpses of himself he caught in the bathroom mirror and the mirrored closet doors, the more his mood had plummeted.

"Look at you," he snarled.

"You're old; look at the lines on that face and the gray in your hair."

And his body, which had once been muscular, was now covered with a layer of pudge.

"You're disgusting," he whispered, sneering at his reflection.

All he was doing was prolonging the inevitable. He would always be alone from now on. There was no hope for him, none. He had only one decision to make now: where to do it. Of course, at first, his plan had been right here in the room. It would be easy and private. No one here to stop him. Yes, there were logistics to work out, but he had the necessary engineering skills, so it would be easy to set everything up. However, lately, he had begun to think of doing it in a much more public place. That bridge between the hotels looked like a very viable option. It was always crowded. Of course, there was the possibility that someone could see him and try to stop him before he had accomplished the deed, but if he played it right and executed it quickly, it would all be done before anyone would have a chance to make a move. Doing it in public like that would also preclude the possibility of him losing his nerve at the last minute. Once he started, once the gun was out, he would have to move, move, move so no one stopped him halfway. Alone in the room, on the other hand, it would be easy to hold off, to delay even at the very last second. It wasn't like he hadn't had the gun out before here in the room. He had many times. He had pointed and aimed it several times and still, like the pussy he was, he hadn't completed the act, hadn't even moved close to the window. Yes, a public place might be the best choice. No, not during the day, though, later at night. What did they say—the freaks come out at night? No need to traumatize a young child who might wander by during the day. Do it later at night; that was the way to go. Half or even more people would probably be drunk, and darkness would give him more cover. No one would pay him any attention. Not that anyone ever did anyway. The more he thought of it, this, this was the way to go.

"Tomorrow night," he said out loud.

He would go to the bridge in the morning to scope it out again. He hesitated momentarily as he thought of tomorrow, but then shook the thought away. He had waited long enough. He would get everything ready. It will all be over tomorrow. Tomorrow is our last day, he thought grimly.

♦   ♦   ♦

Jim opened and closed the two cases, leaning against the windows. It was impossibly early, not yet 6 a.m. Still, Jim was wide awake and planning. He stroked the item inside each case. The handgun was flung haphazardly under the small table near the window. He didn't need to try to hide any of the items anymore. He had put the Do Not Disturb sign on the door and even went so far as to affix it there with a small piece of tape so that some drunk would not wander by and knock it off. He had also called down to the lobby and requested that housekeeping not disturb him for the rest of the day and night. He had mumbled something about a big work project to finish.

The front desk clerk said, "No problem, sir," quickly and crisply.

Jim, however, could not help but wonder how many people came to Vegas and stayed in the rooms, working. Probably not many. No matter, the desk clerk seemed not to care what he was doing. *I guess she'll care later*, he thought snidely, but it would be too late by then. Everything was ready and in place. Now he just had to wait till evening for the sun to set. He had hours to wait and waste. Downstairs for some coffee, he decided. He had a loose end to tie up. Better to get it over with early rather than later. Nothing or no one would deter him this time. He was so ready.

CHAPTER 23

"HMMM," DEBRA SAID, considering her next words as she looked up at John. It was bright and sunny on the bridge between their two hotels. It was warm even this early in the morning. They were each holding a cup of coffee in their hands. It had been so cold inside the coffee shop. The air conditioner was turned down to a polar temperature. Debra had shivered.

John noticed and said, "Let's go outside. It's too cold in here for even a polar bear!"

She laughed and nodded in agreement.

As they made their way outside, John mentioned his son again.

"Did I ever tell you what my son called polar bears when he was small? He always said powder bears, and when we asked him why, he said they were white like his powdered donuts." John smiled, and they stopped walking in the middle of the bridge, sipping their coffees.

Debra hesitated. They were careful about saying too much about their past and families. Debra could feel the caution and hesitation from both of them. Debra knew she was pretending to be divorced from Ron. She had to be careful not to reveal too much, to keep her story straight. The last thing she wanted was the flurry of questions that she knew would come if John knew that Ron had died. Debra did not want to relive Ron's last days or her role in his demise. Debra, however, was curious about something concerning John and his son. John noticed her hesitation and looked at her with a curious expression.

Oh, why not, she finally thought to herself, and without further preamble, she said, "John, you always say *my son* when you talk about your son. You never call him by his name. I was curious as to why that was. Or maybe you aren't even aware that you are doing it?" she said with a question.

John shrugged, but he looked down and away from Debra, as he frequently did when discussing his son.

"I don't know," John said, slowly sipping his coffee. "I never thought about it. I call him *son* when I talk to him, too. I think it makes me feel closer to him."

Debra nodded and then asked, "What is his name?"

John looked directly at her, staring without saying anything for so long that Debra began to feel uncomfortable when he finally opened his mouth to answer. At that moment, his phone pealed out a tone. He grabbed it out of his pocket, flicking the screen on. "It's him," he said, and chuckled.

"What timing," Debra said, "just when we were talking about him."

John moved away from Debra, crossing to the other side of the bridge to take the call. As he walked away, Debra heard him say in a light, cheerful voice, "Hey, son!"

Debra watched him, sipping her coffee. He seemed to be listening much more than talking, Debra mused. The kid is probably telling him his plans for the day. Finally, she observed John nod and say something into the phone. She noticed that he was looking over at her from across the bridge. As he moved to hang up the call, he inadvertently pressed the speaker instead of the end call button. The couple beside him looked up at the noise. "Press one if you would like a special life insurance quote formulated just for you!"

John fumbled hastily to mute the speaker. Thankfully, Debra was too far away to hear. He returned the phone to his pocket and crossed back to Debra, smiling at her as he approached.

"He says it's going to be hot. He's going to the pool with some guys he met yesterday."

Debra nodded, and before she could say more, John chuckled and said, "First, we were cold, and now, standing here, it's starting to feel like Death Valley, which is not that far from here, I guess. Anyway, want to go back inside? Let's see if we can find a happy medium somewhere between Antarctica and the Gobi Desert!"

Debra nodded, "Let's go.".

John had now stared piercingly at Debra twice while they were having their coffee and had pursed his lips as if he had something to say, but then he had never said anything. Now they were on a long walk, looping up and down the strip, which was not crowded.

"Doesn't your son wonder where you are always off to?" Debra inquired.

"Oh, he knows," John said quietly. "He knows where I am all the time."

"He's not jealous that you are not spending more time with him?"

"Nah," John said, looking down. "He..." but then he stopped. "Look, we have to leave Vegas soon. We actually will be leaving later tonight. I mean quite a bit later."

Debra nodded, so that must have been what he had wanted to say to her.

"I understand," Debra said, trying to smile but realizing the thought of him leaving made her sad. She wanted to continue the connection. Did he want to do so too, or was he looking forward to being rid of her? "Are you leaving before dinner?"

"No, much later, after dark."

So, they were probably taking a red-eye, Debra thought.

"John," Debra said tentatively. "I don't want to be too bold, and maybe you have too much packing to do or want to be with your son, but I thought you might want to meet for one last dinner?" Debra looked at him hopefully.

John hesitated.

"If you don't have time, I will completely understand."

John looked thoughtful, as if seriously considering something, then he said in a rush of words, "You know what? I would love to, Debra."

Debra smiled. So, if John was leaving, it meant it was time for her to complete her plan. She could do it tonight after dinner or at the latest, tomorrow. John's leaving was just the push she needed to move the plan forward.

John and Debra parted in the early afternoon. They had made a reservation at the Italian place they liked for that evening. Debra returned to her room and gazed deeply into her eyes in the bathroom mirror. What was she doing? She had been enjoying these few days being with another man. She almost felt as if she were cheating on Ron. *What is wrong with you*, she thought severely; it is less than one year since he died, and you are running around with some guy like you — you, of all people, deserve to be happy. You are disgusting. Debra curled her lip at her reflection in the mirror. She moved out of the bathroom, jerking the closet door open with force and angrily keying in the code for the safe. The safe opened with a beep, and Debra removed all the pill bottles stashed inside. If she swallowed handfuls at once mixed with liquor, surely that would do the trick. She certainly had a significant amount. She had counted them several times, over sixty, and a nice mix of painkillers and benzos. Once she started taking them, she would have to do so quickly so as not to lose her nerve or to risk becoming sick. "Do it now. Do it now. Do it now. Do it now. Do it now." A voice she could only describe as evil sang in a singsong in her head. "Why bother with dinner, Debra? John is leaving anyway," the voice in her head taunted. She grabbed all the pills, clutching them in her hands. She entered the bathroom, looking once again in the mirror, and placed the pills next to the sink. She thought of John. I want to go to dinner tonight. "I want to go to dinner!" she said out loud. *Oh, why not?* came the next thought. It would be her last meal, plus she could drink at dinner and purchase another bottle of liquor downstairs before returning to the room. She lined up the pill bottles in the bathroom. She would not return them to the safe. They would stare at her when she returned to the room tonight. She would see them, and no matter what, tonight was the night. She would put the "Do Not Disturb" sign on the door before she left to ensure that housekeeping did not enter, which was improbable at best in the evening, but still, she would do so to be safe.

♦ ♦ ♦

John closed the door of his hotel room quietly. He stepped into the adjacent bathroom and flicked on the fluorescent light. He stared at his reflection in the mirror. A man with graying hair at his temples stared back, but this man also had a slight smile. As he thought of Debra and tonight's dinner, the smile increased. He leaned closer into the mirror, surprised by how happy his reflection looked. He heard a door slam and, startled by the noise, glanced away from the mirror and out toward the room. "Hey, son," he said out loud. "You won't believe this, but I met someone. I met someone. She is great. She's kind and a lot of fun to be with. Are you ok with this? I mean, is it alright? I don't want to hurt you by being with someone other than your mother. Do you understand? Can you possibly understand?"

There was silence in the room. Absolutely no answer from his son. John found his silence aggravating and could feel his temper rising.

CHAPTER 24

JIM STARED AT HIS REFLECTION in the hotel bathroom mirror. The bright, fluorescent light was not doing him any favors—the streaks of gray in his dark hair showing right up. The wrinkles around his eyes were easy to see. As he stared deeper into his eyes, he improbably smiled instead of glowering or cursing his familiar image. He shook his head. His daughter would be an adult on her next birthday, only a month away. No longer the young teenager that he saw in his mind so clearly. The last time he had seen her; she had been a young teenager. Could she possibly forgive him for the mistakes he had made now that she was older? Or would she always despise him for what he had done? He did know one thing. He had never meant to hurt her. He had, though, violated her with his words and his deeds. He had tried to get her back many times, but she always pushed him away. Did she look different now? he wondered. His wife had sent him last year's school picture, and she looked much the same, just with a more mature-looking hairdo. His wife probably shouldn't have let her wear that low-cut shirt for the picture. He could see cleavage, which had startled him. She had not looked womanly when in the house with him. She had looked like a child then. His wife and daughter had moved near New York City over two years ago. He knew so little about their life there. He had thought of writing a note to his wife, but now he wasn't sure; maybe the note should go to his daughter instead. She was now old enough to handle it. She would be able to understand his words. He would write the note. Yes, that was the way to go. He would try to explain it all to his daughter. Maybe he could finally give her some peace of mind.

CHAPTER 25

JOHN WAS FEELING STRESSED. Before tonight, he had things to do that were more important than seeing Debra one last time. He should probably cancel with her, stay in the room, and finish his tasks. He had Debra's cell number in his contact list. He snapped off the bright bathroom light and crossed to his phone on the wood veneer table. He picked it up purposefully and thumbed until he came to the Ds for Debra. He clicked on her name, but his finger hesitated before hitting the phone icon to connect. With a start, he realized he did not want to cancel with her—all these years of hesitation and indecision. He was estranged from the people he loved the most and never knew what to do or what was right. This! This! He wanted to go to dinner with Debra. He did not want to cancel. Well, why not? Why shouldn't he go then? His son had gone out again and wasn't coming back anytime soon. If he could have some fun, some respite for a few hours, why the hell not? He clicked out of the directory and back to his home screen. Besides, Debra deserved a proper goodbye, didn't she? Lovely lady, he liked her, maybe more, a voice deep in his head replied. "Don't be ridiculous," another voice sneered. John looked up and heard a slam from right outside the door. The sound was so loud it sounded like a gunshot. Was his son coming back early? He thought in anticipation, only to realize just as quickly that he was wrong. It was just other guests passing by in the hallway. John looked at his watch. It would soon be time to meet Debra on the bridge.

CHAPTER 26

DEBRA MET JOHN on the bridge between their two hotels. They had both dressed up more for dinner tonight, having done so without planning it. He was wearing a tie and a very neat-looking black leather jacket. He whistled when he saw her in her frilly black dress and heels.

"Look at you. You look stunning," he said, smiling. He reached out his hand toward her, but did not touch her.

"You look nice too," she said, smiling.

"We have a few minutes before the reservation; Debra, look at this." He gently grabbed her shoulder and turned her toward the strip. It was dusk, and the lights from the bridge were blinking brightly, as if every casino in view was coming to life, its neon greens, pink, and red glow blending into a panoply of color.

"It's beautiful," Debra exclaimed. "In all the times I have crossed the bridge, I have never stopped to take in the view."

"It's so easy to miss the beauty right in front of us, always hurrying off to the next thing like them," John said, gesturing to the growing crowd surging rapidly around them.

Debra agreed, nodding without speaking.

Carefully, slowly, John placed his arm around Debra. She felt his hand at her waist. She let her arms dangle helplessly, unable to reciprocate the hug, feeling her breath quicken. His physical closeness was not unpleasant, but suddenly she became acutely aware that he was not Ron, and she stepped quickly away.

John turned to follow her just as a large group of young men and women with tall drinks in their hands and a long selfie stick began to pass by rapidly. The man with the selfie stick was walking backward and stumbling as if he were pretty drunk. The selfie stick was aimed right at Debra's face.

"Hey, watch out!" John called, grabbing Debra and pulling her toward him as the man stumbled by, narrowly missing a direct collision and a sure hit to the head with the large selfie stick. "Watch out, what's wrong with you!" John said, with an anger entering his voice that Debra had never heard before.

"Sorry, man, sorry," the young man slurred. "Salright, is salright."

John nodded at him, focusing his attention back on Debra. "Are you ok?" he inquired solicitously.

"I'm fine," Debra said, feeling warmed by his obvious concern.

"He could have hurt you," John said, shaking his head.

Facing each other, they stared into each other's eyes without moving. Suddenly, John inclined his head slightly, bending to give Debra a gentle kiss. The kiss was tentative and tender, and at first, Debra stood statue still, but as the kiss continued, she found herself reaching out and pulling John into an embrace. The kiss deepened, and Debra pressed her body slowly against John's. It felt good to be held. To feel the warmth of another human. The kiss intensified; a longing seemed to be present on both their parts. *It has been so long*, Debra thought. Ron had been so sick, so weak, she had cared for him like he was a child. He had been fragile like a china doll. There had been no possibility of physical affection from him for the last six months, maybe eight. Ron! All at once, his face appeared like a mirage right before Debra's closed eyes. Not the sick, dying man but the strong, vibrant man she had loved for all those years. She suddenly realized how different John felt; his shoulders, waist, and lips were so different from Ron's body, which had a familiar, comfortable feeling. Oh, what was she doing? She hadn't come here for this. She didn't deserve to feel any physical comfort. Ron's face would not dislodge from behind her eyes, and she pulled away from John, pushing him away and whispering "no, no," each succeeding negative becoming more strident. She put her hands to her lips as if she could not believe what she had just done.

"Debra," John said softly.

Debra shook her head violently as tears began to spill from her eyes.

"NO, no!" she repeated. She turned from John and fled. She ran off the bridge, flinging herself through the casino doors, past the food court vendors, and heading down the stairs through the casino, which would lead to the elevators and then to the hotel rooms.

"Debra, Debra, wait!"

She heard John's strangled cry. "I'm sorry," she thought she heard, but as she heard his voice, she quickened her pace even more so that he could not catch up to her. She hadn't run this fast in years, probably not since Devon was a child. Devon had escaped, running down the block, and Debra feared out into traffic. She bumped into people but still ran headlong, almost to the elevators. She did not turn to see if John was still in pursuit. She punched the button repeatedly at the elevator bank as if this would hasten the elevator on its way. Thankfully, she heard the ding, and the doors slid open. She entered the elevator alone and pressed the button for her floor. Once on the floor, as she walked down the hall, she allowed herself the luxury of looking back once to ascertain that John was not behind her. She was alone. She pulled the key card from her purse, waving it over the door with a shaking, unsteady hand. She entered the room, locked it, and then immediately went to the bathroom. She felt so ill, as if she might throw up. She held on to the sink but would not allow herself to gaze at her reflection in the mirror. She knew she would hate what she saw looking back.

After several minutes of standing in the bathroom, Debra exited shakily and went to the bed, sitting down and holding her head. She kicked off her heels. She could not stop her hands and her body from shaking. Just then, she heard a loud rap on the door, a loud staccato knocking. She willed the person to go away. She knew who it had to be; who else could it possibly be? How had he found her room? She rose from the bed and moved toward the door.

She heard a muffled "Debra, please," and his voice sounded upset.

She closed her eyes. The rapping on the door continued. He wasn't giving up. She didn't want to answer, but how could she hurt yet another man? John had done nothing wrong. She was the one who was callous and evil. She would provide him with a quick explanation and send him on his way. She moved to open the door.

"Debra, I am so sorry." He began apologizing in a rush before she could utter a word. "The last thing I meant to do was upset you. You said you only wanted to be friends, and I overstepped."

Debra looked at his pained, sad expression. She opened the door wider, motioning for him to enter.

"Please forgive me. It shouldn't have happened. I didn't mean to ruin our last dinner."

"How did you get my room number?" Debra inquired.

John looked down, then smiled ruefully. "It's easy to get what you want if you ask confidently. I told the woman at the desk that you were my cousin, and I had forgotten your room number, but I knew it was on the fifteenth floor."

"How did you even know the fifteenth floor?"

"I made it to the elevator just as the door was closing. I saw you in the bank of elevators that said 15–20. I took a wild guess, and I was right. I will leave if you don't want me here," John said seriously. "I just needed to apologize, and I wanted to ensure you were alright. You got so upset."

Debra closed her eyes.

"It's a long story, John, but I am ok now and sorry I reacted so dramatically. It's been a while. I haven't been with anyone in quite a while."

"I haven't either," John interrupted.

"I am too tired to explain now, John. I can't, I just can't."

He nodded. "I think we have both had a lot of sadness and pain in our lives. That's why we both reacted as we did. Believe me, I know a relationship is not in the cards for me. I'm going to be leaving very soon now, Debra."

"I am leaving, too, John. Very soon," Debra agreed.

They stared at each other as if they had more to say. Debra opened her mouth as if to speak, but then hastily looked down. They both stared at the patterned carpet.

"I should go," John said solemnly.

Debra nodded.

"Could I use the bathroom before I go? It's a rather long walk back to my hotel. I'll cancel our dinner reservation on my way back."

Debra nodded. "Of course," she said and gestured toward the bathroom. Debra moved away from the door and looked out the window onto her splendid view of the hotel's air conditioning units. She turned as she heard the bathroom door open, and John stepped out. He looked at her and ran a hand through his hair, leaving it to rest on the back of his neck.

He looked at her quizzically, disturbed, said, "Debra," then shook his head. "I have to go," he said, crossing quickly to the door. He slammed the door and was gone before Debra could even cross the room.

CHAPTER 27

DEBRA HAD TO ADMIT she felt better now after John's apology. She knew she would not see him again and that it was better that way. Her time here was ending. Why wait? Why not execute her plan right now? She entered the bathroom, turning on the light and allowing herself to look at her reflection in the mirror. An older woman with sad, sad eyes stared back at her. Debra looked down. *No, no, oh, no,* she thought. Her heart quickened as she took in all the pill bottles lined up like soldiers on the counter. One or two were slightly out of place as if they had been recently picked up. John must have seen them all when he used the bathroom. What had he thought? She was ill and keeping it secret, but if he had picked up any of the bottles, he would have seen the name Ron Myers, not Debra. What was he thinking? Had he figured out her plan? Was that why he looked so strange when he exited the bathroom? Was that why he had left so quickly? What was he going to do? Was he going to tell anyone? Inform the hotel or the police about a possible suicide? Or did he think she was sick and would keep the information to himself? Now she had no idea what to do. She couldn't risk the authorities coming to her door. She couldn't lose her pills; surely, they would try to hospitalize her if they knew her plans. Now what to do? She didn't even have any liquor in the room. She would have to go downstairs to purchase liquor or call room service, and how long would it take for them to arrive? What was she to do? And then she saw it! The expensive watch she had noticed and admired on John's wrist was lying just to the side of all her pill bottles. He had taken off his watch. Why? It must have been when he washed his hands! Had he forgotten the watch in his confusion when he noticed the army of pill bottles? Her heart was racing, and her mind was pinging from possible scenario to possible scenario. She picked up the watch and held it in her hand. She would return it. She would go to his hotel now and give the watch back. She would find out what he thought the pill bottles were for. If she went now, she could avoid any possible consequences of his calling anyone. She would make up some bullshit story about the bottles not being what they looked like. It was her only choice. She scooped up all the bottles to return them to the safe. She didn't know John's room number either, only that it was in the hotel on the bridge's other end. He had found her room easily enough. She was sure she could do the same. She pocketed his expensive watch, threw a black wrap around her shoulders, and was off.

CHAPTER 28

THE HOTEL RECEPTIONIST FROWNED, regarding her with disdain. This was turning out to be more difficult than she thought it would be. She had tried to approach the desk confidently, but when she asked if there was a guest named John Waggoner, the man had sighed, punched his computer keys desultorily, and then said briskly, "No, no guest here by that name."

Debra's stomach fell, and she almost walked away. Then, she turned and said, "Are you sure? You must be mistaken."

The man seemed to take this as a personal affront and said, "No, ma'am, I am not mistaken."

Debra thought quickly and said, "But he is registered here, I know it."

The man sniffed and looked at her as if she were a stalker or hooker.

"Please," she forced herself to smile at the man. "It's important. He's my brother, and my daughter left her medication in his room, and I need to get it from him. It's time for her to take her pill, and she can't miss it."

The man sighed and looked at her skeptically. "Then, why not call him on the phone and have him bring it to you?"

Debra thought quickly and sighed, "He's not answering his phone. Believe me, I have tried. You know, old guys either ignore the phone or do not even have it turned on," Debra said, trying to forge some sense of camaraderie with the young desk clerk. Debra thought she was out of luck once again when the man snorted and gave a half smile.

"Yes, I know," he said. "My father is like that. We yell at him about turning off his phone or not having it on him all the time. Let me look again."

He stabbed the keys and stared at the computer screen. He looked up at her, shaking his head. "Ma'am, we do not have a John Waggoner registered. We do, however, have a Jim Waggoner registered."

"Oh, that's him," Debra said quickly with a confidence she did not feel.

"MMM," the clerk said, shrugging and saying, "1113, Midway tower."

"Thank you, thank you so much," Debra said.

She walked quickly toward the bank of elevators marked "Midway." She punched the button, feeling completely unsure if she was going to the right room or whether she was headed to a stranger's room. She would have to be careful. However, how much she cared about being careful wasn't even truly clear at this point.

CHAPTER 29

Location: Massachusetts, Devon

"ANYWAY, DAVID," Devon, Debra's daughter, said to her husband, speaking animatedly and waving her arms as he held the door for her as they entered the coffee shop. "Dad said that we could all come for Christmas. I heard Susan screaming with delight in the background when he said that. I love having little sisters," Devon said, smiling.

David frowned, "What about your mom, though?"

"Oh, I asked him to be sure, and he said there was no problem with her coming. She was more than welcome and always would be."

David continued to frown. "Okay, it's okay on his part, but what about on your mom's part?"

"What do you mean?"

"I don't know, Devon, your mom did not seem comfortable last time we were there on the Fourth of July. It may be ok with your father, but I don't know if your mom likes being around him."

"David," Devon said with exasperation. "Ron had just passed; of course, she seemed uncomfortable and sad."

"I think it was more than that, Devon. Are you sure of everything that occurred between your mom and dad? Maybe there's more than she is saying. He used to drink, didn't he? How do you know that he wasn't mean to her—maybe even beat her?"

"That's a little dramatic, don't you think?"

"Please do me a favor and talk to her again before you say we are all going. Get her thoughts. Make sure she is ok with it."

"Ok, David," Devon sighed, "but it is so much better having a big family get-together than just being the three of us sitting around and looking at each other on every holiday. The kids and all the commotion make the holiday, and besides, a big family has always been what I wanted, and my mom knows that."

"Just talk to her, Devon. Have a private conversation before you go ahead with all these plans."

"Ok, David," Devon sighed as they moved up the coffee line.

After receiving their coffees, they turned to look for a table, and Devon exclaimed, "Oh, look, I don't believe it, but there's Kathy over in the corner. I wonder when she got back from Vegas. My mother didn't say that she had left."

"I thought you only talked to your mother once since she's been gone."

"Yeah, I have, and she didn't have much to say. I'm surprised she's there alone, even if only for a couple more days."

"Hi, Kathy!" Devon yelled, waving vigorously, causing several other patrons to stare. Kathy tore her eyes away from the laptop they had been focused on. When she placed Devon in the crowd, she smiled warmly and motioned for them to come over. She pulled out the chair at her table for David and patted the seat next to her for Devon to sit down.

"I'm surprised to see you here," Devon said.

"Yeah, I know, I just got back," Kathy said, "but running into you is great."

"Are you tired after your trip?" Devon questioned.

Kathy looked momentarily puzzled but then nodded. "You could say that. All we've done is run, run, run. I thought it would never end."

"It sounds like you had a fun time then."

"Very productive. We accomplished a lot."

"How was the hotel? Nice?"

"Oh, it was ok, nothing special."

"I thought it was quite plush," Devon stated.

"Nah, I've been in better."

"Oh, ok," Devon said, shrugging.

"How was the weather?" David inquired.

"Not bad. I had to wear a jacket most days, though."

"That's a surprise. I thought it was much warmer there this time of year."

"No," Kathy said, frowning.

"What was your favorite part?" Devon inquired.

Kathy thought. "Well, I guess I must say the food. We did go to a nice steak restaurant one night."

"The food there is fantastic. I remember that from the time that David and I were there."

"Have you and David been there before? I didn't know."

"Of course, we have," Devon said, looking at David confusedly. "We went there on our honeymoon, don't you remember?"

"No, Devon, I'm sorry, I must have forgotten that."

"So, Kathy, how is my mother?"

"I must admit that I haven't talked to her much lately. She seemed sad the last time I spoke with her. I hope she's doing better now."

"Did you have to leave early due to work?"

"Well, yes, I did. I am preparing for yet another business trip right now. I leave early tomorrow. It's just one thing after another. David knows what I mean," Kathy said, smiling. "Owning your own business means the work never stops. Never time for a break."

David nodded.

Then, Kathy looked suddenly sad. "Devon, I am sorry your mom is still not feeling so well. Losing Ron was hard on her."

"Did she talk about him a lot while you were together?"

"She spoke of him a little last time I saw her."

"But she was happy part of the time? She went to the steak restaurant with you, didn't she?"

Kathy shook her head and looked at Devon, confused.

"No, Devon, she didn't go to the restaurant with me."

"But why not? She isn't just sitting in the room moping, is she?"

"Devon, why would your mother have been with me on my business trip to Baltimore?"

"Oh, Kathy, no, I don't mean the trip you are preparing to go on now. I mean Vegas. How was my mother in Vegas? Was she happy?"

"Devon, I'm sorry, I'm confused. I haven't talked to your mother in over a month now."

Kathy looked up toward the ceiling. "I'm not proud of that, but between all the traveling and work commitments . . . Also, lately, she hasn't answered the phone even when I call. I should try harder to be more supportive, but I have been so busy." "Wait," Devon said, holding up her hand. "I'm confused. I'm talking about the last two weeks, when you were with my mother in Vegas."

"In Las Vegas! Devon, I've been in Baltimore doing business for the last two weeks. I just got back here last night, and as I said, I head out to Cleveland in the morning."

"But you went on vacation to Las Vegas with my mother. You left Monday a week ago and decided to stay one more week this past Saturday."

"The last vacation I had time to go on was over two years ago, Devon, honey."

"But you were just in Vegas with my mother? You are supposed to be there with her right now," Devon said stubbornly, her voice rising as Kathy emphatically shook her head.

"Devon, sweetie, I am not in Vegas, clearly, and I haven't even seen your mother in two months."

"But, but.." Devon sputtered.

David stepped in, "Kathy, Debra told us you both were going to Vegas for a vacation. She called from Vegas a week ago to say you both had arrived. She left a message for Devon two days ago saying that you had decided to extend your stay for a week. Now you say you have not been in Vegas and haven't even seen Debra?"

Kathy looked up with a disturbed look on her face. "That is exactly what I am saying. Debra never talked to me about any trip to Vegas, and she never invited me to go on a trip to Vegas with her."

In a low, quiet voice, "Kathy," Devon said, "What is my mother doing in Las Vegas all alone?"

Kathy shook her head, "I don't know, Devon. I have no idea."

"Is my mother even in Vegas?"

David looked at Devon and grabbed her hand. "Something's not right, Devon, something is wrong, and I think we had better figure out what is going on right away."

Devon swallowed as if her throat was sore and then nodded vigorously.

CHAPTER 30

JIM STARED OUT THE WINDOW, looking down on the front of the hotel as taxis pulled up and then away. People walked in and out of the hotel in a constant stream; from this high up, they looked like little ants moving and scurrying about. They certainly did not appear to be real people. Jim sighed and picked up the gun. He aimed it out the window, then pointed it toward the cars and the people. Suddenly, it seemed like they were all just moving targets in a video game. He looked at the two cases leaning against the chair across from him. Both long and rectangular in shape. It occurred to him to remove the objects inside to look at them again, but although he looked over, he did not move from his position in the chair. He turned the gun around, quickly pointing it at himself, opening his mouth as if to force the barrel inside, then moving it to his chest, then his temple. He should get up the courage to move. He put his feet down firmly on the floor, taking one last look out the window. It was time, time to do it fucking now. He stood up forcefully but stopped as he heard a gentle tapping on his door. Someone was out there. *Go away*, he thought angrily. The tapping increased in volume until it was no longer tapping but knocking, rising in intensity. He was feeling angrier and angrier, 'stop!' his mind shouted. If the person didn't stop, he was going to go to the door with his gun and take the godforsaken annoying knocker out. In fact, that annoying scumbag could damn well go first. He crossed the room, his feet falling hard on the rug, and his anger increasing with every step.

CHAPTER 31

JUST BEFORE HE OPENED the door, he squinted to look out the peephole. He made an intake of breath. Debra, what was she doing here? The anger that had been coursing through him just melted away. He looked around wildly, and he ran back across the room, throwing the gun down under the coffee table between the two chairs. He combed his fingers through his hair, unsure whether he looked presentable. She was still knocking. He opened the door.

"John," Debra said, "I thought maybe you weren't in, or I had the wrong room."

"No, I'm here," John said, finding his words gummy and sticking to the roof of his mouth.

"Is something wrong?" Debra questioned.

"No, no," he said, shaking his head.

"I…" she hesitated, "I have your watch."

She held it out to him.

"You left it in my room, in the uh bathroom."

He nodded at her and held out his hand. Part of him wanted to say thanks and close the door, but as he looked at his new friend, he saw the kindness in her eyes, and something broke inside him, something that made him want to help her. Could he help save Debra somehow? He could not let another person die.

"Come in," he said, gesturing, "thanks for returning it."

"You're welcome, but you certainly were not easy to find. You are not registered under John."

"Yeah," he said, providing no additional information.

"Debra, I need to ask you something."

Here it comes, Debra thought. He is going to ask about the pills. He motioned with his hand as if he was inviting her to sit down on the bed, but she moved past the two double beds and headed toward the sitting area facing the windows, and just like that, she looked down suddenly, taking in the gun thrown so precariously under the coffee table. She stopped, then her eyes scanned the two larger objects leaning on the chair, pointing toward the window. He heard her make an audible intake of breath. She stepped back, taking two steps backward as if to exit the room, but John was behind her, blocking her path.

She shook her head, "No, no," she said. "Oh, John," she said as she whirled toward him, and he saw abject fear in her eyes. "You, you are planning a shooting, you want to hurt people," she said, and she looked around him as if searching for a way out.

"What," he said, stunned. "Hurt people? What do you mean?"

"John," she whispered, "there is a gun under the table, and you have two more rifles pointed at the window."

CHAPTER 32

Two years prior

JEANNINE STARED AT HER FAMILY seated around her in the half-moon-shaped booth. She touched her wrist to the restaurant table and pulled it away when she realized it was slightly sticky. The breakfast restaurant was busy early on a Friday morning, and Jeannine realized they would probably have to wait a while before getting their order. Jeannine looked at her fourteen-year-old daughter sitting beside her, with her long hair cascading down and partially covering her face. Jasmine was quiet, having remained so since they picked Justin up from rehab. Justin had just turned eighteen, but had already been through so much. Jeannine wished she knew what her daughter was thinking. Her gaze moved over to her husband, Jim, and her son. Seeing them seated next to each other, it was clear how much they looked alike. They had the same coloring and features. Both had light sandy hair and an easy smile that was impossibly handsome. Both were talking animatedly, seemingly oblivious to all else around them. Her husband was extremely happy, talking a mile a minute to his son. He had been so excited from the time they had driven into the parking lot of the rehab where Justin had completed his extended ninety-day stay. Her husband had been close-to-jumping-up-and-down happy, Christmas-morning happy. Jeannine, in contrast, was subdued, as subdued as her much more introverted daughter. People had often remarked on how ironic it was that Justin resembled his father both physically and in personality, while Jasmine resembled her in both ways. Her husband laughed loudly in response to something funny that her son had shared. She had not heard his comment, so she did not share in the delight. Jasmine had not heard either. She glanced at her brother and father, but neither laughed nor smiled. Her mouth remained in the same straight line it had been in ever since they had seen Justin striding down the hall toward them. Jeannine wished she could be as happy and carefree as her son and husband, but she couldn't. She was just too wary of the future. Eighteen and already in rehab? Would he be okay this time? Were they still on the hamster wheel of addiction that they now knew all too well? Jeannine didn't want to think this, but at the last two sessions Justin had with his parents, his proclamations of remorse did not ring true to Jeannine. Had he learned what he needed to, or was Justin parroting the words he needed to say to please those around him and get out and be free once more? Jeannine wasn't sure. She had tried to share her doubts with her husband, but it had not gone well.

"What do you mean?" Jim had inquired, seeming stunned that she would even think such a thing.

"Ninety days, Jeannine! He was there for ninety days. That's a hell of a long time for a young kid. Of course, I know that he is better. Sure, he made some mistakes and got in over his head, but it's ended now. You have to be supportive, you know. He needs to feel that we believe in him."

Jeannine had only nodded, incapable of finishing the thoughts she so longed to say. She wanted to believe in Justin more than anything but worried it was not over. She did not want to be negative, and the last thing she wanted to do was doubt her son! But some of his answers were just too smooth, too pat. She no longer knew who Justin was, and it scared her. Her other concern that sometimes she did not feel Jim shared was Jasmine. Poor Jasmine, so young, had been forced to go along on the ride of her brother's disease since she was only twelve years old. What must she think! It didn't help that Jasmine was the opposite of Justin's glibness and loquacity.

Jasmine was measured and quiet in her speech; she almost always thought things over carefully before letting the words tumble out of her mouth. Jeannine had to work hard to get her daughter to share her most closely held thoughts. She also noticed a slight distance between Jasmine and her dad, which disturbed her. Jasmine had idolized her father as a little girl, always jumping on him and begging him to pick her up. Naturally, this would change as she aged, but sometimes Jeannine worried it was more than that. Jeannine was worried that Jasmine might feel her father preferred her brother's company to hers. Jeannine was confident that Jim loved his children equally, but they were very different. Jasmine once mentioned, "Yeah, and I'm not Justin, the favored son."

Jasmine had been angry about some perceived slight; Jeannine couldn't even remember what it was, but she wondered if Jasmine honestly thought that. She had tried to talk about it with her once, but Jasmine denied having such feelings and simply said, "I was mad," refusing to elaborate further.

Jeannine now knew that Justin had begun smoking pot and using pills at thirteen, younger than Jasmine's age right now. Jeannine was always watching Jasmine. She was almost waiting for her to make the same mistakes as her brother, yet Jasmine was quite different.

"Mom, Mom, halloo," Justin yelled across the table, frantically waving his hand when she looked up, and Jasmine did, too, at the commotion.

Justin held up his spoon, pretending it was a microphone. He said in a deep voice, "Paging Mom and Jasmine, Mom and Jasmine, please report to the table at Murphy's Pancake House. We request your presence at an important, official family celebration. Jasmine and Mom, we need you here now."

Jeannine looked at her husband, laughing hysterically at Justin's antics. All Jeannine and Jasmine could muster was a weak smile.

Justin put down his spoon and seemed ready to say something, but the server burst upon them.

"Sorry about the wait, but here comes your food now. I can guess who ordered chocolate chip pancakes," she said jocularly, treating Jasmine like a much younger child.

Jeannine glanced at Justin. Everyone else was looking at the food and the waitress. For a second, just one second, she saw a look of distress enter his eyes. Without blinking, she continued to stare at her son. Just like that, the look disappeared, replaced by a broad smile.

"Bring it on," he said heartily.

"Guard your food, family, because I'm so hungry I could eat it all!"

She watched her husband clap him on the shoulder with a big smile. Jeannine looked away.

CHAPTER 33

JUSTIN HAD ONLY been out of rehab for one month. Jeannine was becoming increasingly convinced that something was wrong with him. She didn't want to voice what she was thinking. She didn't even want to say the words in her head, but she was so scared that he was using again. So many of the signs were there, and now here he was, staggering as he opened the door and entering a half hour past his curfew again.

"Hey, son," Jim stood and said the greeting warmly, but she could tell that Jim was looking at Justin, wondering if he was altered, had been using just as she was wondering the same thing.

"What's the matt..." Jim had started to say, but Jeannine interrupted him.

She didn't want to hear another excuse from Justin. They had been coming fast and furious the last two weeks—"I lost track of time, I have a terrible headache, I had to help a friend, the car broke down, but it started again and is ok now." Twice, she had smelled mouthwash so strongly on his breath that it almost seemed he must have bathed in it. Was he covering up alcohol on his breath? She also knew that he had withdrawn over $500 from his bank account within the last week, yet he was sporting no new clothes or technological gadgets. Where had the money gone? What was it being used for? She was sure that Justin did not know that she had the password to his account, and he would probably be mad if he thought she was monitoring him. She hadn't even told Jim about this discovery. She didn't want to hear him defend Justin once again. Perhaps she could have asked him kindly and gently where he had been or if something was wrong, but she knew that was what Jim would do. They were getting no answers this way. If the kid needed to return to rehab, let's do it now, not wait until when? When he collapses in the hall again? When he overdoses? Without giving Jim time to get the rest of the words out of his mouth, Jeannine said firmly, "Justin, where have you been? You are late again! Have you been drinking? This time, I want a straight answer." Maybe her words sounded harsh when she meant them to be forthright, but she needed answers; they needed to know what was happening!

"Am I drinking?" Justin repeated, and his voice rose higher on the second syllable, sounding slightly slurred.

She felt her stomach fall as if she had been going down the hill of a roller coaster. *Oh, God, I'm not wrong*, she thought sadly, sickly.

"Jeannine," Jim said in a hushed whisper, and Justin toggled his head over to his father as he reached out to rest a hand on the couch for support.

"Son," Jim said, but this time Justin interrupted him before he could get the words out.

"Am I drinking?" Justin yelled with uncharacteristic fury.

"What the hell, Mom? I just got out of fucking rehab! Why would I be drinking? You think I'm using drugs! I can't believe this! This is the support I get from my own family!"

"No one mentioned drugs, Justin," Jeannine said, trying so hard, oh so hard to remain steady and strong.

"You guys think I'm an addict! Your own son! I cannot believe this! How can you treat me like this? I work so hard, and this is what I get. I went to rehab. No, Mom, I haven't been drinking. I do not do DRUGS!" and he screamed the last sentence at such a decibel level that

Jeannine was sure that the neighbors next door must have been able to hear his protestation.

He was denying it so strongly, a line from Shakespeare's Hamlet flashed through Jeannine's mind: "The lady doth protest too much." *Only the guilty get that upset*, Jeannine thought, staring at the carpet and her feet.

"I am clean," Justin affirmed. "Please believe in me, not sabotage me. Why would I want to stay clean when I get accused of things I don't even do? If you must know why I was late, I had to drop John off at his house. He had been drinking, and I would not let him drive. I drove him home, and you know where he lives, twenty minutes away. No way could I make it home on time."

"Why didn't you call?" Jeannine questioned.

"Mom, always a question, huh? I guess I can't do anything right, can I? Do you want me to be drunk? Is that it?"

"Justin, Justin, now calm down, son, calm down. I can see why you might be upset, but you shouldn't be around kids who are drinking, huh?"

"Dad, you are as bad as she is. I was at the hamburger place with the guys, and John showed up like that! So now I am in trouble for being completely sober and helping a friend. Thanks for your support."

"Justin, you don't seem right. You've been very irritable for the last two weeks. Are you feeling ok?" Jeannine inquired.

"When I get treated like this by my own family, why wouldn't I be irritable? I have a terrible headache! I need to go to bed."

"Justin," Jeannine had almost gathered her courage to ask him about the money. She noticed he was staring at her with a sullen and belligerent look.

Jeannine opened her mouth, but before she could get the words out, Jim said, "You know, maybe Justin is right, Jeannine. Maybe we need to give him a little more slack," he said, and turned toward his son.

"Do you think a later curfew would make it easier for you? And, son, you need to know that I do not doubt you are sober. It is admirable that you went out of your way to help a friend."

"Thanks, Dad," Justin said. "I need to know that you believe in me."

"Jeannine, you need to back off and give the kid a break. He's had a hell of a year."

Jeannine glared at her husband. It would be one thing if he shared these sentiments with her, away from Justin, but to say the words right in front of him, he was making her look like the bad guy, like he had no doubts about his son at all.

"I need some sleep," Justin said, looking down.

"You get to bed, son, get your rest. Everything is fine."

"Thanks, Dad," Justin said.

He walked past his mother without saying goodnight. They both watched him walk down the short hallway. He seemed to be walking ever so slowly, ever so deliberately; right before he entered his room, he staggered into the doorjamb as he turned into the room. Jeannine looked back at her husband with a question in her eyes.

"Jeannine," Jim sighed, "he said he had a bad headache. He's overtired, that's all. It's all good, it's fine."

Jeannine felt something inside crumble into pieces, and then, worst of all, she found herself doubting the reality she had seen so clearly just moments ago in front of her face.

CHAPTER 34

JEANNINE STARED after her husband and son. Justin had just closed the door, and it made a soft whoosh. She shivered as frigid air from the front door briefly surrounded her, then rapidly dissipated. As she turned from the door, she heard a voice barely above a mumble say something that sounded like "he's a liar." Jeannine turned toward her daughter, seated on the far end of the couch, her face buried as usual in the screen of her laptop.

"Jasmine, did you say something?" Jeannine inquired.

"He's a liar," she repeated, still at a barely audible level.

"Who is? Who's a liar, Jasmine? Your father?" Jeannine questioned, stunned. Jasmine had been quiet lately, barely participating in anything with her family. Jeannine hoped that she would stay in the living room to eat the pizza that Jim and Justin had gone to pick up, knowing that it was equally likely that she might attempt to take a piece and run to her room.

"Jasmine, look at me. Talk to me," Jeannine commanded. "What are you talking about? Why is your father a liar?"

"No," Jasmine said, a look of irritation moving across her face. "Not Dad, I'm not talking about Dad. Justin. Justin is a liar."

Jeannine perched on the green easy chair perpendicular to the couch.

"Why, Jasmine, why is your brother a liar?"

Jasmine took in a large gulp of air and met her mother's eyes for the first time.

"I heard all the screaming when he came in last night. How could I not?" Jasmine challenged.

"Jasmine," Jeannine said in a hushed, serious tone. "Do you know something? Is your brother using again?"

Jasmine shook her head no. "I mean, I don't know for sure, but I know he lies. He acts weird, Mom, like all the time, he acts weird. He forbids me from going into his room. Did you know that? The other day, I was looking for the laptop charger and opened his door. I didn't even know he was in there. When he saw me, he screamed at me to get out, and he threw something that looked like a pill bottle into his drawer. He yelled at me so loudly; he was so angry. He said he would kill me if I ever came into his room again. I wasn't even in the room, Mom, I was in the hallway. And, at school, he doesn't hang out with the football players like he used to. He doesn't hang with Mark, hardly ever. He is always with the druggies, and especially he is always with John, and everyone knows that John is a huge user. A lot of kids say that John deals, too. When he said last night that he was with Mark and John showed up drunk, that's not how it happened. Cara was there with her brother, and she told me."

Both women looked up as car headlights shone into the window as a car entered the driveway. Jim and Justin were back with the pizza. Jasmine looked down. Jeannine reached out, touching her daughter's knee.

"Jasmine, tell me the rest later. And Jasmine, thank you for being honest."

Jasmine nodded silently.

CHAPTER 35

JEANNINE COULD NOT BELIEVE she had been forced to wait an entire week before telling her husband what Jasmine had said. First, she had to wait for a private moment so Jasmine could tell the rest of her story. Then she had wanted—needed—to find a time when both kids were out of the house so she could have a frank, serious discussion with Jim without interruption or the possibility of being overheard. But now, finally, Jasmine was spending Friday night at Cara's, and Justin had said that the guys were meeting for a pickup basketball game. Jeannine had not been able to take her eyes off Justin since Jasmine had shared her stories, and the words that she had said reverberated through her head repeatedly: "He's a liar, Justin's a liar." Jeannine felt that now Justin was becoming aware that she was watching him— twice in the last day, he had looked at her and had said, "What, Mom?" She had had to deny that anything was wrong. And now, finally, they were alone, and she could share her concerns and fears with Jim.

"Really, Jeannine, that's all you've got? I thought you had something terrible to say about Justin. I thought you found drugs in his room or something, but this is all you have to say. You act like you've solved some big mystery. Give the poor kid a break, will you!"

"You think Jasmine calling her brother a liar is nothing? Did you even listen to the stories I just told you?"

"Of course, I heard. An older brother doesn't want his kid sister anywhere near his room, and she thinks she might have seen him throw something in a drawer. In what reality is that a big deal? Additionally, you mentioned that you've been violating your son's privacy by sneaking around his room. Nothing, Jeannine, you admit that you found nothing."

"Then," Jim held up his hand as if counting off items on a list, "Jasmine says that Justin is hanging with a bad crowd at school. Are you sure she knows, or is this just some kids gossiping and telling rumors? Jasmine doesn't hang with seniors; most of their classes aren't even in the same wing. How does she know what he's doing? She's hearing stories. Look, Jasmine could be jealous of her brother. He's been getting a lot of attention. If you play into this, her stories will only get bigger and more dramatic. When will you start supporting your son?"

"Jasmine doesn't lie, Jim, you know that. She is not a gossip, and she is not overly dramatic."

"Yeah, well, your son doesn't lie, either. This is getting ridiculous. You need to have his back like I do, not wait for him to make a mistake. None of this translates into Justin being a liar," and Jim actually made air quotes as he said the phrase! — "And the money you say is missing from his bank account? It could be missing for any reason. Maybe he's buying a present for someone, even you, or more likely, he's seeing a girl and buying something for her, and he isn't ready to tell us yet."

"Explain what happened at the hamburger restaurant, Jim. I want to hear you justify that one."

Jeannine could tell that what she wanted to be a simple discussion was rapidly turning into an argument with Jim on one side and her on the other. This wasn't what she wanted.

Jim sighed, "Ok, tell me again. Tell me what happened at the restaurant. Tell me exactly what Jazzy told you."

"Jasmine's friend, Cara, was there with her older brother. Maybe Mark had been there earlier, but he wasn't with Justin when Cara and her brother arrived. Justin was there with John. John didn't come in drunk like he told us; they were there together."

"Go on," Jim said tightly.

"Cara told Jasmine both John and Justin were loud and disruptive. People were looking at them. Cara told Jasmine that both boys went to the bathroom five or six times. The manager eventually came over to them and asked them to leave. Cara said that Justin was loud and very obnoxious. Cara said hi to him one time as he passed by their table. She said he looked at her like he didn't even know who she was. When Cara said to her brother, 'What's wrong with Justin?' he said with disgust, 'They're high.'"

Jeannine finished speaking and looked questioningly at her husband. Surely, this proved that Justin was in trouble. He had indeed lied about who he had been out with that night. Instead of agreeing with her as Jeannine suspected her husband would, he shook his head and said, "Sounds like more gossip to me, Jeannine. So, they were having fun and got a little rowdy; that place is always like that. Maybe Mark had just left, and Justin didn't want to tell us how long John had been there because he knew he shouldn't be hanging out with him after he had been drinking. Cara and her brother are kids, not drug counselors, so what qualifies either of them to make a judgment of whether someone is high or not?"

Jeannine opened her mouth to reply, but Jim's words continued. "And he didn't recognize Cara, so what? He's supposed to remember all of Jasmine's friends."

"Jim, stop," Jeannine said, startled and shaking at her husband's skewed perspective. "Justin has known Cara since the girls were in preschool together. She has been coming over to this house since she was five years old. He most certainly should know her."

Jim shrugged.

"He's in trouble," Jeannine said quietly. "I know he's in trouble, whether you will admit it or not."

"Why won't you even give him a chance, Jeannine? He needs to know that we believe in him." Jim held up his hand, gesturing once again to make his point. She looked at her husband and could tell without a doubt how much he fervently believed in his son.

"You watch him, Jeannine, just waiting for him to make a mistake."

"Did he say something to you?" Jeannine inquired. "Did he say something about me?"

She had been observing Justin since his return from rehab, but she hoped she had done it without him noticing that he was being watched. And there was no way that any of the family could know that she went into his room, rifling through his drawers and the clothes in his closet to see if anything, any drugs, were stashed away. She always entered his room with laundry to be put away or would grab his wastebasket as if she were cleaning up; no one could know she was looking for something that she, more than anything, did not want to find.

"No, he hasn't said a thing, but I know you well, Jeannine. I can tell how you feel without you having to say the words. If he thinks you don't have his back, if he finds out, well, he will be crushed."

"I have his back," Jeannine said now between clenched teeth. She did not intend to get angry, but she could feel anger flaring hot and deep in her stomach. "I have his back," she repeated, "we have his back. This whole family has always supported him and had his back! Jim, you can't just support and agree with him unquestioningly. You can't let him snow you. Remember before he left for rehab? Justin stood right there," and she pointed to a spot in the living room in front of the couch, "and made an impassioned speech about how he was sober and had been for months. Two nights later, he passed out in the hallway right in front of Jasmine. He almost overdosed, if you remember."

"If I remember? What the hell, Jeannine, of course I remember. And he is not snowing me."

"What did they say at that family session at rehab? Do you remember, Jim? Never trust a person with an addiction."

"He's not an addict," Jim snorted.

She could see that he was getting angry, too.

"He's an 18-year-old kid! Look, I did my share of drugs in college, and I could probably drink him under the table if I were his age. Look at me now, I am perfectly fine. No, I didn't take pills, but they weren't around when we were in college. I certainly would have if they had been around. He's a normal kid, that's all. They go overboard at rehab. It's all doom and gloom all the time. Ok, he started young. He took it a little too far. He's over it all now. I know. I can tell."

"You can't know, Jim, you can't be sure."

"And you are so sure he is using then, are you? Do you have any proof?"

"No, no, I don't," Jeannine said, looking down.

"Then why can't you believe in him? You must stop resenting him for something that is not his fault."

"How, Jim, how is his drug use not his fault?"

Jim ran his hands over his face and abruptly stopped speaking. Then he said quietly, "No, Jeannine, not the drug use. I think....."

Jim hesitated, "No, never mind."

Jeannine stared at her husband, her eyes never leaving his face as she watched him look everywhere but directly at her. "Say it, Jim," she said in a voice just above a whisper, "if you have something to say, say it." She wasn't sure what he was going to say, but she thought she knew what he was referring to.

He sighed deeply and said, "Look, I understand it. You were extremely disappointed. The money for the trip to Bermuda covered his extended rehab stay."

His words felt as real as if he had slapped her in the face. She could not even speak at first, but then the words tumbled out in a louder and angrier voice than she wished. "Jim, you think I wanted to go on a vacation instead of helping my son. I resent my son because I didn't get my vacation. What kind of person do you think I am?" She looked at him challengingly. He did not speak. Jeannine had no more words to say. She walked away.

CHAPTER 36

JEANNINE FELT HER HEARTBEAT speed up as she heard Jasmine's feet pound down the stairs. Justin was out at a team meeting, and Jim had finally agreed to listen to the story Jasmine had told her one week ago. Perhaps hearing directly from Jasmine might convince Jim where Jeannine's own words had been unable to. Jeannine was sure that Jim had been avoiding this discussion. He was busy when Jasmine was home or too tired after work for a discussion. Jeannine finally pinned him down and insisted he listen to Jasmine's story. "Justin is fine," Jim had repeated just moments ago, right before Jeannine called Jasmine to come downstairs.

Could saying Justin was fine make the words come true? If so, then Justin would be fine. Jim honestly believed his son was well, that his drug use was over, done. But were words enough if the reality did not match? Jeannine would have wished her son well, too, if she could, but she could not. She could not believe so easily and so fully as Jim did. Only last night, when Justin had come home, missing curfew yet again, Jasmine had looked at him, grabbed her laptop, and fled the room, knowing what was coming before any voices were raised. Jasmine was hiding in her own home. Jeannine's heart was breaking for both of her children. On some level, she knew that she was losing both of them.

"Dad," Jasmine started, looking down at the floor. Her mother patted her shoulder encouragingly.

"Go on, tell him exactly what you told me. You're not in trouble. I already told you that."

"What, Jazzy, what is it?" he said, smiling and encouraging her.

She glared at him in response. He had forgotten again that she no longer wanted to be called Jazzy. Suddenly, the nickname had become babyish overnight. It would always be a sign of his affection for her, and he couldn't see what was so bad about the name. It wasn't as if her nickname was Pooh Bear, which was precisely what they had called Justin when he was a toddler.

"Jasmine, Jasmine," he repeated, clearing his throat and looking at her seriously. "Please, tell me what you think is important for me to know."

Jasmine sighed, looking over at her mother once again for support. She rocked back in the chair, causing the old springs to squeak.

"Last Saturday, I said I was spending the night with Cara?"

She said it as a question. He nodded.

"I was with Cara, but we weren't at her house initially. We went to a party. One of the seniors on the football team."

"Why were you at a seniors' party? You know you're not supposed to attend house parties. I am assuming the parents weren't there."

Jeannine placed a hand on his knee to stop his words. She pressed a finger to her lips to admonish him to listen. Jasmine looked down.

"Yeah, well, it was a lot wilder than we thought it would be. We wanted to leave, but we had to wait for a ride from Cara's brother, who had just dropped us off. There was a lot of drinking, bottles everywhere, people smoking, and yes, Dad, I mean weed. And pills—there were candy dishes of pills. It was gross. So many people were wasted."

"You shouldn't have been there," he interjected.

"Let her finish," Jeannine forcefully said.

"I know that, Dad, and I didn't like it there. Not one bit, but it's not just that."

She hesitated.

"Did something happen? Did someone hurt you?" He felt bile rising in his throat at the very thought.

"No, Dad, but someone was there."

"Who?" he said, although deep in his stomach, he already knew the answer.

"Justin, Dad, Justin was there."

"Ok," he said. "So, Justin told us no more parties, and he went. He is a senior," and he looked imploringly at his wife.

"Jasmine, are you telling us all this to get yourself out of trouble, ratting out Justin before he rats you out for lying?"

"Dad," Jasmine said, looking at him with something close to disgust on her face. "It's not about me."

Now she was angry, and her words were spilling out rapidly.

"Justin wasn't just there. He was using, carrying around a fifth of whiskey by its neck, clearly wasted, Dad. I watched him, and so did Cara. He was taking whatever he could get his hands on. He was so out of it, he didn't even know I was there. He's still using. He's not clean like he says."

"Are you sure he wasn't just having a couple of drinks?"

"NO! Dad, he was so high. Talk to Cara if you don't believe me."

"He's in trouble, he needs help," Jeannine interjected. "It is getting worse every week. He's escalating, Jim."

Jasmine nodded. Jim ran his hand through his hair and sighed.

"Thanks for telling us, Jasmine."

"I don't even know if you believe me, Dad, you are disgusting," and her lip curled as she looked at him. She jumped from the chair, and he heard her feet pounding loudly on the stairs.

Jeannine sighed loudly and slammed the book she had been reading closed. With reluctance, Jim placed the Popular Mechanics magazine he had been pretending to look at on the arm of his chair. He looked over at his wife. She shook her head. "Jim, we must talk about Justin and what Jasmine told us."

Jim nodded, swallowing and looking down at the same time.

"He's in trouble. We have to help him before it's too late."

"Too late, Jeannine? That's a little dramatic, don't you think?"

She knitted her eyebrows together and gave him the same harsh stare Jasmine had earlier. "No, it is not a little dramatic, Jim. He could die. Millions of people do every year."

"He promised me he wasn't using anymore, though!"

"But Jim, Jasmine has given us concrete evidence that that is untrue. Maybe he can't stop even if he wants to. We can't sweep this under the rug. Doing nothing is doing something, you know. Doing nothing allows the problem to continue. I think he needs rehab again, whether you think so or not."

"I'll talk to him. I've known all night that is what I need to do. Let's see what he says before jumping to conclusions."

"When, Jim, when will you talk to him?"

"He should be home in an hour. I'll speak with him tonight, I promise."

"Don't let him gloss it over like he always does with you."

Jim could feel anger rising deeply from his belly.

"I said I'll speak with him unless you want to, if I am so incapable and useless!"

"I didn't say that, Jim. He will respond better to you; you have always been close."

"Jeannine, I'm unsure how to say this, but I think it must be addressed."

"What?" she responded, puzzled.

He rubbed the back of his neck and focused on the magazine resting on the arm of the chair instead of on Jeannine's face.

"Well, this story is all coming from Jazzy about this party. You know as well as I do that Cara and Jazzy are great kids, but let's face it, neither one of them is exactly part of the popular, 'in' crowd."

"And what does that have to do with anything?"

"What they saw might have looked worse because they are innocent and don't hang out in those circles. Look, you know I was just like Justin in high school. Yeah, we got a little wild. We drank, we partied, we smoked. Pills weren't that big, but when some acid came around, we tried it. If and when they were around, the kids like Jazzy were always horrified at us, like we were the big, bad derelicts. Well, I turned out fine, as did most of my friends."

"So, let me get this straight: because Jasmine is not that popular, she can't see things get out of control at a party?"

"Jeannine, you know that Jazzy is like you as well as I do, and Justin has always been more like me."

"Jim, it seems like you're digging a deep hole here, but go on."

"You and Jasmine are wonderful. You know how much I love both of you. But when you were young, when I met you, you were pretty much a straight arrow, and so is Jazzy. You don't think seeing kids doing shots or smoking would be a little bit frightening to those girls? You had your first shot with me, and you choked so much you almost threw up all over the bar, you must remember! Justin is a popular senior who plays all sports. Yeah, he does remind me of myself. I was wild, too, and I turned out fine. Look, I am sitting here with you. I'm not an alcoholic or a homeless heroin addict. I think Justin is partying and finding his way, and yeah, I think Jazzy might have misinterpreted what she saw."

Jeannine shook her head. "You are unbelievable. You think because he is popular, he is somehow immune to having a drug problem. And what you think of Jasmine and me is that we are losers with no social skills who can't even fit in at a party."

"Jeannine, I never said that! I take what she says with a grain of salt, though, and I believe that Justin deserves the benefit of the doubt, not a rush to judgment."

"Jim, drugs are different than when we were kids. Everything, even pot, is stronger now; it's nothing to mess around with."

"I know that, so I will talk to him tonight. If you want to be here while we talk, feel free."

Jeannine sighed and shook her head, her lips curling slightly as she looked at him. "No, Jim, you talk to him alone. I'm getting a terrible headache, plus I'm sure an unpopular loser like me could not possibly understand what a party for popular kids might be like."

"Jeannine," Jim sighed and reached out his arm to touch her, but she brushed past him quickly, knocking the magazine still on the arm of the chair to the floor. He heard her footsteps run up the stairs in a staccato rhythm like Jazzy's had.

Great, he had managed to offend her in so many ways, and he had no idea whether he was right or wrong about Justin.

CHAPTER 37

JIM AWOKE WITH A START as he heard the key in the lock. He had fallen asleep waiting for Justin. He checked his watch. Justin was fifteen minutes past curfew. Not perfect, but not that bad. Jim rubbed his eyes and took a deep breath. He said a silent prayer that Justin would enter the room sober and not chemically altered in any way. He moved to the edge of his recliner, swiveling his head to view Justin directly. Justin was humming tunelessly as he entered the room, looking down and not noticing his dad's presence. Jim's heart leapt. He was fine! Jeannine and Jasmine were overreacting. He wasn't high! But just as those thoughts flew through Jim's mind, he watched Justin stagger and grab for the wall to steady himself. Jim's heart plummeted.

"Justin," Jim said quietly.

"Whaa..," he slurred, looking toward Jim and squinting, becoming aware of his father's presence for the first time.

"Justin, come here," Jim said solemnly. "We need to talk."

"Dad, now?" Justin said. "I'm tired, exhausted!"

His voice sounded funny, as if he were trying with all his might to control something.

"Yes, Justin, I think we need to talk now. Please sit down, only for a few minutes, then you can head to bed."

Jim tried to put a smile into his voice. He was extremely glad that Jeannine was not there. She would be judging Justin, maybe even yelling at him already. At least with it being just the two of them, they could have a normal conversation. Jim tried to ignore the clumsy way that Justin moved over to the couch, hanging onto the arm of the piece of furniture for support. Once seated, Justin looked at his father with half-closed eyes.

"Justin," Jim sighed. "Have you been drinking?"

Justin held up a hand. "Ok, ok, Dad, I might as well admit it. I had a couple with the guys. Just a couple. They hit me pretty hard since I haven't had a drink in a while. I was fine driving, but I only noticed that I was feeling it slightly as I walked in the door."

"Nothing else, Justin? Have you taken any drugs?"

"No, Dad, I swear. I am done with that shit, that stuff, sorry Dad. I promised you, remember?"

Jim nodded.

"What?" Justin questioned.

Jim sighed.

"Jasmine says she saw you last week at a party and that you were really out of it, definitely high."

"What! And she waits a week to tell you! What party?" he said, looking confused.

Jim furrowed his brow. The comments did not seem to match. Either he didn't know about the party, which would make "What party" the correct answer, or "Why did she wait a week," which sounded like he knew, maybe even that Jasmine had been there. The two comments didn't jibe.

"Justin, were you at a party a week ago, and did you know your sister was there?"

Justin sighed, "Ok, ok, I went to the party. It was for Sam and the last party before they move away. All the guys were after me to go. How could I say no?"

"Damn it, Justin, our deal was no more parties—too many temptations. If you needed to say goodbye to Sam, we could have worked something out if you had told me. I could have picked you up and dropped you off—less time for you to be there and be tempted."

"Right, Dad, I want to go there, but then I have to leave because Daddy is out front. I'm not thirteen years old!"

"You knew your sister was there? You didn't do anything about it at a wild party like that?"

Justin snorted. "I don't know what she told you, but it wasn't a wild party. It was a get-together to say goodbye to Sam. There was a tub with a few beers, but that was about it."

"Justin, Jasmine said there was booze everywhere and all kinds of drugs, bowls full of pills."

Justin snorted again. "Man, that kid has an active imagination, huh? It was nothing like that. It was very low-key. I didn't even know why Jasmine and Cara showed up, though. They didn't stay long. Looks to me like they got bored pretty quickly. We were all just sitting around talking about the team, football plays, and so on. I didn't say anything to protect Jasmine. She's the one who is not supposed to be at senior parties, not me."

"You aren't supposed to be at parties at all, Justin."

"And I wasn't at a party technically, Dad, because I wasn't drinking or using. I was saying goodbye to Sam. I don't know what Jasmine saw or what she thinks she saw, but it was nothing. Nothing happening there at all!"

"Justin, if I tell your mother that you've come in tonight after drinking, you know she'll say you need rehab."

"Dad, two beers, and I didn't finish the second one. I am clean! Come on, you understand better than they do. Give me a break. You know what it's like to be young and on a team. They don't. I can't believe you don't trust me. Mom, I understand. Jasmine, she's so innocent; she would probably think a party with some parents' beer in the fridge was too much. I swear to you, Dad, I am clean. I'm slightly buzzed right now, but that's because I haven't had a drop in months. That's why it hit me so hard. Come on, Dad!"

"Justin, if I keep this from your mom, you have to promise me right here and right now that it will not happen again. No drinking, not even a sip, until graduation."

Justin raised a hand as if taking an oath. "I promise, Dad. No more. It won't happen again. I am fine."

Jim nodded, allowing himself a slight smile for the first time. "Ok, Justin, we'll let this time slide. Just promise me that you're ok."

"I am fine, Dad, for sure. There's no problem here."

"Ok, son, get to bed," Jim said, rising from the chair.

Justin stood too, but his knees buckled slightly, and he almost fell back onto the couch.

"I'm tired, Dad," Justin said in response.

CHAPTER 38

"HE MISSED CURFEW AGAIN, JIM. How long are we going to let this go on? He didn't come home last night at all."

Jeannine's words were clipped, and her gaze at him contained barely contained anger, even fury.

"He is not getting better or trying to change, needs to be given a break, or any other platitudes you like to mouth about his situation. Jim, something needs to be done now. It has needed to be done for months, but you bury your head in the sand."

"Are you even sure he isn't home, Jeannine?" Jim challenged. "I just walked by his room, and the door is closed. Are you sure he isn't in there? He always leaves the door open when he goes out. Why would he close it this time?"

"He used to leave the door open, you mean. He has been closing his door all the time for the last few months, and you know it, Jim."

Jeannine slammed her coffee cup on the counter.

"He is not home. I was awake all night—all night, Jim—every minute listening for the car in the driveway, and he, I repeat, did not come home. Unlike you, who has no worries about your son, I didn't sleep at all."

Now, Jim was angry at the direct challenges and how dare she say he wasn't worried about Justin? Of course he was—any father would be!

Suddenly, Jazzy appeared in the kitchen, her hair still tousled from sleep. She wore rainbow leggings and an oversized t-shirt with a bear winking and waving. The outfit made her look much younger than her fourteen years. She looked at both her parents, and her mouth turned down in dismay when she realized they were arguing again. His happy family had turned angry and surly almost overnight. "Jazzy," Jim said, trying to smile and remembering at the last minute how she now hated the old nickname. "Do me a favor: Go to Justin's room, open the door, and tell me if he's sleeping there."

"He's not, Jim," Jeannine said.

Jasmine stopped and looked at her mother as if she were questioning whether his directive deserved to be followed.

Jeannine glared at him but then said, softening her voice, "Go ahead, Jasmine, check his room."

Jasmine turned and scooted out of the room. He heard Justin's bedroom door open. He realized he was holding his breath and praying that she would return to say that he was sleeping or that he would hear Justin yell out, "Leave me alone." He closed his eyes, and Jeannine continued to stare into her coffee cup without drinking. Jasmine re-entered the kitchen. She was shaking her head.

"No, Dad, he isn't there, and his bed is made. Looks like he hasn't slept in it at all."

"I told you," Jeannine said.

Jim ran his hand through his hair and moved out of the kitchen into the living room, opening the blinds to let the morning light in and give him something to do. He stopped with the blinds only partially open. In the driveway, parked right next to his van, was Justin's car, pulled straight into the space. The vehicle wasn't askew or crooked as someone drunk might have parked, but pulled in precisely and straightly. Jim cleared his throat, feeling his stomach make a happy jump. Justin was fine! He was home! So much for Mrs. and Miss Gloom.

"Jeannine, Jasmine," he called out. "He is home—his car's in the driveway. Everything's fine. You're sure he wasn't in his room, Jasmine?"

"Dad," Jasmine whined, "He wasn't in there, ok? What do you think I'm stupid?"

"Ok, ok," Jim said. "He must have slept in the car; I'll get him."

"Slept in the car, Jim, and why do you think he would do that? Because he was too drunk or too stoned to make it into the house. That's still a problem. Damn it, Jim, just because he's home doesn't mean everything is ok."

"Let me get him and we'll talk," Jim said, opening the front door, jumping quickly off the two steps, and crossing the grass to the car. He would shake his son awake if he were still asleep. He would get him in the house, and it would all be over. Hopefully, he wouldn't be too noticeably hungover. So what if he had to cover for the kid once again? He was sowing some wild oats. It would all stop soon enough, and he would come to his senses. Jim pulled open the car door. Yep, Justin was right there in the driver's seat. Jim noticed his head slumped over at what appeared to be an uncomfortable angle. He whispered loudly, "Justin, wake up."

There was no response, no flutter of an eyelash or intake of breath. He touched his son's shoulder. Something didn't feel right. He pressed harder, yet Justin did not move or flinch away from him at all. Suddenly, Jim felt a sense of unreality, as if he were out of his body and watching himself from a distance.

"Justin," he said louder, shaking his son's shoulder. Justin did not feel right! There was no movement in his body and no warmth. He placed another hand on his son's chest. He felt cold and hard. Jim shook him harder, watching his head loll to one side due to his abrupt movement. As Jim pulled on him, his head flopped toward him, and he saw blood pooled on the side of his face. Frantically, now, he clutched at his arm. It was so, so cold on this warm spring morning.

"NO, no, Justin!" Jim heard a voice repeating and only then thought, Oh, that is me. He continued to touch his son, willing him to be something other than what he was, cold and unmoving, lifeless. He felt for a pulse, but there was no sign of life moving through his son, through his baby, through his firstborn. He heard an ear-curdling scream directly behind him. He turned to see Jeannine collapse into a heap in the driveway, almost as if she had no bones in her body. He saw Jazzy approaching the car.

"Jazzy, no, no," he barked, "turn around, go back!" Jazzy continued toward the car with a look of determination on her face. As she reached the car, she began to sob. Jim reached out an arm toward her, but at the same time began to be blinded by flashes of black. The next few minutes—or were they hours?—flew by in a haze. Later, all that Jim could recall about that time was an image of himself sitting on his butt in the grass as ambulance lights flashed and two men loaded Justin into the ambulance in a body bag.

CHAPTER 39

JIM SAT AT THE FUNERAL. It didn't seem real; it was like a movie playing before his eyes. There was Justin's coffin and Justin lying there as if asleep. They were seated on the side in the family section, separated from the other mourners by some weird, ugly beige curtain. Jim could see some of the mourners and tell by the buzzing and whispering that many more people than he could see were present. He heard stifled sobs. He looked at Jeannine and Jasmine, watching them cry openly as they hugged each other. Jim sat in the chair, immobile. They did not reach out to him, and he did not try to touch them either. He sat silently, unmoving, his eyes never wavering from the coffin. The minister was saying something, but Jim was unable to decipher what any of the words were. The receiving line after the service was the worst. There were so many crying, some stoic and solemn, many work colleagues and kids from school, plus both Jazzy and Justin's friends. Justin's entire football team came through with their enormous crush of bodies towering over Jeannine and Jazzy. So many people gripped his hand solemnly and repeatedly told him to take care of Jeannine and Jasmine.

"They'll need a lot of help," they would intone solemnly. Ok, OK, he got that! But what about me? He wanted to scream. Even the damn minister imploring him to look after the girls, "they need you now." Didn't he need any help? Why were they all so sure that he was fine? Just because he wasn't crying, sobbing, or showing any emotion didn't mean he was fine. Are you people fucking stupid? he wanted to yell. He wasn't fine; he was far from fine. Something was so broken inside him that he couldn't believe others couldn't see the jagged edges running through him. But apparently, no one could see; they were all blind, including his friends, family, and the minister. No one could see what was raging quietly inside him, and no one was coming to help him put this raging fire out. He stared into the distance, nodding solemnly from time to time. How could no one know? Why wouldn't anyone come to help him?

♦ ♦ ♦

The service and the reception were over. Leaving Justin in the graveyard had been grueling, had made it seem all too real. No more pretending that he was still alive now, was there? He had been doing that a few times this past week. Jeannine and Jasmine didn't know that he was doing the pretending, but if he could make the pain lessen for even a few seconds, it seemed somehow worth it. Everyone had left. The minister was approaching them to say his goodbyes. *Good,* Jim thought, *please go.* He had a banging headache and only wanted to return home. When they returned, he wanted Justin to be there, splayed out on the couch and saying, "What took you guys so long? Can we get a pizza? I'm starving!" The minister gave Jeannine a warm hug. He clapped Jim on the back, then grabbed his hand. "Justin will always be with you," the minister intoned solemnly.

What the hell, was this guy somehow reading his thoughts? That was way too creepy! "Always be with me," Jim thought as he nodded silently at Reverend Jeremiah. He thought, *What crazy shit is this guy droning on about?*

But now, months, almost a year after Justin had gone, he did understand. He now knew what the Reverend meant because he felt Justin was there. He was often nearby, standing beside him. He took great comfort in talking to Justin on the phone or in person. It soothed him to know that Justin was there.

CHAPTER 40

One year prior - Debra

DEBRA SAT QUIETLY looking at her husband, not crying, but staring fixedly. She watched him take first ragged breaths only moments before, followed by more shallow breaths. And now, nothing, total cessation. She knew he was gone. She should have called Devon and David to have her daughter and son-in-law here with her, but it was so impossibly early, or was it impossibly late? Either way, Debra had not wanted to call them, even when she knew the end was coming for Ron. Debra had wanted, no, needed, to be alone with Ron. It had been the only way, and now it was all over. Debra basked in the quiet, knowing there would be no peace for the next several days or weeks as soon as she moved to the phone. Debra also knew that once she saw her daughter and best friend, Kathy, she would cry and mourn for the man she had been married to for over thirteen years. Right now, though, she could only stare at the body of the person she loved so much. She looked at him lying in the hospital bed, and still, without crying, she whispered, "Forgive me, Ron."

"David, David, get out here," Devon yelled through the door at top volume.

"Devon, I'm in the shower," David yelled back. "What could possibly be so importa—" but before he could finish saying the word, he heard a sob right outside the door. David immediately turned the water off, jumped out of the tub, and grabbed the adjacent towel. As he opened the door, he saw Devon perched on the edge of the bed, her phone in her hand, but crying too much to talk. She looked up at him as he quickly strode over to her, bending down and placing his hand on her knee.

"Your mom?" he whispered. Devon only nodded. Suddenly, David knew what was happening, and feelings began crashing through his mind like loosened bricks from a collapsing wall. David gently pried the phone from his wife's clutching hand and held it to his ear.

"Debra?" he inquired softly.

"Oh, David," she said in a surprisingly clear voice unmarred by the tears or sobs he thought he might hear.

"David," Debra repeated, "I've upset Devon terribly. I feel so bad."

"Is it Ron?" David whispered, unsure why he thought it was appropriate to keep his voice so quiet.

"Yes, yes, it is. Ron is gone," Debra affirmed.

"Are you sure?" David questioned. "Do you need to call the rescue? Is he in a coma, maybe?"

"No, David, he's gone. I know that for sure. Can you two please come over now? I know it's early, but..."

"Of course, we'll be right there. Are you alone? Is anyone with you?"

"It's just the two of us, Ron and I," Debra said, but stopped abruptly. "Oh, yes, it's just me," and David heard his mother-in-law's voice break for the first time.

"We're on our way," David said firmly. "We'll be right there."

CHAPTER 41

"IS SHE SLEEPING?" Devon whispered as Debra's best friend, Kathy, exited the bedroom. It was just approaching afternoon. The mortician had removed Ron's body from the house over an hour ago and taken it to the mortuary. Both Devon and Kathy had helped Debra make the needed calls. Devon had called Kathy after arriving at her mother's house.

"I'm leaving for a business trip tomorrow," Kathy had said before realizing what had happened. Kathy hastily canceled the trip to help Devon and spend some time with her best friend, whom she hadn't seen in months. Kathy shook her head.

"I got her to lie down at least. I handed her a pill, but she put it down on the dresser, so I don't think she took it."

"Kathy, she seems messed up," Devon said sadly. "I know she's upset. Of course, we're all upset, but she is acting so weird."

Kathy nodded, then moved closer to where Devon and David held hands on the sofa. She whispered, even though the bedroom in the large house was too far away for Debra to hear any words they were saying. "Maybe it was too much for her. Maybe it was all too much for her. She was taking care of Ron by herself for all those months. She pushed us all away. Maybe I should have tried harder to connect with her." Kathy shook her head.

"I think being alone was what Ron wanted, but was it really what your mom wanted? He was so sick. I don't think he realized how hard it was for Debra."

Devon looked over at her husband. "We were thinking the same thing! She seems so out of it, so off and disconnected. I know Ron just died, but still."

Devon started to cry again.

"She hasn't cried either, at least not in front of us. Has she cried with you?"

Kathy shook her head. "She might be in shock, Devon. We don't know what happened during Ron's last moments. She'll get better, Devon."

Kathy attempted to soothe Devon. "She just needs some time."

A shadow passed in the hallway, causing all three of them to look up, and then suddenly, Debra entered the room.

"What are you doing up?" Kathy said kindly.

Devon stood as if to go to her mother. Debra smoothed her hair.

"We need to go to the funeral home now."

Kathy frowned. "No, Debra, they said to come first thing in the morning."

"You should sleep now, Mother," Devon said worriedly. "You look like you haven't slept in weeks." Devon approached her mother to give her a hug, but Debra moved away, patting her daughter's shoulder instead.

"I can't. I can't sleep. I just can't."

"Did you take the pill, Debra?" David inquired gently. "It might help."

Debra shook her head and said firmly, "No, I will not take a pill. Kathy, please help me. First, we need to select a suit for Ron. You know he will want to look nice. Then, we have to coordinate everything. You know how meticulous he was!"

Debra started to walk back in the direction of the bedroom. Kathy began to follow, but then turned to look back at Devon. Devon shrugged.

"Of course, honey," Kathy said, moving after Debra.

"My mom is acting so strange," Devon whispered to David. "I can't lose her, too!"

"I know, I know," David murmured, enveloping Devon in a hug.

CHAPTER 42

DEBRA SIGHED AND RUBBED the spot above her nose, right between her eyebrows. She had another headache, but was so glad to be home. She had seen how Kathy had looked at her with so much pity in her eyes.

"It must be hard to go home alone now, Debra. Isn't it?" Kathy had said, patting her arm.

Debra had to use every bit of strength to stop herself from flinching away from the gentle touch. Instead, she only silently nodded and wished again to talk to the only person who had understood her, Ron. But he was gone now, wasn't he? And really, he had been unable to help her or talk to her for the last few months. And if he could speak to her, would he want to now, after what she had done, how she had behaved? If she believed in ghosts, and she most decidedly did not, how could he possibly comfort her or offer her words of wisdom as he had done so many times before getting sick? Of course, no one knew or could understand, but she had not been the caretaker or the loving wife they all thought she was. She wasn't worried that Ron's ghost would come back to haunt her; she was more worried that if there were souls in the afterlife, his would ignore her, pretend she didn't exist. After all, she had done that for him when he was here, right? Debra knew that her friends, even Devon, thought she should be recovering from her loss by now, moving on, getting over it. Most people think grief and death are like a bad flu: you are treated kindly for about two weeks, and then it's "buck up, ok, let's get over it now, move along, move along." No one wanted to talk about her feelings; they only wanted to pay lip service and talk about something else. That way, they felt better; they had paid their respects, but then they could talk about another topic entirely. If Debra brought death back up, more than one friend would grip her hand, pat her, and say sympathetically, "Let's talk about something else," as if ignoring her feelings, her grief, would make it all vanish right away. If it was this hard for them even to acknowledge death, there was no hope that there was anyone to have a substantive conversation with about deeper, more complicated feelings, such as, "Yes, I sucked as a caretaker, you have no idea. He's dead because of me." If she had said those thoughts, their heads would probably have blown away in a puff of smoke. Debra had tried to see someone at Kathy's suggestion. Yeah, right, that had worked out well as she needed to drive through the city in heavy traffic. Ron had always driven into the city; she had never had to, so she was on edge before arriving there. Once there, to have some lady, younger than her, who probably hadn't even had anyone close to her die, stare at her for fifty minutes or ask her in a hushed voice how she felt. "How do I feel, dear? I feel like shit! What do you think about that?"

"You have to try, Mom," Debra heard Devon's strident voice in her ears.

Well, she had tried. She had even bravely brought up the medication. Of course, she had danced around the topic, but she had been partially truthful. She had mentioned how constant and how fatiguing it had been the last few weeks, giving Ron the pills, remembering to give Ron the pills on time, then monitoring the pills' effects: was he in too much pain, had she given him too little, or had she given him too much, would he go into shock as he had twice after taking the pills. The doctor said that his weight was fluctuating so much and his body was breaking down so quickly that it was hard, if not impossible, to gauge if a dose would be correct or too much. And when the medication pump had finally arrived, well, that had been no better. She was constantly aware that she probably had the power to end his life at any moment. She had been under constant wear and tear, watching death approach, and then, if he was having a better day, watching it recede, but still there, lurking never far away. She had wanted to be a good caretaker, but it was emotionally, mentally, and physically fatiguing. She had just wanted it to be over. She had stopped there and looked up at the therapist, who had only smiled at her gently. Smiled! She wasn't talking about a good sale she had found on shoes. She stopped and said no more, and the therapist maintained the silence until Debra rose from her position on the brown couch surrounded by all those damn pillows and walked out, never to return.

CHAPTER 43

"OK, DEBRA, I didn't see anything in the backyard. I shined the light everywhere, and with that recent rain, it is muddy enough that I think footsteps would show up if someone had been walking around. I checked the door and all your windows, and everything is secure. It doesn't look to me like anyone has been back there. Are you sure you heard a knock at the back door?" David questioned.

Debra had called Dave and Devon in a panic about an hour ago. She had become convinced she had heard someone at the back door trying to get in. She had crept toward the door, staying far enough back that she was sure she couldn't be seen through the glass. She had heard the noise a second time; it had sounded like a knock, and she was sure it wasn't the wind. This time it was accompanied by what sounded like a low wail. She remembered the old urban legend about serial killers who would record crying babies and then place the recording next to women's doors to entice them to fling the door open without further thought. It occurred to her to call the police, but what if she was wrong? What if it was nothing? She would look like a fool! But what if it was someone? Her thoughts were complicated by the situation that had occurred that afternoon. She was reading when she heard a car door slam in the driveway. She had jumped up to peer out the window and had observed two men exiting a rather beat-up-looking black car. They were walking quickly to her door. Her heartbeat thumped out a quickening rhythm. Her stomach clutched as she realized for the gazillionth time how very much she missed Ron. She hadn't realized how she had let him answer all the phone calls and the infrequent visitors to their door. All she had to do was yell, "Ron, phone, Ron, door," and he was there. It had been that way for so long that she had taken it all for granted. It started a long time ago. Devon was still a young teenager. She had had difficulty getting rid of an overly persistent telemarketer. Both Devon and Ron had stood in the doorway laughing at her inept attempts to hang up the phone and get away while still being polite, of course, oh, yes, of course, always so polite. She remembered Ron, a much younger Ron, so handsome in her mind, striding over, grabbing the phone from her hand, and saying briskly and firmly, "We're not interested, goodbye now!"

"You better let me handle unwanted visitors and calls from now on," he had said, chuckling.

She did, for years, but now there was no one here but her to answer, and she didn't want to hide. What if they were burglars? Then they would start trying to get in. There had been two raps on the door while she had been lost in thought. She inhaled and strode toward the door, opening it and immediately and obviously locking the screen door as a barrier between them. She didn't say anything but just looked at them purposefully—at least she hoped she looked purposeful.

"Afternoon, ma'am," the taller one said pleasantly. The older, shorter man with glasses leaned on the side of the porch.

"We were just in the neighborhood today and wondered if you might be interested in solar panels. They are great energy savers. Several of your neighbors have them."

Debra shook her head, checking that the screen door was securely fastened. They wore no worker uniforms, and the seedy, old car was far from a work van.

"No, thank you," she tried to say firmly, but even she heard a stutter and a squeak between her words.

"May I ask why not, if I may be so bold?" the taller man said, smiling.

She noticed his partner was not looking directly at her, but casting his eyes around the yard and the contours of the house. Ok, they were starting to creep her out.

"No," she said more firmly this time. "It's not a suitable time," and she emphasized, "WE are not interested right now."

"Okay, energy is expensive, and these can be real money savers. Perhaps I could explain the technology to your husband."

Now they were trying to find out if someone else was home!

"My husband can't be bothered now, and I need you to leave."

Of course, he can't be bothered, Debra, he's dead, a sarcastic voice in her head taunted her.

The older man shrugged and turned to go. The younger one continued to smile and said, "You have a blessed day now," as he turned away.

She quickly slammed the door shut, peering out the farthest window, and watched the car drive away. They had freaked her out! You would have thought she would have had time to adjust in Ron's year of sickness to taking care of all this, but it had been different when he was alive. There was still another person in the house, and when he was better, she would constantly consult, asking for his opinion. She had not realized how much she had relied on him. He had always seemed like an expert, maybe because he was so much older than she, fifteen years. He had never been controlling but always willing to help her handle things when she asked; apparently, she had asked a lot without even realizing it! Debra had stayed freaked out by the men for probably half an hour, and after checking the driveway several times and not seeing them return, she had relaxed and forgotten about the incident.

The night—everything was always worse at night. Ron had been sicker; his pain had been worse in the dark of night. Knowing that she wouldn't easily reach a doctor had made her monitoring of Ron even more critical. Even after all these months, she still hated to see darkness fall. It was two a.m. when she first heard the knock, then the strange noise, the wail, the soft yowl. Her heart quickened, and she grabbed her phone. She thought of the police, but what if it was nothing? She would look like a crazy old lady. She immediately remembered how the last time David had left with Devon, he had placed his hand on her shoulder and said, "If you ever need anything, Debra, you call us. I mean it, anything."

She listened and heard the rustle at the door once more. She flicked the phone on and called Devon and David's number without another thought.

"Thank you, Dave, thank you so much."

He looked perplexed but said kindly, "Debra, you're sure you heard someone at the back door?"

"Maybe it was the wind, Mother," Devon said tightly.

"No," Debra shook her head firmly. "It was more than the wind. Two men were here earlier today trying to sell me something; they creeped me out."

"Mother!" Devon said, now clearly exasperated, "You should have called the police. What was David supposed to do if a bad person was back there anyway, shine his flashlight at them? Blind them by shining the light in their eyes!"

Debra looked down. She knew Devon sounded harsh, but she had always gotten this way when she was scared, and now, she could tell that Devon was scared both for her and for Dave.

"It was probably nothing. I guess I was wrong. I shouldn't have called. It might just have been that old gray cat of Mr. Moore's. He has been prowling a lot lately."

"A cat? After all this, you think it might be a cat."

"Dev, calm down," David said, touching her shoulder.

Devon angered quickly, just like her real father, whom she didn't even know. How much of the emotion of anger was genetic? Debra wondered.

"Mom, David has to get up in — oh, look — three hours now. He has that big presentation for that new customer."

"Oh, David!" Debra said, looking concerned. "I am so sorry. I forgot all about that."

Devon sniffed. Debra looked at them. David was wearing pajama bottoms under his jacket, and Devon, who usually always dressed to the nines, had on sweatpants, and her hair was falling out of a messy ponytail. Clearly, Debra had called them over, and they had been sound asleep in bed, and now she had disturbed David and ensured he would be tired for his important work presentation.

"I am so sorry," Debra said, looking stricken.

David shook his head. "Stop, Debra, we will be here for you anytime. Don't worry about it."

Devon was still glowering, then she spoke. "Mother, if you are afraid to be here, maybe it's time to consider moving out of the house and getting an apartment. You would be around other people. You could even find a place with security. Ron has been gone long enough now. You need to start getting over it all and move on."

"Devon," David said, frowning at her. "Don't push your mother. It's no problem."

Devon sighed heavily. "Okay, Mr. Nice Guy, be all Mr. Perfect here and complain about everything when we get in the car, David, like you usually do."

Debra looked down, crestfallen.

"We have to go," Devon huffed. She gave her mother a half-hug and walked out the door. David looked down, too. He looked up at Debra.

"Are you okay to be alone? You can come home with us. She worries about you a lot; you know how she is."

Debra nodded. She was trying to hold back tears.

"David, I didn't realize it was so late."

"Again, it's no problem."

"But your presentation?"

"I'll be okay, Debra. Family comes first."

"I'm fine now," Debra mustered, trying to smile. "Good luck tomorrow."

David patted her hand and walked out. Debra felt sure there would be little, if any, sleep again tonight.

CHAPTER 44

DEBRA SIGHED LOUDLY. It had been two more long months. Debra still missed Ron terribly. She felt a physical ache in her chest when she thought of him. Now she was driving to a place she wasn't sure she wanted to go. She checked the rearview mirror for the third time before changing lanes and moving onto the exit ramp. The drive into the city had only become hectic in the last ten minutes, so it hadn't been as bad as she thought it might be. She rubbed her hands over the steering wheel, feeling them slide as the wheel was slick with sweat. The traffic wasn't so bad, but that didn't mean she hadn't been nervous. She had always hated driving in traffic, and Ron had always driven whenever they went into the city. Debra felt comfortable and safe in her little bubble of suburbia, where they lived, but the traffic and noise of the city intimidated her and had always done so. Ron had always been happy to drive, even taking her places she needed to go, although she could have gone by herself. He had continued to drive even after he had gotten sick, until he was unable to drive anymore, and by then, he was so ill that neither one of them left home unless it was for a visit to the local doctor or hospital, which were both near their house, thankfully. As Ron had grown sicker, they had both become virtually housebound. Debra had left a few times for errands, but with so much of life now being completed online, she found no need to go out. Groceries and food were delivered; banking was done online, and even some of their doctor appointments had been completed via video.

"4550, 4550," Debra now repeated to herself, reciting the number of the building she was looking for.

"There it is," Debra said aloud, putting on her blinker to turn into the adjacent parking lot. She noticed that several other cars were turning in as well. It was too late to back out now, she thought as she looked left and right for an open parking space. A grief group, she couldn't believe she had come! This meeting in the city was the closest one to her house. Both Kathy and Devon had urged her to attend. She had been putting it off for months. She didn't know if her best friend and daughter had been encouraging her attendance because they noticed how sad and lonely she was, or whether they just wanted her to stop talking about Ron. And yes, she did talk about him a lot. What else was she supposed to talk about? She still rarely left the house. They had been together, married for thirteen years, and had known each other for fifteen years. She couldn't just forget he existed. Everyone else, except Debra, was over Ron's death. He had been gone for over four months. Devon rarely spoke of her stepfather anymore; maybe this was to spare Debra, but Debra thought it was more likely that Devon had just moved on and had other things on her mind. Kathy, her best friend, had mentioned that she might go with Debra to the group at first, even though she hadn't lost anyone.

"I would come for moral support," she had said kindly. However, after Debra had located the grief group, entered the address into her GPS, and informed Kathy of the date and time, she demurred.

"I fly out on a business trip that next morning, and Debra, maybe I shouldn't go anyway. I won't have anything in common with those people; they might not even want me there."

You have me, you have me in common, Debra had wanted to say, but had remained silent instead.

So, now here she was sitting in the parking lot looking at the strange, unfamiliar building. She had come this far. She couldn't just drive away, although part of her wanted to. Debra's heart raced, and she felt her hands and underarms perspiring again. It was so hard to walk into a strange place. Where would she sit? Would the people be kind, ignore her, or be hostile to her? *Stop, Debra, don't be a fool*, she thought. Debra had always been shy, but Ron had given her the strength and confidence she needed.

"You can do it," he would always say. "You'll be great, everything will be fine." Platitudes, sure, but his encouragement, his love, had been her strength. But apparently, she had only been parasitically using his strength and confidence because now that he was gone, every bit of confidence, strength, and efficacy in the world had disappeared along with his physical presence. Only her awkwardness, shyness, and hesitance remained. The group started in ten minutes. She had to get out of the car now.

◆　◆　◆

Debra cast her eyes around the circle of people gathered in the slightly uncomfortable chairs in the center of the room. She was also seated in this circle, next to the group leader, Casey, a younger woman who greeted Debra warmly and led her to the chair next to her own.

"You can speak if you want or listen to the others; it is entirely up to you."

Debra had nodded mutely. There were only twelve of them, so it was not a large group. Three of the women were older than Debra. They looked like they could be in their seventies or even eighties, Debra thought. Another woman, about Debra's age, had a glum, almost angry look on her face, and Debra quickly looked away from her. There were two men. One was a man with a large, muscular build and sandy hair. *He looks about my age*, Debra thought. The other man was young. He was quite thin, with both arms covered with tattoos. He looked serious as he stared into the cup of coffee he held. *"Who had he lost?"* Debra thought. He was so young, she felt bad for him. As Debra continued to glance around at the people in the circle, her eyes came to rest on the man about her age once again, and this time he caught her looking and smiled kindly as he nodded his head slightly. Debra quickly looked away.

"Ok, everyone, it's time, we should get started," Casey said authoritatively. "We have two new people with us tonight. We'll have them introduce themselves in a bit if they're up for it, but let's start with one thing we are grateful for this week. Tell us one positive thing that happened to you this week."

The woman about Debra's age let out a large sigh, and Debra turned toward her, waiting for her to speak.

"Casey, again?" the woman said, irritation oozing between her words. "How is that nonsense supposed to help us? We only have an hour here, and you want to waste time with all that superficial bullshit, hearts and flowers crap. I am probably going to lose my house, you know. Without my husband's income, my life has gone to hell!"

Casey held up a hand.

"I understand, Diane, but sometimes thinking about the good helps; it can even calm the brain and help you formulate solutions to problems you would never solve if you only focus on the negative."

Diane snorted loudly, like a horse, Debra thought in response.

"I'll go," the young man said quietly. "My daughter called me Dada for the first time this week."

Two of the older ladies made an "aww" sound in response.

"It's great, you know," the young man said, "but man, there is so much I don't know about taking care of her. I mean, I read the books, but sometimes I feel so lost. I wish my wife were back to help care for her so much."

The young man started to cry and hid his eyes behind his arm.

"I'll go next," the man about Debra's age said. "I went outside and looked up at the sky and the clouds, and I thought, you know, there is beauty out there; all we have to do is notice it."

"Thank you," Casey said without further comment, as Diane, the unpleasant woman, snorted again.

"Before we get into anything else, maybe we will let the new people introduce themselves now. Ladies, please introduce yourself and share a little about your background. If you aren't even comfortable with that, say pass. Who wants to go first?"

One of the older ladies spoke up immediately.

"I'm Barbara, and my husband, Harold, well, he passed just three weeks ago. We were together for over fifty years. I do miss him."

Silence.

Debra saw Casey cast a glance in her direction. Oh, no, she didn't want to say anything! The silence continued.

Debra inhaled. "I'm Debra. My husband...," and suddenly she felt a large lump in her throat that might cut off all her breath.

"My husband died," she finally choked out. "I can't say more, not yet."

"That's fine, Debra," Casey said gently. "That was great."

She sounded so tongue-tied, so awkward. *What a goof they must all be thinking*, Debra thought. She stared very purposefully at her boots.

"Ok, now let's talk about any challenges we had this week. Diane, I know you mentioned something."

Debra looked up and noticed the man about her age was staring at her. Before Debra could look away, he nodded subtly again, smiled, and winked an eye at her. Debra glanced away. The group continued. Debra was trying to focus but felt so buzzy and lightheaded that it was hard to make sense of any words. He would greet her with a smile whenever she glanced in the man's direction. Debra remembered that he had said his name was Mickey at the beginning of the meeting.

Debra found herself casting more frequent glances in his direction. He was definitely about her age. He was also good-looking, dressed neatly in a black leather jacket. He had kind eyes. She hadn't come here to meet anyone. She couldn't imagine dating, but as she thought that, she realized, Oh, maybe I just did.

Diane, the complainer, monopolized the time, droning on about her finances and how her husband had left her in an impossible situation. Debra glanced back at Mickey again. He raised his eyebrows in response, then smiled once more. This time, Debra smiled back. Ok, so even if she wasn't interested, at least this man seemed to find her attractive. Maybe all hope was not lost if there was something desirable about her, even now.

"Diane, we'll have to continue that at the next meeting," Casey said.

"Ok, folks, stop for coffee and cake before you leave."

"I never get to finish a thought here, do I?" Diane snarled.

Everyone began getting up and stretching, and most were moving back toward a large coffee urn and slices of cake set out on a table at the back of the room. The younger man threw on a motorcycle jacket, said, " gotta get home to my kid," and whooshed out of the room. Debra followed the others back to the table, more to be sociable than anything else. She looked longingly at the door the young man had just exited through. She was ready to go, too.

"It's chocolate, I should have known," the unpleasant Diane remarked.

"Casey, you know I have an allergy."

"Sorry, Diane, we'll have another kind next week," Casey said, seemingly unperturbed by the criticism.

Debra leaned over to pick up one of the smaller pieces of cake. Only then did she notice the man, Mickey, right beside her. He was holding two cups of coffee in his hands.

"One for you, Debra," he said politely.

"Thank you," she said, juggling the cup and the cake.

He touched her gently on the shoulder.

"Here, let's sit down over here, we'll be more comfortable."

He pointed to two adjacent chairs with a small table between them. Debra put her coffee down gratefully.

"Look, Debra, I've been coming here for a while," Mickey said, leaning toward her. "It's so hard at first. You did great tonight."

"I did not do great; I could barely get my name out!"

"You should have seen me," he laughed. "I didn't say anything for three months, not one word. Casey was starting to think I didn't have the power of speech! Your husband…," he said and trailed off.

Debra wasn't sure what he was asking, but feeling emboldened by his attention, she said, "Ron, his name was Ron. He died of cancer."

"Oh," the man said immediately. "What a coincidence, my wife, Patti, had cancer, too. Hard, isn't it?"

"I took care of him mostly by myself," Debra shared, unsure why she was telling this stranger so much!

"Wow," he said, shaking his head. "Me too. I took care of my wife without help, too."

He reached and picked up his Styrofoam cup of coffee. He grimaced as he took a sip. "This coffee is terrible. I bet mud tastes better, although I can't say I've ever tasted mud, so I guess I wouldn't know."

He smiled and gently touched Debra's knee.

"It is pretty awful," Debra agreed.

"Hey, you know what?" Mickey said, leaning toward her. "Why don't we get some decent coffee? I know a cute little shop not too far from here."

Debra hesitated.

"Oh, I'm sorry. Did I overstep? I know, I know, I'm a stranger, but our experiences are so similar. We could talk more. It's so nice to meet someone who understands. I'll drive, or you could take your car."

"I'll take my car," Debra said immediately.

Mickey smiled. "Great, you're going then. Come on, let's get out of here."

Most of the other group members had already left. Debra was surprised to see Casey frown briefly as they walked by her.

"I hope you'll come again, Debra," she said.

Casey only nodded at Mickey. They exited to the parking lot. It was colder than when they had arrived, and Debra shivered.

"Darn," Mickey said, "I left my jacket on the chair. I'll be right back."

He skimmed his arm across her shoulder as he walked away, which Debra was unsure if she liked. Should she even be doing this? she wondered, but the attention felt good. She had felt invisible for so long now.

"Donna, Donna, I need to talk to you," she heard Diane call.

Debra looked around to see who she was yelling at, but they were alone in the parking lot. Diane crossed right to Debra. "Look, Donna, I know you don't know me."

"Debra, it's Debra," she said.

"Oh, right, whatever, sorry about that. Listen, Debra, that guy Mickey, I wouldn't go with him if I were you. I know it's not my business, but none of us thinks he is who he says he is."

"What do you mean?" Debra inquired.

"He hits on all the new women, and none of us even knows if his story is true. What did he tell you his wife's name was?"

"It's Patti, he said, it was Patti."

"Yeah, right," Diane snorted once again. "Some weeks, his wife's name is Paula, and once, he called her Polly. His story doesn't jibe in other ways, too. I mean, it's none of my business. Do what you want, but just thought you should know."

She walked away quickly. Debra was so confused. Should she believe this unpleasant woman who had been nothing but negative throughout the whole meeting, or should she believe this guy she felt was just a little too touchy, even though he had done nothing untoward? Nothing yet, a voice said inside her head.

"I'm back," Mickey said, smiling broadly, and Debra turned toward him, startled. "Did I scare you, hon? I'm sorry." He smoothly put his arm around her, attempting to pull her close.

Debra pulled quickly away from him. "I'm sorry. I can't. I can't go with you."

"Why, what happened?" he said.

"I forgot, I have to meet my daughter right away."

"You seem upset. You want me to drive you? Maybe I should follow you home? Make sure you're ok?"

"No, no, I'm fine. I need to go."

"Ok, ok. Another time, then. Let me get your number."

"No, I'll see you at the next meeting. Please, I have to go right now."

"Debra, did something happen? Did something change?"

"No, please, I need to leave right now."

She jumped into her car, hoping he didn't notice how quickly she engaged the door locks. She pulled out of the parking lot, watching him frown in the rearview mirror as she pulled away. She couldn't trust this man! He was a stranger. What had she been thinking? The only man she had trusted was Ron; even with him, it had taken her a long time. She couldn't believe she had been so foolish as to consider going somewhere with Mickey. For all she knew, this Mickey was another Gary, her first husband and Devon's father. She shuddered and rubbed her jaw, suddenly feeling so much pain rushing through her body. She knew better than to trust men. She had put herself at risk. She could be hurt all over again. It wasn't safe. She wasn't safe.

♦   ♦   ♦

Three blocks away, right before the exit leading her to the freeway and her home, she pulled into a parking lot. She looked around, making sure she was not being followed. She waited a few moments, just making sure, but then she put her head on the steering wheel and allowed, finally, a sob to burst from her throat as tears began to run from her eyes. Yet another thing that had not worked out. She knew she would never return to the group. Why had she been so foolish to think that someone normal or nice would be interested in her? Why had she thought she deserved to feel better? She did not deserve to feel better after what she had done! She only deserved this. To feel alone forever. Then she heard it once again. The mean voice snarling, "End it! What have you got to lose? You have nothing. You will always have nothing from now on. No one wants you. No one will ever want you again. End it, end it!" the voice chanted.

Debra looked up, wiping her tears with the back of her hand. She had a long drive home through traffic.

CHAPTER 45

IT WAS NOW APPROACHING the six-month mark since Ron's passing. After the debacle of the grief group, Devon and Kathy had encouraged Debra to try church, and she had grudgingly agreed.

Debra took a large breath and briefly hesitated before flinging open the large church community room door. She had been participating in the women's group here at the church for almost two months now. She would never have come, but both Devon and Kathy had urged, no, exhorted her to attend. She was also going to Sunday services. She had convinced Devon and David to go with her once. Devon had seemed decidedly uncomfortable and was now busy on every succeeding Sunday. This was the same church she had attended irregularly with Ron when he was alive. Ron had grown up attending church, and although they hadn't participated anywhere in years after they had married, Ron had expressed interest in attending once again when he retired, so they had done so sporadically, mostly on holidays, and then had stopped altogether when Ron had gotten sick. And now, Debra was once again forcing herself to participate in an activity she was not particularly interested in, if she were to admit it. The grief group she had tried had been a big bust. All she had done was attract the attention of some creepy guy. No way could she ever go back there. She hadn't told Devon or Kathy why she would not return to the group, only demurring and saying it wasn't for her. Their new thing, both of them, was that she should get involved in the church group.

"It would be good to see people, Debra, more people than just Devon and me," Kathy had said.

"Mom, you went to that church before, and you'll meet women your age. You can talk."

Debra wasn't sure and almost wanted to ask both of them, "Do you want me to go because you don't want to be bothered by me anymore? You want me to talk to, or call, someone else?" She was careful with them, never acting too upset, being too sad, never crying, and never saying how she felt. Maybe she talked about Ron too much, but what else was she supposed to say? Were they trying to get rid of her? Pawn her off on different people! She would never know because she wouldn't ask them and could not possibly share her true feelings.

Anyway, she had been attending this women's group for almost two months. It was primarily a social time, with people taking turns bringing dessert. They would do a Bible reading and then participate in or set up participation in various social projects. Debra had enjoyed sorting food for the food bank and had helped stuff bags of essentials to be handed out to people without housing. Debra liked the projects that could be completed during their weekly meeting time the best. The social interaction exhausted Debra, and she wasn't sure why, but she was always so glad to get home. She knew that some women participated in every opportunity, going to the homeless shelter to pass out sandwiches or make evening meals. Debra was finding that she did not like to drive at night, ever since her abrupt and hasty exit from the grief group. She could still see that creepy guy, Mickey, standing in the parking lot. Sometimes when she was driving, she thought she saw him in the rearview mirror and had to look back quickly to ascertain that it was a mirage; it wasn't real, although it was all too real in her mind. She knew that each member of the women's group was supposed to take a turn working in the thrift shop, but this had seemed too much for Debra. There were too many people, too overwhelming, and this Saturday was the bazaar. Everyone had signed up for shifts to work.

"Even if you only do an hour, ladies," Carol, the group leader, had intoned loudly and somewhat insistently. Debra hadn't signed up yet, but she knew she should probably do so today, reluctantly. Debra wished she felt more comfortable with the group of women, and she was sure it was her, not them, but she felt awkward and not truly accepted into the group, even though she was always polite and as friendly as she could be. Debra grabbed a cup of coffee from the table, declined the offer of a cinnamon roll, and took her seat in the circle next to an older woman, Hazel, whom she had sat next to several times before. She noticed the leader, Carol, frown at her as she sat down and then shift her gaze to Barbara, seated beside her. *Did she give me a look?* Debra thought with a start. "Don't be paranoid, Debra," the mean voice in her head snarled. That voice had become a constant companion lately. Debra smiled at Hazel warmly.

Hazel smiled back and said, "Hello, dear. You must be new. I haven't seen you here before. I'm Hazel, and you are?"

"Oh," Debra said, momentarily taken aback. She had sat next to Hazel at least three times, and yet the woman had no recollection of her! Oh, well, maybe she had some memory issues.

"I'm Debra," she said pleasantly.

"Well, nice to have you, Dawn. We can always use new members. We participate in a lot of service projects, Dawn. We can use your help."

"I know that," Debra said and nodded. Should she correct the older woman, restate her name, or let it go? Before Debra could decide, Carol clapped her hands loudly, and all the women quieted immediately.

"We have a lot to talk about today, ladies," Carol proclaimed.

"We are starting several special projects and need your participation to succeed."

Debra tried to maintain her attention and focus but found herself staring at the other group members. One of the older women appeared to be asleep. Two of the younger women were silently talking behind their hands, seemingly uninterested in what Carol was saying.

"So, I need a volunteer to coordinate and be responsible for all the homeless shelter meals," Carol said, looking around the circle severely.

Debra looked around the circle, too. She could help, but hadn't been here long enough to be a coordinator. Suddenly, she felt a pull on her arm and looked to her left, surprised. Hazel was raising Debra's arm and had a tight enough hold on it so Debra could not easily yank her arm down.

"Dawn volunteers," Hazel shouted. "Dawn will do it."

All eyes turned to look at Debra. Debra felt blood rush to her face, and she looked down. Her heart was beating loudly. She didn't want to do this! It was too much! She looked at Carol, expecting her to decline the offer, which wasn't an offer because Debra's hand had not been raised by choice.

Instead, Carol boomed out in a loud voice, "Excellent idea, Hazel. Debra, what a great opportunity for you. Can't think of a better way for you to get to know all the members of our group."

Debra found herself completely panicked. She felt sweat beginning to pour off her body. Everyone in the room was staring at her! She had to say something; she had to do something. If she meekly said OK, it would only be worse later. She did not know how to do this job. It would be a nightmare. She just was not ready. Staring, they were still all staring at her. Debra flickered her eyes closed, opened them, and, taking in a large breath, said in a voice that was at first almost as quiet as a whisper, but then she looked right at the intimidating Carol and said clearly, "No, thank you, I'm sorry. I'm just not ready for that."

For an uncomfortable moment, Carol continued to stare at her without saying anything, then she cast her gaze around the circle.

"Well, then, anyone else?"

Everyone was silent, and no one else raised a hand. Debra felt awful, but a wave of relief shuddered through her body.

"Ladies, we need to fill these positions. Let's take a break. Everyone, get some more coffee and another cinnamon bun. Then, we'll come back together for the Bible reading and see if anyone has had a change of heart."

Debra stood up and fled to the bathroom outside the community room without looking at anyone. She rubbed cold water on her face, still trying to calm down. She entered the back stall, flicking the lock just as she heard voices outside the door. Looking down, she saw Carol's shoes, but she would have known it was her even without seeing them by her loud voice. Two other women accompanied her. "Well, I wouldn't feel bad," one woman said. "I don't care if she looked uncomfortable," the other woman said. "She is picking and choosing what she wants to do. She doesn't even seem aware that the rest of us are doing it all. We are doing everything, even Hazel." This voice was so clearly Carol's.

"How long has she been coming here?"

"Two months at least," the other one answered.

They are talking about me! the voice in Debra's head thundered.

"Sure, I know she's done some charity work, but if we all did as little as she does, nothing, I mean nothing, would ever get accomplished. Even Emily, who works full-time with two toddlers, is doing more than she is. What's her deal anyway? She's so quiet. I bet she thinks she's better than the rest of us. Did you see that address she listed? She lives in Graymaron Estates. You know how expensive the homes are over there! Let's see if she steps up when we come back together, even without Hazel's help. God bless her."

They all laughed. Debra heard the door open and footsteps recede. She was immobile, standing silently in the bathroom stall. Suddenly, she flung the door open, grasping at her purse on her shoulder to ensure it was there. After leaving the bathroom, if she turned right, she would be back in the community room; turning left would take her through the glass doors and outside into the parking lot. Debra turned left and walked to her car with increasing speed. In the last few steps, she almost ran, her feet hitting the pavement with force. She didn't need more judgment, more negativity. She could stay home if she wanted to feel this bad about herself. She turned the car's ignition. Another activity that had not worked out.

CHAPTER 46

DEBRA HEARD THE FRONT DOOR bang open and the sound of heavy footsteps walking quickly down the entryway and hall. Devon had been loud since she was a young child. Debra rubbed her forehead. She had been thinking about Ron and finding it difficult to believe he had been gone for over a year; time had gone by so fast, and at the same time, unbearably slowly. She missed him so much. She wondered if the physical pain she felt would ever subside.

"Mom, you won't even believe what happened!"

Devon exclaimed excitedly as she entered the kitchen where Debra was sitting. Debra had a terrible headache and had been contemplating lying down when the door opened and both Devon and David burst through. Devon had a huge smile on her face, so at least Debra knew whatever her news was, it was good news and, God forbid, not more tragedy.

Debra smoothed her hair and did her best to hide how awful she felt, instead replying, "What, honey? I can't wait to hear."

"Well, you know how I have been looking for my birth father? I just posted a couple of updates and scanned the old picture of him that you had given me. I searched him through the town hall and genealogy records, but found nothing."

Debra nodded. She was not in the mood to talk about her long-ago ex-husband, but oh, well. Devon continued.

"Anyway, I go on Facebook just messing around, wasting time, and there it was! A post from a woman claiming to be married to Gary Robinson. She said she recognized his picture and spoke to him, and she is sure I am his daughter. I yelled for David, and you know David, he was cautious at first."

David said, "Make sure you're not getting played."

"So I asked her every question I knew about my father, even though it was hard, because, Mother, you told me so little. She could answer all the questions, and the two that she couldn't, she went and asked her husband, and he answered right away. We took the conversation to Messenger, and she gave me her phone number. I called her yesterday, and she's great, Mom - so nice and pleasant. We talked for almost an hour. She said her husband wasn't home at the time, and I wasn't sure if I was ready to talk to him anyway, so she suggested I arrange a time and call back when her husband, my dad, was home. I didn't tell you anything because I wanted everything to be straight before I told you."

"David did some more investigation to be sure she was who she said she was. And she is. Anyway, an hour ago, I called, and he was there. I talked to her first. Did I say how nice she is? Her name's Colleen. Anyway, we talked for a few minutes, and then she handed the phone over, and I talked to my dad."

Devon finally took a breath as she beamed. She looked then at Debra's face, and her look of radiance began to dissipate like a balloon slowly losing air.

"What, Mom, you aren't the least bit happy for me?"

Devon's words cut into Debra like a knife.

"No, Devon, honey, it's not that at all. I know you're an adult and you can handle things, but your father, your real dad..." Debra realized she was feeling so awful because she had always considered, somehow, that Ron had been Devon's dad. He had certainly acted like one, unlike Devon's biological father.

"What, Mom, spit it out!" Devon said impatiently.

"Your birth father, Gary," — Debra felt a choking in her throat just repeating his name — "wasn't a nice man. He had some problems. I haven't told you, but.."

Devon cut her off before Debra could continue.

"He told me all about it, Mom. He admitted that he wasn't nice to you. He even admitted that he had a drinking problem when he was young. He says he knows he made a ton of mistakes. He's been in AA now for almost ten years. Then Colleen came back on the phone, and she confirmed that he was completely sober now. He said I should tell you he was sorry, and they both seemed upset to hear about your husband, too."

My husband, Debra thought. *Oh, Devon, that is all Ron was to you.* She felt the stab of the knife in her stomach once again.

"Mom, I haven't even told you the best part! He and Colleen have three kids together. I have little sisters! Isn't that great? The youngest just started middle school. You know how I always wanted to have siblings. They only live an hour and a half from here. They invited David and me to visit. I can't wait."

Debra tried to smile, but she was sure she wasn't quite pulling it off. She felt sure her smile was wan at best.

"That's great, honey," Debra said.

"Look, Mom, I understand why you might not be thrilled, but what happened between you was long ago. You were both young, and he has changed."

How should she say this? Debra wondered.

"I would keep my expectations down for now, Devon, and you should be careful."

"Oh, Mom, I know all that. I was hoping you would be happy for me."

Debra sighed, "I am happy for you, Devon. There is a lot, though, I never told you about your biological father."

"See, David? I knew she would be like this. I knew you would try to bring me down. Mom, you can be such a downer lately."

"Devon, it's difficult for your mother to process; give her a break," David asserted.

"I know, I know," Devon said. "Anyway, we should go. We're meeting Tim and Sally for dinner in a few minutes. I was so excited, I just wanted to stop and tell you."

"I am happy for you," Debra said, blinking rapidly to keep the tears that so wanted to come from overwhelming her eyes.

As the door banged closed and the silence again enveloped Debra, images from long ago appeared before her eyes. She remembered all too well bouncing off the wall and careening into the crib where Devon lay, unaware, blissfully asleep. Debra doing her best to push her husband out of the room so as not to disturb her sleeping infant. There was so much Devon did not know about her father. Debra had never wanted to tell her, but now this. So much was roaring back into her head. She looked down, realizing her body was shaking, and her hands were clenched into tight fists. She could feel her jaw aching, and she remembered all that she had done to protect her baby from her husband's unreasonable rage. Debra sat down heavily in the rocker in the living room. Her ears rang with shouts and screams that she thought she had forgotten long ago.

CHAPTER 47

DEVON WAS SEATED at Debra's kitchen counter with a steaming cup of coffee in front of her. Debra could not ignore the huge smile that was lighting up her face. She looked happier than Debra had ever seen her. *Certainly, happier than when she lived here with Ron and me*, Debra thought glumly. She closed the refrigerator and plunked the creamer on the counter before sitting across from Devon with her cup of coffee. Debra inhaled silently, prompting herself to keep her face neutral or happy, willing her features not to betray the trepidation and unrest she felt coursing through her body.

"So, how did it go, Devon? I want to know all about your visit with your birth father."

She could not bear to say his name, Gary, did not even want that name in her mouth, and she would not just say father because Ron had been Devon's father as far as Debra was concerned—certainly not this, this sperm donor who had never tried to contact his child when she was young. Devon did not seem to sense any of Debra's inner turmoil, and she plunged right in, happily describing the visit in detail.

"Their house is small but so nice. Colleen is so warm and funny, and she ran right out the door to meet us when our car pulled up. My Dad was inside in the living room, and he seemed nervous at first, pacing back and forth, but Mom, do you know what we all noticed right away? I look very much like him; our hair is the same color, and he's tall just like me. I told him I towered over you by the time I was thirteen, and he chuckled, saying how petite you always were. I always felt like a big monster walking down the street with you, but I didn't feel too tall beside him. He's probably a couple of inches taller than me, certainly taller than David. Anyway, the girls came out of their bedrooms and were initially shy. Sarah was working and wasn't home, but I'll meet her next time. Susan and Tiffany are only a year apart, blonde like their mom, and so pretty. Tiffany is autistic, on the spectrum, they say. They were thrilled to meet me, and by the end of the visit, Susan, the youngest, was talking to me nonstop about everything. She wouldn't let me out of her sight, even my dad and Colleen said she had taken a shine to me. It felt so good to be with a large family. It's what I always wanted. The visit could not have gone better!"

"Did he talk about the past at all?" Debra inquired.

"Yes, he did. He admitted to having a bad drinking problem when he was young. He said he had no secrets from his kids and hoped they would learn from his mistakes and not repeat what he had done. He attends AA meetings, and he even sponsors a fellow member. Colleen said he drank a little when they first married, but she got him to go to AA, and he completely stopped. He showed me his 10-year medallion."

"Did he have anything to say about me?"

Devon looked at her mother and frowned, but continued.

"He said that you both got married so young, and then you got pregnant immediately. He said that you fought a lot, and he was certain that the fights were his fault a lot of the time. He said he wasn't ready for a baby at twenty-three years old, but that was no excuse for the fights or his behavior. He apologized for leaving me and said he should have stayed, and it was something he would always regret."

Debra hoped that Devon did not notice the slight shudder that came over Debra like a wave at the thought of him staying around.

Additionally, in this version, she wondered who had left whom. Debra had walked—no, run—away from him to protect Devon. He hadn't just walked out. She had hidden from him for over a year, terrified that he would return. Sounded like this part of the story had been omitted.

"Did he say anything else?"

"He said he felt awful that he had lost touch with you, but since he had still been drinking then, he didn't care. But after he met Colleen and got sober, he was ashamed to pursue us after so much time had gone by, and he had no idea how to find us. He said he looked up our names online every few months, but nothing ever came up. He understood it all after I told him we had unofficially changed our last name to Ron's, even before you married him, and he officially adopted me."

"Anything else?" Debra pressed again.

This time, Devon looked exasperated and even started to get angry quickly, as she often did. Debra pulled back slightly as she saw Gary's eyes in her daughter's eyes and even in her exasperated demeanor.

"How many times are you going to say, 'anything else,' Mother? He said that he was sorry a million times. He admitted he made mistakes. What else do you want from him, Mother? He said he would like to apologize to you in person one day and knows that he needs to make amends."

Debra shuddered at the thought of ever seeing Gary again. She stared into her coffee cup. Should she tell her daughter the truth? Should she tell her the number of times she had bounced off the walls of their small apartment? Should she tell her how often she had been pushed into the wall or slapped across the face? Should she tell her daughter the reasons, the specious reasons for the violence—breathing too loud, taking too long at the store, coming home late from work when she had only been five minutes past her regular time. How about the last time, the last time before she had left the following morning with only the clothes on her and Devon's backs, pretending she was taking Devon to daycare and going to work, but instead driving as far and as fast as she could to save her baby. Should she tell Devon why she had left, when it sounded like Gary's version was that he had walked away? He had been so drunk that night, holding onto the wall to remain upright, when Devon had started to cry. Gary hadn't let go of her arm so that she could go to Devon. Instead, he repeated—slurred, actually—"shut that kid up, or I will," but he held on to Debra even as she tried to get away and go to her daughter. He had pushed her aside with such force that she had fallen into the coffee table. He had been in Devon's room before she could rise from the floor. She had begun to crawl toward Devon's room as fast as she could, only managing to grab his ankles just as he reached out toward the crib and the still-crying baby. What had he meant to do? Bounce his infant daughter off the wall as he often did with her?

"Shut up, bitch!" he had screamed at the baby in the crib, but Debra's ankle grab threw him off balance, and he turned his attention back to Debra, kicking her hard in the face.

He had turned toward Debra as if he had forgotten about the baby. "You're not worth it," he screamed, seeming to be addressing both of them. He staggered from the room; Debra still curled on the floor, inching closer toward the crib. She heard the refrigerator open and then heard the pop of a beer bottle being snapped off. She heard the TV and prayed he would pass out soon. Then, she knew what she had to do to save her child. She thought of trying to leave, running out of the apartment right then. Still, she was too scared that he would try to follow them, so instead she had waited until morning, and as they both got ready for work, Debra pretended she was going to work but actually made plans to drive away with Devon. She had no choice, no choice. She had to save her baby. Did Devon need to know this story now? What would it prove?

"Mother!" Devon yelled, and Debra jumped, almost spilling the coffee.

"What is wrong with you? Did you even hear me? Dad and Colleen have invited all of us, including you, to their house for the Fourth of July. They said you were more than welcome. I said we would go. It would be great to spend a holiday with a lot of people instead of just us for once. Will you think about it or not? David said it was a lot to ask of you, but I won't go if you don't say yes, and I want to. Will you think about it or not? I've already asked you twice. Where is your mind at?"

"I don't know, Devon, I don't know," Debra repeated.

"Mother, don't ruin this for me, alright? I am happier now than I have been in a long time, please? Just think about it."

Debra nodded glumly, watching a smile cascade across her daughter's face again.

CHAPTER 48

DEBRA SHUDDERED and looked down, avoiding direct eye contact with her daughter. Yet again, she was stunned by how much Devon looked like her father: the same piercing hazel eyes and thick, almost jet-black hair. Devon had started gaining height on Debra at thirteen years old and now stood five inches taller than her mother. She was statuesque and well-built, whereas Debra was tiny, slight, with nothing more than a small bump in her bust area. When Debra was younger and in happier days, when she had more bounce in her step and a smile on her face, she was often mistaken for a much younger woman. She had regularly been carded at bars and liquor stores well into her thirties. She and Devon were frequently considered sisters, and they often said Devon was the older sister given her more womanly frame. But those eyes—sometimes, if she stared into her daughter's eyes too long, she would see Gary looking back at her instead of her much-loved Devon. And Devon certainly had the temperament of her father and always had, from a three-year-old chucking blocks angrily when they did not snap together properly to a hormonal teenager slamming her fists on the door because she had been denied the right to go to a party that was not adequately supervised. Devon's anger had always intimidated Debra from an early age, but Ron had been so good at dealing with Devon's anger. He had a gentle, quiet way that could almost immediately calm her wrath. He told her that he had been angry as a young man, which Debra had to admit was hard to believe. Still, he had learned to channel his feelings positively, and that it was consistently more effective to fight for what you believed strongly with words rather than with fists. Ron had helped Devon immensely throughout her teenage years. Devon knew that David was a calming influence on Devon, but today, he was not here, and they were alone. Debra looked back up at her daughter, seeing the flash of anger in her eyes. She could tell by the tautness of Devon's body how much she was trying to control herself, how she wanted to shout and angrily advocate for what she wanted, but she was not.

"I've given you two weeks to consider the trip to see my dad. I need an answer today so I can confirm with Colleen. And now all you do is shake your head no! I deserve an explanation. Tell me why you won't go."

Anger flashed from Devon's eyes, a wordless symbol that was all too real for Debra.

"I don't want to see him, that's why."

"Mother, that is not an answer! You sound like a teenager saying 'cuz, just because.'"

"It's hard for me, Devon. I don't want to see him."

"Ok, but tell me why."

"It has been so many years."

"Was he very mean to you? Because he doesn't seem mean now. He already told me that you both used to fight and that he was very sorry."

"If you think you will keep me from seeing him by refusing to go, I will tell you now that it is not going to happen."

Devon could state what she wanted oh so very clearly. *Why in hell couldn't Debra do the same*, she thought. Debra opened her mouth to reply. Where to begin? How much did Devon need to know, and how much would her words poison her against her father? Surely, Devon had a right to know her father! Maybe Gary had changed, and maybe Debra was being unfair. She closed her mouth.

"Ok, we'll go," she said quietly, acquiescing once more to something she did not want to do but knew someone else wanted so much.

CHAPTER 49

DEBRA TRIED TO KEEP the fake smile pasted to her face as she sat in the back seat of Devon and David's car. Devon continued to chat animatedly and seemed oblivious to Debra's emotions that she was trying so hard to hide. David, however, kept glancing back at her in the rearview mirror as he drove.

"Everything ok, Debra?" he inquired.

"Oh, yes, I'm fine," she said. God bless him; he was so intuitive, knowing something was wrong with her. He was so steady and kind, and he totally understood Devon. He didn't overreact to her bluster; she had seen him more than once calm her down as she began to rage about something insignificant. Again, she offered a silent prayer that Devon had married a kind, gentle man and would not repeat the turbulence of Debra's first marriage and early adult years. Debra did not want to go where they were headed. A Fourth of July cookout at Devon's birth father's house. It was the last place she wanted to be. She had no desire to see Gary again, and although Devon had assured her that everything would be fine, she had no idea how Gary would react to her presence. She had not wanted to come but had felt forced into it by Devon's increasingly urgent entreaties. Devon insisted she would not go without Debra's attendance, so she implored Debra to come with her because she wanted more than anything to be there.

"You'll see, Mom. You'll love Colleen, and the girls are all so cute. They will welcome you, and my dad has repeatedly said he wants to apologize. He won't bother you or be mean. I know he won't. Besides, you can stay close to David and me if you feel uncomfortable. Please, Mom, you must come!"

Debra was sure that if she told Devon the truth, mentioned the abuse even without going into gory detail, Devon would understand her reluctance, but apparently Devon's father had mentioned none of the abuse, just that they had fought, like there had been lapses on both their parts. If she told Devon, would she ruin the burgeoning relationship she was developing with her father? Would she believe Debra and want nothing more to do with him? Or would she doubt Debra's words, think she was embellishing, and pull away from her instead? Debra could not take another loss, so she said nothing and reluctantly agreed to go to this fiasco cookout! At first, she put it out of her mind, pretending that the day would never arrive, but it had arrived. Now here she was unhappily ensconced in the back seat and trying with all her might to hide her feelings of anxiety and near panic as they hurtled closer and closer to Gary and a past that Debra had left behind so many years ago.

♦ ♦ ♦

Debra peered at her face in the mirror in the bathroom in her ex-husband's house. She looked normal, she decided, even though she felt awful, with stabs of pain zooming through her body. She would feel pain in her stomach, a knot in her chest, and then a sharp pain in her head as if she were being stabbed. Her skin felt creepy and crawly, and she would feel first hot and then cold. Worst was the sudden pain in her jaw, which felt so much like the pain she had felt after Gary had slapped her all those years ago. But even though she felt as if her head might burst off or explode at any moment, as she looked at herself, she appeared to look completely normal. Devon had been right. Gary's wife, Colleen, seemed to be a kind, warm person, and her girls, Gary's girls, were polite and beautiful. Colleen had given her a warm hug immediately and had introduced the girls. Debra had seen Gary lurking in the doorway to the kitchen out of the corner of her eye. His bulky frame was taking up the entire doorway. Debra had avoided him for as long as possible, but as they all lapsed into silence, Colleen had gestured for him to come into the room and said, "Well, now, here's Gary. Come on, Gary, come on in and say hi to Debra."

For the first time, Debra had looked directly at him, feeling her hands and armpits beginning to sweat profusely and even seeing flashes of light in front of her eyes.

But he said softly and shyly, "Hello, Debra, it's nice to see you. Been a long time."

He smiled and looked down, running a hand over his balding head. He looked so much older than the young, robust Gary that she saw in her mind. Only his build, the largeness, was the same. His face looked so much older, and his hair, which had been thick and dark the last time Debra had seen him, was now practically nonexistent! Debra had instinctively moved closer to David as Gary approached her, and David threw an arm around his mother-in-law's shoulder. He must have felt her body shaking. *How could he not? If he tries to hug me, I'm going to run or kick him,* Debra thought unreasonably, but instead he stretched out his hand, leaving a good deal of physical space between them. He did not grab her hand but waited patiently for her to react. Although she wanted to recoil, she stuck out her hand, and his much larger hand enveloped hers, and they shook. She pulled her hand away as quickly as possible without it being too noticeable.

"I'm glad you could make it," he said solemnly. "My wife—I mean, Colleen—and I are so happy to have you. We were very sorry to hear about your husband. Please accept our condolences."

Oh, he was so polite, wasn't he? Just the perfect gentleman.

As an awkward pause developed, Colleen said, "Hey, this is a barbecue, we're not going to hang around the kitchen all afternoon.

Gary, get the grill fired up. The girls and I will get the salads out. Go on now! Debra, Devon, could you help Susan chop up the veggies for the salad?"

Debra knew she couldn't stay in the bathroom much longer without drawing attention, so she flushed the toilet she had not used and then turned on the water in the sink. So far, so good. The food had been good, and Colleen and the girls were talkative and funny. Debra could see how much Devon liked being with and talking to the three younger girls; they all seemed to gravitate to her. It had been easy to stay away from Gary, and she had done so with relative ease. It would all be over soon. She took a deep breath and opened the bathroom door. She could hear all the talk and laughter from outside on the deck. Devon, David, and the girls were about to start a volleyball game. It was quiet inside the house.

Debra smoothed her hair, and she heard a deep voice say solemnly, "Debra."

She reeled back. She had not seen Gary standing in the hallway just outside the bathroom door. She looked around. The voices suddenly seemed so far away. No one else was in the house. It was just her and Gary.

"Oh," she said, trying to keep the fear from entering her voice. "Do you need the bathroom?"

"No, Debra, I wanted to speak to you."

Debra felt her heart quicken, and she took a step back. Why the hell had she come into the bathroom? She should have stayed outside next to Devon and David. "Where's Colleen?" Debra inquired, her voice choked.

Gary shrugged.

"She's putting the dishes in the dishwasher, I think."

Did he know, could he tell that she was still scared of him after all this time? This was one more time when she wanted Ron more than anything. Of course, if Ron were alive, she would never have been here in the first place. She would never have agreed to this trip with Ron encouraging her and making her strong. The silence between Gary and Debra enveloped them like a slow-moving fog.

Finally, Gary spoke.

"I won't keep you long, Debra. Look, I know, I can tell that you don't want to be around me, and I get it. I do. But all I want to do is apologize to you. I was wrong to leave all those years ago. I was wrong to drink when I should have been a responsible husband and father. All the fighting was so wrong, and even though Devon was just a baby, it was something that she should have never heard or seen. I apologize, Debra. I apologize for all of it."

Ok, so to an outsider, it would probably seem that he was accepting responsibility and admitting his mistakes, blah, blah. But, my God, he was apologizing for drinking, for arguing, but what about the hitting, the pushing, the abuse? And fighting, he somehow made it seem they were both at fault!

"We were young, Debra, it's not an excuse, but hey. All we can do is try to do better now, right?"

And not a word about how she had raised Devon alone all those years, struggling to get by for over 10 years. Her life only became easier after Ron had come along. How about that?

"Do you accept my apology because I am sorry," Gary asked.

Debra made a large intake of breath. The fear of him that she had felt earlier was being overtaken by anger. He was glossing over it all, but if Colleen were here, she would have probably thought it was a perfect apology. Just how much did Colleen know? Did she even know the brutality her husband was capable of?

"Anything else, Gary, are you sorry for anything else? Is there anything else you did that you regret?"

Now it was Gary's turn to make a huge intake of breath.

"Ok, Debra, yes, yes, there is. I was never sure how much you knew, but I wasn't only drinking, I was using drugs as well. Unfortunately, almost anything I could get my hands on. I was wasted out of my mind a lot, and we had a baby in the house! I will regret that for the rest of my life."

"And?" she said challengingly.

"I should have tried harder to find you instead of leaving both of you. I should have paid child support for all those years. I guess your husband had some money, but you must have struggled in the years before you met him."

"I, we did, Gary, we struggled quite a lot."

"Again, I am sorry, Debra, I was wrong."

"And the fighting, Gary, do you remember the fighting?"

"Of course, I remember the fighting. It was wrong, and I guess it became physical a couple of times, but you gave as good as you got if I remember correctly."

He started to smile but stopped when he saw the serious look on her face.

"You do remember who left who, right?"

"Debra?" He looked at her, somewhat perplexed.

"I walked out and never looked back. It was wrong."

"What about the abuse?"

"Abuse?" he questioned. "The fighting was wrong. I already said that, but abuse—that's a little strong. Married people do fight. I wouldn't call a little push from both of us abuse, do you, Debra?"

Debra shuddered. It had been so much more than one little push, and it had happened repeatedly.

"I think I'm done with this conversation, Gary. I need to get back to Devon and David."

"Debra, I never contacted you because I was messed up when I was younger. Devon didn't need to be around a father like that, but now that I am clean and sober, and now that we have found each other, I very much want to be involved as her father. I know she wants that. I hope you are mature enough not to try to stop it by bringing up old, meaningless grudges from the past."

"I need to go, Gary," she said tightly, sidling carefully, always so carefully, past him. She shuddered. Impossible. It was an impossible situation. If he didn't acknowledge the truth, didn't admit that he was an abuser, was it even the truth? Was any of it even real? What made her truth real and what made his truth a lie? Less than half a day in his presence, and already all she could do was doubt her every move, her every thought, once again as she had done those many years ago.

CHAPTER 50

Debra 2 months later

"MOTHER!" DEVON QUESTIONED BELLIGERENTLY. "Do you have something to say or not?"

Debra shook her head. When Devon and David arrived to have dinner with her this evening, she had had every intention of telling them that she was not going to Christmas at Gary's. She had even rehearsed the words. "It's just impossible, Devon. You two go and have a good time. We'll celebrate before or after—whichever is better for both of you."

See, she would still be accommodating but would not put herself through the torture of sitting there with Gary pretending that everything was ok, that he wasn't a selfish abuser who would have probably abused his own daughter if given the chance. Did she care if he had reformed himself? Frankly, the answer to that question was no, not really. He hadn't ever really apologized to her; he was denying her reality more than anything, and seeing him turned her stomach, but now with Devon and David right in front of her, the words were not flowing out of her mouth as she had hoped. Devon was looking at her impatiently, waiting for her to say something, so she did what she so often did, which she had done for years. She lied easily and facilely.

She said, "I was just wondering what I should bring for Christmas dinner at Colleen's." No, no, this was not what she wanted to say.

David looked right at her and raised one eyebrow. *He knows that is not what I wanted to say*, Debra thought morosely.

Seemingly not noticing, Devon said, "Oh, anything you want to make, Mother. Colleen won't care. She says the girls eat everything, and she says Gary never saw a food item that he didn't like. Are you getting as excited to visit as I am? I can't wait," Devon said giddily.

"Yeah," Debra said, trying to smile and trying to make her voice show an excitement she did not feel. "It will be fun," she said, looking directly at David. She knew that David knew something was up, as she tried to hide, to cover up what she felt once again. Debra seldom lied to benefit herself, usually to benefit others, to make things easier for them, to make them feel better, to validate their feelings, regardless of her feelings. She had lied her way through Ron's illness, telling Ron and Devon she was fine, no, it was not too much for her to care for him, even lying to the nurses, insisting she was fine, she didn't need extra help. It was what Ron wanted, after all. Debra had lied for so long, had tried to read people's thoughts, emotions, and then mirror her thoughts and feelings to coincide with theirs, to please them, Debra wasn't even sure if she even knew what her thoughts were anymore. Debra was beginning to realize that most people lied "up" instead of "down," as she so often did, that is, they embellished details to make themselves look better, not worse. Debra often did the opposite, more likely to provide denigrating information about herself, more likely to remember and retell her missteps instead of her successes. Ron had tried to build her up before he got sick and convinced her she could find independent accounting clients and work independently, which afforded them more time to travel and do what they wanted with no set schedule.

"See what you are capable of," Ron would crow.

"You need to believe in yourself more!" However, as Ron got sicker, all her accounting clients faded away. As she cared for him and he became sicker, Debra increasingly doubted herself. Yet she had repeatedly assured everyone that she was always absolutely fine. Debra wondered if the people who embellished themselves, who made themselves look better, came to believe their lies. Is that what had happened with Gary? Had he told Colleen a fictional story about himself and had told it so many times that he now thought it was true? Did he not remember what had gone on between them, or did he not even know what truth was anymore? Was the fictional version easier to believe, or had he truly forgotten the real story? Was he hiding from reality, or had his fiction become reality at this point? Debra only knew one thing, and that was how sad and hopeless she felt and how sad and hopeless she had felt ever since Ron had died.

"Mother," Devon raised her voice, snapping Debra out of her reverie.

"Do you need David to help you get the roast out or not? Honestly, whenever I come here lately, you seem so preoccupied. What is going on with you? Are you alright?"

Debra smiled. "I am fine. Nothing is wrong. Don't be silly. You two sit down. I've got the roast. I've got it."

Debra slammed the dishwasher open and began to plunk the pans down on the counter heavily. The lid of one of the pans dropped from her grasp and fell with a clatter to the floor; she picked it up angrily, slamming it onto the counter next to the others. "Did that skillet do something to you?" She heard a voice that sounded so much like Ron's saying to her in her head in a light, humorous manner. She stopped and inhaled a deep breath. Ron had always had a way of calming her down, of neutralizing a situation instead of escalating one. Debra shook her head. No, she wasn't mad at the pans; the inanimate objects had done nothing to cause such ire. Devon had just left and had waltzed out the door quite happily after procuring her mother's agreement to attend Christmas at Gary's house. She couldn't go back there again! Why had she said she would! Even thinking of Gary made her stomach curdle, and the visions and thoughts of him were getting worse, not better. The images of the past with him were becoming ever clearer, not receding. Colleen and the girls were pleasant, but she couldn't go there again. She was dreading it already, and Christmas was still months away! There had to be a way out of it. Think, Debra, think, she said to herself. It would be hard to feign sickness, and she didn't want to ruin everyone else's Christmas at the very last minute. Why did this always happen to her? She would have to talk to Devon. It was the only way, but she had only made it so much more complicated by saying yes and now having to rescind. Devon would probably have already called Colleen, and it would be all set up. How could she make Devon understand? How could she get the words out? How could she say what she felt without sounding selfish or foolish? Gary had already said to her, "Don't get in the way of my establishing a relationship with my daughter." How could she clearly state her feelings and possibly say what she meant? How many times over the years had she opened her mouth and no words had come out? How many times had she second-guessed what she wanted, clearly able to see the other person's perspective, and so clearly failing to articulate her own? It was as if she didn't even exist. And then just like that, the thought thundered into her head once again, landing there fully formed and growing stronger, so much stronger each time she thought it. Don't even exist. "It would be better, Debra, if you didn't even exist," the voice said, using her own words. "That would solve all your problems if you just erased yourself from the world." Devon could go on and do exactly what she wanted. She had family now. She had her father, Colleen, and the girls, who were all happy and full of life. David would get no more late-night phone calls. Devon and David would not need to come rushing to her house late at night because she was scared of nothing, of the wind, of being alone. Her circle of friends had grown so small as to be almost nonexistent; she never saw any of those people. Kathy, her best friend, was always traveling for work, and it seemed that she and Debra had less in common each time she called. The conversations were getting ever shorter and more stilted. No one, absolutely no one at all, would even miss her. This one act and all the problems would be solved just like that. Now all she needed to do was come up with a plan. She had fourteen weeks. That should be enough time. It was the only way to go.

CHAPTER 51

DEBRA SIGHED AND CLOSED her eyes tightly against the encroaching sunlight. Lately, in the first few moments after awakening, she would feel the comfort of her bed and then, for a microsecond, would feel okay. She would realize she was home and safe in bed, and she had nothing to jump up to do; she didn't have to check Ron's breathing or hurry to prepare meds. So for that microsecond, she would feel some peace, but as quickly as the feeling had come, bang, it would go away. Of course, she had nothing to do. Ron was gone. Ron was dead. "And you are all alone," the mean voice in her head would sneer. "Ron is gone," the voice now taunted, "thanks to you, thanks to you." Debra scrunched her face, keeping her eyes closed, almost wishing the night would return, although she yearned for the daylight every day as the night approached. She forced her eyes to open and saw bright sunlight peeking through the blinds. Great! She was finding she preferred dark, overcast days to the bright sun and blue sky she would see if she were to open the blinds. The sun, the brightness seemed to be jeering at her, mocking her for her inability to enjoy the nice weather, to go outside, and to go for a long walk as she used to enjoy before Ron's death. The brightness of the day gave her no excuse to mope about inside, and yet to open the shades, let alone the door, seemed a monumental task. Debra pulled herself to a seated position, letting the quilt and the sheet fall beside her. She felt such pain as she hoisted herself to a seated position. Where was it from, and why? Did she have a disease like Ron's? Was an unknown cancer encroaching on her own body? Well, impending death wouldn't be the worst thing that could happen, would it? Instead, the possibility of life seemed much more frightening to her now than death. She was fifty-two years old! What was her average lifespan? Is there any way she could tolerate thirty more years of this, and exactly for what purpose would that be anyway? She wanted to feel better; she did, but she didn't know how to pull herself out of the funk, the smelly, gloomy funk that engulfed her. Some days were better than others, but most days were like this. She knew they, all of them, said that things would get better with time. Devon, Kathy, and David, her entire small, pathetic world of people, agreed that she would feel better soon. Years from now, next week, next decade, exactly what did soon mean? Debra forced her body from the bed into the bathroom to shower. She had read that getting up each day and showering even during abject grief was supposed to help. Yeah, great advice, not working, wise guru, whoever you are! At least when she was alone, she didn't have to pretend as she did when Devon or David were present—or Kathy, too, but Kathy hadn't been around at all lately, and if she did call, the calls were rushed and it was easy, so very easy to pull the wool over her eyes. It was more difficult with Devon and David. Devon knew her so well, and David—well, he was intuitive. She sometimes thought he was more aware of her feelings than even Devon. She would try hard to cover how she felt if they were coming over. Devon had been more patient in the first months after Ron had died, but now she seemed to lose patience quickly with Debra if she seemed mopey or withdrawn. *Guess I passed my expiration date for grief with her*, Debra thought. Glancing at herself in the mirror but quickly looking away, she found it harder and harder each passing day to look herself in the eye. The visit to Gary in July had made everything worse. She knew Devon thought that getting out more was what she needed, and Devon had been excited about the trip, saying it would be good for Debra to be around more people. *Yeah, right,* Debra thought, *spending time with my abuser is certain to improve my mood.* Devon and David were unaware that Gary had confronted her in the bathroom while everyone else was outside. Though he had not been threatening in any way, he had still provoked abject terror within Debra. Okay, maybe his denial, saying they had only fought a lot, was a veiled threat, and saying that he did not want old hurts to endanger his relationship with Devon—well, was that a threat or not? Maybe he honestly didn't remember all the ways that he had hurt Debra all those years ago. Is the truth real, or is it what we choose to believe? Do we create our stories and then fit reality into them? After all, he had seemingly apologized to her. Yet, after she had come home from that visit—more like that horror—she had been utterly unable to sleep for weeks. Even now, all these months later, she would go through nights of not sleeping, followed by a night or two of sleep. And when she closed her eyes, the images that she saw running and blurring before her eyes were all of violence, yelling, and then running with her baby, her Devon, clutched tightly in her arms. Debra could not stop these images; she saw them almost every night. Sometimes, they would be interspersed with dreams, quickly becoming nightmares. She would hear yelling voices and run to Ron, who would be standing to one side, and just before she reached him, he would crumble into pieces and blow away like sand. In another dream, she was running from Gary, but when she pulled the blanket aside to look into her baby's face, it was Gary wrapped in the blanket instead. She would hurl the small body far from her, only to hear an infant's cries as the baby bounced on the ground, and then David would suddenly appear and say to Debra angrily, "Now look what you've done, you've killed Devon."

The nightmares, the images, and the sounds never stopped, and they were getting worse now. Debra could not believe she had foolishly agreed to return to Gary and Colleen's house for Christmas.

"I want to go more than anything," Devon had said, "but I wouldn't think of leaving you at Christmas, so you have no choice but to go with us."

No choice, yes of course, as usual, she had no choice and had to do what everyone else wanted her to do. Debra pulled the medicine cabinet above the sink open with a forceful jerk. She was confronted with the Percocet bottle on the middle shelf with Ron's name on it. This time, she grabbed the bottle out of the cabinet, shaking it. It rattled, almost full of all the painkillers he had not taken. "Do it, do it," the surly voice repeated. Debra crossed out of the bathroom and back into the bedroom, opening Ron's dresser drawer and pushing past all his black socks, which lay still nestled in the drawer. She moved her hand to the very back of the drawer and added the Percocet to the stacked pill bottle collection. A collection of opioids and several bottles of benzodiazepines in her name. She certainly had enough. Devon and David thought she had taken them all to the police station months ago for disposal, but no, she had not, and here they were hidden away, waiting, just waiting. Lately, as time went on, many of the nights when Debra was awake were occupied with thoughts of how she would, how she could do it. What would it be like to take her own life? For her, the pills were probably her best or only option; she had no firearms, she had never been good at tying knots—had failed that unit in Girl Scouts—but she had researched how, how many, and whether to mix with liquor many times late at night. The option was becoming more and more appealing to her each day, and as the season changed and Christmas approached, and the thought of visiting Gary again loomed, especially in the dead of night, it seemed the only option. Not here, though, it couldn't be here, she had thought for weeks. The only plausible response to her demise would be that Devon and David would find her, and she did not want to put them through that. Devon would miss her, but she had David and was so enamored with Gary and his family. Why did she need a sad, pathetic old lady saddled around her neck? The answer, of course, was that Devon did not. Debra thought, though, that she had the answer now. Late last week, as she conducted her macabre research of death and suicide, she had by accident come upon an article about how many people come to Las Vegas with the express purpose of ending their lives. Debra had read the article with interest, her heart thumping harder as she read. Yes, this article was her divine guidance. This could work for her. Vegas was 1,000 miles from here. By the time David and Devon would be contacted and could make their way there, she would be long gone. No way she would have to worry about them finding her and reporting her death; it would all be over before they even knew, and they could continue with their lives. She would miss Devon. It might have been nice to have grandchildren, but it was better this way, easier for everyone, and all her pain would melt away. No one would miss her. No one needed her anymore. Las Vegas had the added attraction of being one of Ron's favorite places. The two of them had been there many times. Devon had even spent her honeymoon there. This could be a strange, quixotic way to honor Ron. She would be in his favorite place. She could go to places he liked to go, and then she would go to the hotel room and do it. It could be penance for what she had done to him, how she had treated him in his last days, and the mistakes she had made then. She counted the pill bottles. She certainly had enough. She just had to set it all up. She looked through the blinds and saw the bright sun again mocking her. It was time. It was time.

CHAPTER 52

"OH!" DEBRA JUMPED, STARTLED.

"Oops, sorry," David said.

He had dumped the bag of canned goods from the grocery store heavily onto the kitchen island, and the loud noise had startled Debra, causing her to jump.

"Mother, they're only cans. You jumped as if someone were shooting at you."

"I know, I know," Debra said, trying to conceal her fear and taking in deep breaths in a vain attempt to slow down her racing heart. "I've always startled easily, Devon, you know that," Debra said by way of explanation.

"I know, Mother, but you're getting worse. Are you scared to be here in this big house without Ron?"

Debra was already shaking her head before Devon had even finished the sentence. She loved her house, and yes, it was way too large for one person, but she did not want to move. Everything in the house reminded her of Ron, Devon, and happier, younger days. The last thing she wanted to do right now was have a conversation about moving with Devon and David.

"I'm not scared here at all. Don't be silly."

"Well, you were months ago when you called us at two a.m."

"Devon, Ron hadn't been gone that long, and you know it hasn't happened since! It was a silly mistake. Everything is fine. I am fine, Devon."

Devon pursed her lips and shook her head as if she didn't believe her mother.

"We have to go, Dev. We'll be late," David said, nudging her.

"Thanks so much for dropping the things by," Debra said, opening the door to see them out.

"No problem," David shouted as he made for the car.

Devon gave her mother a quick hug and an air kiss, and just like that, they were gone.

Debra paced, reviewing the conversation in her mind. She would never call Devon and David at night again, no matter if a mob of serial killers were breaking in, if grizzly bears were swimming in her pool, if twelve bats were hanging in her shower. She made herself smile as she thought up ever more ridiculous scenarios. She was still scared sometimes at night. The driveway was long and isolated, and with the night came quiet. With no one else home to make any noise, she heard every creak the house made, every time the heat turned on and off. She had always been jumpy. Ron and Devon had joked about it for years. Debra had always said, "I've always been like that. I was that way as a kid," but Debra couldn't remember being so jumpy as a child. She secretly thought that it had occurred after Gary. She had always had to be on guard around him, always aware of where he was and what he might do. She had been so afraid after she had left him, so afraid that he would come after her and Devon. She would lie awake night after night, always listening to make sure that he had not found them and was not attempting to come in to hurt her and steal their baby. Although part of her did realize that the possibility that he might want to hurt her was probably all too real, she wasn't at all sure that he would steal the baby, that he even wanted the baby at all. She had remained on alert for years, though, watching for him in stores, at gas stations, when they were out. Her vigilance had paid off in some ways, for he had never shown up in all those years. Debra had been afraid of the dark for many years now. She preferred to sleep with a nightlight on, and now that she was alone and couldn't bother anyone else, she just went ahead and kept the adjacent bathroom light on all night. It shone brightly into the bedroom where she was, and the fact that she could open her eyes at any time and see her surroundings perfectly gave her a small amount of comfort. She knew she had worried Ron when they were first together and had started sleeping in the same bed. She would wake up in a panic, yell, scream, and even try to hit Ron to get him away from her. That had been earlier in their relationship, though, and this had diminished as the years had rolled on. But now, the night terrors were back, and no one else was around to soothe or comfort her. At first, the dreams—the nightmares—had been images of Ron so sick in his hospital bed, or worse yet, his ghost shaking his head and castigating her for how she had treated him at the end. She had thought those dreams were bad, but since returning from Gary's house on the Fourth of July, the night terrors and the fear were much worse. Gary would be chasing her with knives, guns, or other weapons. He would be strangling her—so much violence, always so much violence. Sometimes the dreams were all too real, and she felt that she was reliving violence that had happened between her and Gary: the hits and the slaps and the awful last time when she had grabbed him by the ankle to keep him from advancing into the room of their crying baby. To do what, to do exactly what? The flashbacks were becoming all too real, and she found that they did not easily go away even once she had opened her eyes and attempted to reorient herself to her familiar surroundings. She could still see Gary in front of her, even though she was fully awake. Sometimes, he was the young Gary, strapping and with a full head of thick, wavy black hair, and sometimes the older Gary, gone to seed, balding, and with more fat on his body than muscle, but still, his form towered over her menacingly. Was she hallucinating? Was she cracking up? She couldn't tell anyone about any of this! No one would understand. She had always been able to talk to Ron about anything and everything, but this would have been weird even to mention to him, but no matter, anyhow, because he was gone. Who could she tell—Kathy, Devon, or David? Impossible. No way they would understand. They would think she was losing it. Was she losing it? Was she losing her mind? Would she need to go to a mental hospital? No, no way. She couldn't put Devon through that. Devon was beginning her life. She knew without being told that Devon and David, who had been trying for a baby, had put off Devon becoming pregnant once Ron had gotten so sick. She didn't even know if they were trying again or were waiting for her to seem better, to have moved on from her loss. She had no right to ruin her daughter's life by becoming a constant burden: a sick older woman unable to care for herself and not even all that old, which only meant that she would have many years to worry Devon and to keep her from enjoying life as she so deserved. No, no, Debra shook her head with resolve and stopped pacing. It would be better to go now, to go quickly, to stop all the pain for everyone involved. It was the only solution. It had to be done. It had to be done now before the Christmas holiday and the visit to Gary got any closer. She had been researching where to go for weeks and had almost made a decision. Should she book the one-way flight to Las Vegas?

CHAPTER 53

DEBRA ROCKED BACK and forth in the chair with her arms tightly wrapped around her body. She felt hot at first and then cold. Her heart was beating loudly and uncomfortably in her chest. She knew, however, that she was not ill. It was another panic attack, yet again. They always seemed to happen at night. Everything was always worse at night. She had shoved her half-eaten sandwich on the end table between the two easy chairs. One chair used to be Ron's, the other hers. She tried to control her breathing. "It's not working! It's not working," the voice inside her head screamed. She glanced over at her phone, which was also lying on the end table. No, she couldn't; she would not call Devon again. "Nothing is wrong. It's all in your head. It's not real," she told herself. But the voice, the mean voice, answered back. "Of course, it's all in your head, Debra, because you are losing your mind! But you deserve to suffer, don't you, and you know why." Debra lowered her head until it was practically between her knees. There was no part of her body that did not hurt or feel like it was shaking uncontrollably. She needed help. She had to do something. Her hand inched toward the phone but stopped just before reaching it. No, she couldn't bother her daughter and son-in-law again. A pill, she would take a pill. She certainly had enough of them. She had many leftovers from Ron's illness, and the doctor just last week had given her a new prescription for her preferred antianxiety med. She had barely mentioned how anxious she sometimes was, downplaying her symptoms, the actual attacks.

Still, he had said, "I have no problem giving you another prescription, Debra, you've been through a lot this year. It takes time to heal."

A pill, a pill, she thought again, and with some difficulty, she moved to stand and move into the bedroom where she kept the cache of pills. She stopped and gulped in a huge breath. Had she heard a noise outside? Did she hear movement in the hallway? Maybe she was not alone in the house! She stood immobile but heard nothing but silence. She moved to the drawer, opened it, and extracted the pill bottle. She picked it up and began to unscrew the cap. Her hands shook so much that she dropped the bottle, still capped, and watched it roll with dismay under the bureau.

"No, no," she said out loud.

She sank onto the adjacent bed, placing her head in her hands. Her breathing was worse, coming in shorter and shorter gasps. Finally, mustering all her strength, she dropped to her hands and knees and began to reach under the bureau. Of course, the bottle had been dropped with enough momentum that it had rolled to the farthest back corner. She spied the amber bottle, but it eluded her grasp. She reached again, grasping it and bringing it to her chest. She sat back down on the bed, opening the bottle carefully. She popped the small, round white pill into her mouth, sipping from the nearby water bottle.

"Nothing, it's not working," the voice in her head said. "You're going to die. You're going to die," the voice chanted.

"Maybe I will," Debra said, answering the voice.

Debra repeated the thought, "Maybe I will."

Debra felt her shoulders infinitesimally fall and begin to relax. Ok, so the pill was mercifully beginning to take effect. She allowed herself a more extended breath. She repeated in a whisper, "Maybe I will. Maybe I will die soon."

Why not? It was finally time to die.

"Vegas, here I come," Debra said. "It's time to die. I can't go on like this. I just can't."

CHAPTER 54

DEBRA SIGHED INTO THE PHONE. Maybe she was regressing and becoming a teenager once more. That or she and Devon were already playing out that age-related role reversal where the child begins to act like the parent, and the parent becomes increasingly childlike and in need of care. *But not yet*, Debra thought. *I am not that old.*

"Mom?" she heard her daughter ask, expecting more than a sigh for a response.

"No, Devon, of course, I am not going alone. Kathy has very graciously agreed to go with me for a week. I could use some time away."

"Okay, Mom, I get that; I do. I know it's been a tough year for you. I loved Ron, too, but I know it is different. I cannot imagine what it would be like to lose my husband. I thought Kathy always said it was so hard for her to get away from work, and now she's just zooming off to Vegas with you on short notice for a whole week."

"Look, Devon, all I know is she agreed when I asked. She wants to support me and help me feel better."

"Devon, this trip will be so good for me, and the best part is I won't be a burden to you or anyone else anymore."

"Wouldn't say you were a burden, Mother, I would never say that. But, oh, hey, Mom, someone is at my door. Do you want to hold on?"

"No, Devon, you go. I have to finish packing and call Kathy. The plane leaves early in the morning, and I won't have a chance to speak to you again. But, Devon, please know I love you with all my heart and do not ever feel guilty about anything. You have been the perfect daughter."

Debra could sense that Devon was only half-listening.

"I love you," Debra ended, emphasizing the word love.

"Love ya," Devon shot back perfunctorily.

Debra moved into the bedroom she had shared with Ron. She would not think of him now and let memories engulf her again. She moved to the open suitcase on the bed; bringing that many clothes was unnecessary. She checked the inside pocket of the suitcase, feeling for the multiple bottles of pills. She should have more than enough, and when combined with alcohol, which would be more than simple to obtain in Vegas, her plan should work perfectly. It would all be over soon. She checked the times listed on the single one-way plane ticket. It would all be over soon. She couldn't wait.

CHAPTER 55

Jim one year prior

"JUSTIN LOVES THIS GUY," Jim said, looking up from the TV and chuckling.

"He'll like this show!"

He was enjoying himself watching the slightly profane comedian that Justin loved so much.

Jasmine, sitting unsmiling and emotionless on the sofa next to his chair, jumped from the chair and exploded with words that reverberated across the room.

"Dad, are you crazy? Justin is gone, dead. You talk about him all the time like he's still alive. I hate that!"

She ran from the room, and he heard her bedroom door slam again. Jeannine looked over at him.

"Starting early this morning with the drama, aren't we?" he said.

He was determined to make today a good day, a happy day, if not exactly happy, at least tolerable. Jeannine knit her brows together.

"Jim," Jeannine said gently.

"You do know that Justin is dead. Because Jasmine is right, you do talk about him as if he were alive, as if he were still here. Because if you are becoming delusional, we will need to get you some help."

"I'm not going to see anyone, Jeannine. I already tried that. It didn't work for me."

She nodded slowly.

"Just tell me that you know that Justin is dead. I need to hear you say the words."

Now it was Jim's turn to jump from his seat in the living room. He stood and hurled his empty coffee cup across the room, where it landed in front of the fireplace, shattering into a million pieces.

"I love my son!" Jim yelled passionately, breathing heavily.

Jeannine, who had also risen from her seat when he had stood, now took two steps away, looking at him with something close to fear. She reached out her arm, but stayed far enough away that it was impossible for him to reach her physically.

"We all loved him, Jim," she said quietly, "but he is gone. I need to make sure that you know that. It's been over a year since Justin died."

"Of course, I know that he is not here, Jeannine. Do you see him? Because I don't see him here in the living room? I don't see him in the kitchen, either, and he isn't in his bedroom."

He was trying hard to keep his voice from rising in anger, but it was so hard as so much anger surged through his veins, his body.

"Ok, ok," she repeated slowly.

She was placating him, talking to him like he was a toddler or a mental patient. A mental patient, that was probably exactly what she thought he was!

"As long as you know that we'll be fine. Grief is a process, Jim. It can take a long time to heal."

He closed his eyes. She was about to spout more therapy crap.

"I can't do this right now," Jim said, his words clipped.

He walked away from her and toward the blinds still covering the window on this rainy day. He raised the blinds and looked out at the driveway as he had done that day last year. That day! He looked down the driveway. Justin would be home soon.

CHAPTER 56

"NIGHT, HONEY," Jeannine called warmly as their daughter ran up the stairs to her room.

Jim could not help but notice that again she had failed to acknowledge his presence. He buried the shot glass even deeper into the side of the easy chair he was sitting in, nestling the empty glass next to his hip. He silently prayed, willed that Jeannine would not detect his slightly altered state. He forced his eyes to focus on his wife; unusually, she smiled at him almost kindly.

"Jimmy," she said gently, "you should come with us next time. The group is good. It's not like what you would expect a grief group to be. It might help you."

Jim shook his head and concentrated on not slurring his words. He choked out, "nah, I'm fine."

The kind look vanished from her face.

"You're many things, Jimmy, but fine is not one of them. You can't deny forever that he is gone, you know."

Jim looked down, blinking rapidly. He looked back up at his wife. The kind look had returned once more to her face.

"You have to forgive yourself," she said gently.

Something about the kindness hurt him more than her usual tacit disapproval. He jumped up violently from the chair, exiting with such force that he dislodged the shot glass that had been buried at his side, and it rolled obscenely across the floor, stopping only inches from

Jeannine's foot. He staggered slightly, and as he did so, he saw all the hatred and disapproval roar back into his wife's face.

"That," she said, pointing at the shot glass, "will totally help you," she said sarcastically. She sighed. "You'll lose everything, Jim, as if you haven't lost enough already! Keep it up. It all goes. We go. You must know that."

He bent to pick up the glass and walked wordlessly out of the room.

CHAPTER 57

THE CAR GAVE A STACCATO BEEP as it backed up and pulled out of the driveway. Jim gave a halfhearted wave that, of course, could not be seen in the dark. He staggered up the steps, feeling his body list to one side. Just before his hand closed on the doorknob, he realized confusedly that he had lost the small bag from the hardware store. He patted his coat pockets but could feel only emptiness. Damn! Jeannine would probably be mad that he was not returning with the washers and screws that he had gone out for. Of course, she would probably be mad anyway because it was now quite dark and late. The hardware store had probably closed hours ago. He was relieved to find the door unlocked. He felt unable to grapple with his keys. He staggered in the door. Suddenly, he realized it was pretty late and he was quite drunk. Much more than he had thought. He had left the house hours ago, probably around 3 or 4 p.m., to obtain the parts needed to repair the leaky kitchen sink. He should have driven to the big-box home improvement store. It was closer to their house, but instead of turning left, he turned right and aimed the car at the smaller mom-and-pop hardware store in the strip mall. Yes, it was fifteen minutes further away, but he had convinced himself that he was going there to support a local small business. It would be a good deed. He could not, would not admit to himself that two doors down from this business was a small, somewhat seedy bar. He had gone into the store and had picked up the supplies he needed, but as he exited and crossed to his car, he looked up and suddenly decided to enter the bar. Why not? What could one drink hurt? He was thirsty, and he just needed to relax. There was so much tension at home. It never stopped, never let up. How could having one beer hurt? But now, it was hours later, what was it? He couldn't read the clock in the hallway. Even as he squinted, the numbers were jumping around. He leaned over on the nearby coat rack to steady himself, almost knocking it over. 10 p.m., 11 p.m., he wasn't sure? For the first time, he noticed Jeannine standing in the doorway with her arms crossed, looking at him disapprovingly—no more than disapprovingly—more like he was pond scum or something even worse.

"Please tell me you didn't drive like that!" she said solemnly.

He shook his head no.

"NO, no I dinnit," and he could tell how thick his tongue felt, and he knew that his words would be slurred. "No," he repeated, "sum, sum guy…" he trailed off the words.

"Some guy?" Jeannine repeated. "Some guy you know?"

He shook his head again.

"Some strange man that you just met at a bar? You let a stranger drive you home? You let some strange guy bring you home with your wife and teenage daughter here? Jim, they have Ubers for this kind of thing! You don't get in a car with a stranger or bring that stranger to your house. You're putting us all in danger!"

"It's ok," Jim slurred, "he only wanted to help."

"Or come back later and murder us all in our sleep," she snorted.

"Lil dramatic there," he retorted.

He moved into the kitchen; maybe he would try to make coffee if he could figure out how to work the Keurig. Jeannine followed him.

"I won't even ask if you made it to the hardware store because clearly you didn't."

Jim saw a foil-wrapped dish on the counter and, distracted by it, went to lift the foil to see what Jeannine had made for dinner.

"I wouldn't eat that if I were you," she said, her words clipped and short.

"It's been sitting on the counter now for hours, and there's sour cream in it."

He replaced the foil.

"Jim, you have a drinking problem now, too," she said, sighing.

NO!" Jim said, raising his head to look at her and realizing he was glowering angrily.

"Jim, for God's sake, get help before it is too late. I'm going to bed. There are pillows and blankets on the couch for you. Please don't come upstairs and disturb us."

She walked away. He stared after her. He picked up his foil-wrapped meal and hurled it toward the garbage can, plate and all.

CHAPTER 58

JIM HESITATED, remaining seated in the car even after turning the keys off in the ignition. He hated the driveway. It reminded him too much of Justin, and just sitting here reminded him of that awful morning when he had found Justin sitting in the car in the driveway. He shook his head to clear the visions and the memory. He needed to go into the house and apologize again to Jeannine and Jasmine. He had come home drunk again last night. He thought he had waited long enough, and they both might be asleep in bed, but as the Uber rounded the corner, he saw all the lights in his house blazing. They had both been seated in front of the TV in the living room, and both had looked up at him disapprovingly, judging him again as he entered. He had raised a hand in greeting, hoping to hide the fact that he had been drinking, although when he would have to request a ride to work from Jeannine in the morning, that would be a dead giveaway that he had gone out with some of his coworkers after work. If he had only left the bar at the same time they had. Tom had said he would give him a ride home, but he hadn't been ready to go. He didn't have enough of the familiar buzz that would wash away the memories of Justin for a few moments—a few hours if he were lucky. Anyway, he had tripped over the rug as he had entered the living room, throwing him off balance and causing him to crash into the wall.

Whoops! he had said, trying to be lighthearted. "Little clumsy tonight," he had said, trying to smile.

Jasmine had jumped from her seat on the couch and headed for the stairs. She had to pass by him to reach the stairs, and he grabbed her arm. He wanted to say "Please, Jazzy, I love you, don't leave," but instead he had just slurred,

"Where ya goin'?"

And she had let out a muffled yell, "Ouch, Dad, stop, you're hurting me!"

"Jim!" Jeannine yelled.

Jim let go of his daughter in shock. He hadn't meant to hurt her. That was the last thing he wanted to do!

Jasmine gave him a look of disapproval and ran up the stairs as fast as her feet would take her.

"What are you doing? What is wrong with you?" Jeannine said, and he heard such fury in her voice.

He was ashamed that he had startled Jasmine, which somehow made him feel such anger at himself, but instead, he directed this anger at Jeannine.

"I didn't do anything to her," he yelled. "I just wanted to talk to my daughter! What is so wrong with that?"

"Then come home and talk to her, don't go out drinking all night. Jim, I can't believe this is happening again."

He felt such a surge of rage flood up from his belly. The rage was so intense, he found it scary. He turned toward Jeannine, wanting to tell her how he felt and how scared he was, but she did not shut up. Now she had raised her voice.

"It has to stop, Jim, and stop now!" she shouted at him. "We can't live like this anymore."

It was like she thought he wanted to do this! Well, he didn't want this! He didn't want any of it!

"I have told you we won't continue to live like this, but no, you…"

He couldn't take it. No more words, no more noise.

"Shut up, shut up, you bitch," he screamed with so much force and so much anger—more than he even knew he was capable of. He slammed his hand on the wall and watched Jeannine move away from him in fright. He didn't know what to do. There was no more to say. He staggered past Jeannine, watching her move even further from him. Did she think he was going to hit her? He hadn't hit anyone since college! He half fell onto the sofa, covering his face with his hands. He heard Jeannine's footsteps run up the stairs just as Jazzy's had a few moments before. He slumped onto the couch, pulling the blanket over him, now that the couch seemed to be his new permanent bed. He had woken at 5:30 a.m. feeling headachy and sick, but he had washed up in the downstairs bathroom and grabbed clean clothes from the laundry room. He took an Uber back to work that morning.

He hesitated in the car for one more minute, then exhaled with a sigh. He owed both of his girls a huge apology. He would tell them he was done drinking. He would tell them things would get better. It had been a long, miserable day at work. He had felt hungover for most of the day and snapped at his coworkers again. But maybe it was all for the best because he felt so awful that he had made a vow never to drink again. All he had to do now was apologize to Jeannine and Jasmine, and they could all start over. Opening the door, he almost tripped over the two large suitcases. He stared at them uncomprehendingly as if he didn't know what they could mean. Jeannine appeared, rounding the corner with her purse and Jasmine's backpack.

"Going on a trip?" he said solemnly.

"Oh, Jim," she said, and he watched her attach the purse and the backpack to the top of each suitcase.

He stood there glumly, staring at the luggage without looking up at Jeannine.

Suddenly and without warning, he felt hot pinpricks of tears appear in his eyes. He cleared his throat without speaking.

Jeannine looked at him, and he saw resolve and seriousness on her face so clearly. "Jim, Jasmine and I are moving out. I've tried to help you in every way I know how. You refuse to stop drinking; you won't go to thera..."

He cut her off before she could finish the word.

"I tried therapy, Jeannine, you know that. I couldn't do it. It's not for me."

She shook her head.

"I have tried to give you time, but the drinking, the anger, the delusions. It's too much. It's not healthy for Jasmine. She's so young, and she has been through so much. She has her own healing to do. I can't, Jim, I won't. I won't lose another child. I have to save Jasmine."

Now Jim was crying. This couldn't be happening! This couldn't be real!

"You don't have to go."

He choked out the words, and as he looked at Jeannine, he saw she was crying too.

"We can be a family again. I'll change! I was going to tell both of you, no more drinking. I'm done. I am. We can be a family again. I know it! We can do it. Just the four of us!"

Jeannine took a step away from him.

"The four of us, Jim? There aren't four of us anymore! There are three of us, and that's the problem right there! Jim, get some psychiatric help before it's too late."

She shook her head, picked up the suitcases in one fluid movement, and slammed the door.

As he heard her car start up, Jim realized that his daughter was already gone and had left without a goodbye. He had no idea where they were going. He stared at the closed door. Had saying four been a slip of the tongue? He realized he was unsure. He continued to stare at the door until his legs felt weak and he felt a wave of dizziness so strong that he was forced to sit down on the bottom stair.

CHAPTER 59

JIM RAPPED SHARPLY on his boss Don's office door while opening it, not caring if he was interrupting or being invited to enter. Social niceties just weren't important to him anymore. He approached Don's desk, only then realizing he was on the phone.

"Call you right back," Don said to the person on the line.

Jim did not greet his boss but immediately said, "I need to take a few days off. I have to go somewhere. I'll be back next week."

Don stared at him, and it seemed to be taking a long time for him to answer or respond in any way to Jim's request—or was it a demand?

Jim shrugged at him and frowned.

Don sighed loudly.

"Again, Jim?" he intoned solemnly. "I know you've been through a lot, but you are taking a lot of time off, more than almost any other employee."

"I only need a couple of days, Don, ok? I'm not even asking for a whole week," Jim snarled. He had no intention of backing down and acquiescing to someone who had no idea what it felt like to be him, how hard it was to be him, to live!

Don sighed again, which was actively beginning to piss Jim off.

"Jim, take as much time as you need."

"Ok, then," Jim said and turned to leave the office.

"Jim, wait, understand me. Take all the time you need, but don't bother coming back here after that."

"What?" Jim queried.

"We'll pay you for your hours worked, and you can use the rest of your sick time—that is, what little of it, if any, is left. Your health insurance will continue to be covered because that is the law."

Jim held up his hand to stop Don before he continued droning on.

"You're firing me?" Jim said incredulously. "After all these years?"

"Jim, please understand, this is not something I want to do. The higher-ups and I—well, you should know it has been discussed for a while now. I've tried to protect you. I really have. I've explained all the emotional turmoil you've gone through, and everyone has been more than sympathetic to how hard it must be for you. But, Jim, the new hires who don't know you and don't remember you before all your troubles. Well, many of them are actively afraid of you. You are not easy to be around. The rage, the anger, it's not socially acceptable, and it seems to be getting worse with time, not better. And it's not just how you are socially; we have other employees who are not exactly socially nimble, so if it were just that, we could probably work around it. But your work, Jim, has been shoddy for the past year. Someone must redo your plans before they are sent out to customers, and forget about having you interact with any clients. You would probably curse at them or scare them away. We have all been covering for you for a long time. I am unsure if you are aware of this, but it can't continue. I am under increasing pressure from upstairs to take action regarding you, and now you are requesting even more time off. Do you even have a good explanation for the time off? Are you going away to get help or something?"

Jim knew he could have lied and said yes. Maybe even that lie would save his job, but he didn't feel like it.

"I told you I need to go somewhere," he snarled.

Don shook his head. He looked up at Jim with a steely, unyielding expression.

"Ok, then, Jim, take the time, do whatever you need, but don't come back here. Please clear your desk now and leave within the hour; otherwise, I will have security escort you. I'd get busy right now if you don't want a scene. Are we clear?"

Jim nodded and slammed the door as he stomped back to his cubicle. Ok, he and Justin could stay in Las Vegas as long as they wanted. He would not be rushed to return to the architecture firm. It was probably better that way.

CHAPTER 60

"IS THERE SOMEONE I can call for you, sir? Is there anyone you would like to come and stay with you? The doctor should be in soon to explain your test results, and sometimes it helps to have an extra set of ears to listen," the nurse said, smiling at him kindly.

Jim looked down at the thin, white blanket draped over his lap as he lay on the uncomfortable gurney. What was this thing made of? Rocks or a concrete slab? It wasn't possible that he could be more uncomfortable! Jim looked up at the young nurse, who was still smiling at him expectantly. He shook his head no, and only then did Jim realize with certainty that there was no one. There was no one for her to call to be with him. Jeannine and Jasmine were a state away, and Jasmine wasn't even speaking to him. He guessed Jeannine might come if she were called, but it would take her hours to get here. Plus, he wasn't sure, but he thought she might be seeing someone. On their last phone call over a month ago, she asked him if he was seeing anyone.

"NO," he gruffly replied.

"Jim, I…" she had started, and somehow, he felt sure she was going to say she had met someone. He hadn't wanted to hear it and had cut her off.

"I have to go, Jeannine."

He had slammed down the phone. No, there was no one to call, no one who would want to come and be with him, no one who would want to see him, and no one he wanted to see.

"Ok, sir," the nurse said, touching his hand gently, "the doctor should be in soon."

Was he mistaken, or did he see a glimmer of pity in her eyes? How dare she pity him! He hated people, all people, these days. He somehow attempted to adjust himself on the gurney to find a more comfortable position. He should get up, put his clothes back on, and leave this hospital. But still he waited. He mustn't be having a heart attack. There were no monitors on him now. The EKG had been done, and no one was rushing in. It had been months since he had walked out of Laney and Broadmoor Architecture with his box of personal items under his arm. Laney and Broadmoor had been his workplace for almost thirty years. Thirty years and what did he have to show for it? Absolutely nothing! He had opened the car door and thrown the box in the back seat with such force that most items had bounced out and even now lay strewn across the back seat. He had awoken this morning, and a fog had settled over him as soon as he realized that he had nowhere to go, nothing to do. Maybe he would go to Vegas with Justin, as he had said months ago. He would research flights this afternoon. Suddenly, though, he felt a need—no, greater than a need, an urgency, a compulsion—to get out of the house. He would go to the bank. He would need funds for the trip. He dressed quickly, drove to the bank, and realized that he felt incredibly dizzy as he approached the teller. He shook his head to shake the feeling off. He hadn't eaten any breakfast; that was all it was. He waited in line behind an older man, feeling the line move at a stultifyingly slow pace, sweat breaking out under his arms and on his forehead. Finally, it had been his turn, but as he approached the teller, he had stumbled and felt an awful wave of both nausea and dizziness.

The teller, not noticing, said, "May I help you, sir?"

Jim had begun to thrust the withdrawal slip in her direction, but then had had to close his eyes as the waves of dizziness only grew in intensity.

"Sir," the young teller said, noticing something was wrong with him. "Are you alright?"

Jim felt as if he had lost the power of speech. He looked around desperately and choked out "Go ahead" to the woman standing behind him. He staggered back to a green couch abutting two chairs, where people waited to do business with one of the bankers. He sat down, putting his head in his hands, willing these awful feelings to disappear. The waves of nausea had not subsided, and then he had felt an uncomfortable pressure in his chest. He grabbed at the front of his shirt, feeling his heart beat out an ever faster beat, faster than he had ever felt it before.

"Sir," a young banker with slicked black hair and impossibly shiny shoes stared down at him as he forced his eyes open. The light was so bright. His eyes hurt so badly!

"Are you ok?"

Jim wanted to stand and run from the bank, but doubted his legs would hold him up.

"Are you ok?" the banker repeated stridently.

"Don't feel so well," Jim gasped in a voice that did not sound like his own. He grabbed his chest again.

"Are you having chest pains?" the young banker repeated, raising his voice on the word pains.

Jim gave a half nod, and just like that, the young banker yelled out, "Doris, call 911 now."

"You're ok, sir, you're ok," a young woman in a navy-blue suit soothed.

Where had all these people come from, and they were all surrounding Jim. He might be going in and out of consciousness, for chunks of time seemed to be missing. The next thing he remembered was two EMTs arriving with a loud walkie-talkie squawking on one of their hips.

"Alright, alright," Jim remembered slurring, but the next thing he remembered, he was in the back of the ambulance with houses and trees passing by so fast that he had to close his eyes again to stave off the nausea. And now here he was, lying on this concrete slab of a gurney. He had had a few tests; they had taken blood, and he was waiting for a doctor. He breathed in—no, no pain. What was he doing here? He needed to leave.

Whoosh, a doctor in a white coat with green scrubs underneath bustled in, moving the curtain surrounding Jim's gurney aside.

"Mr. Waggoner," he said briskly.

Jim nodded dumbly.

"All your tests and your blood work have come back. Your heart appears to be in good condition. Pulse ox rate is good, and there are no signs of any infection," he said, looking down at his papers. "You appear to be just fine physically. Has anything happened recently to you that is particularly upsetting?"

Jim laughed harshly, causing the doctor to look up at him for the first time.

"Like losing my job of thirty years recently? Would that qualify?"

The doctor nodded and said, "Uh-huh. Mr. Waggoner, in my opinion, you had a fairly severe panic attack, which is understandable given the circumstances you just mentioned. There is no reason to keep you here, although I will send you home with a few benzodiazepines just for the next couple of days. If you continue feeling anxious, you might want to find someone to talk to."

"No," Jim barked, causing the doctor to frown.

"Ok," the doctor said, sighing. "I'll sign the release form, and you can pick up your prescription at the pharmacy. You can have it filled downstairs, so it shouldn't take long. Any questions?"

"No!" Jim repeated forcefully once again.

"You can go ahead and get dressed. Mr. Waggoner" — the doctor hesitated before parting the curtain — "you'll be ok, you'll see," he said softly and kindly.

Jim snorted, "Yeah, right, what do you know?"

The doctor shook his head and was gone.

Jim dressed quickly, and as he fastened his belt, he looked up toward the ceiling. Justin, he said silently to himself. We're going to Vegas. We'll leave tomorrow. Now, all he had to do was go home and gather all the necessary items. He would get the rest of the things he needed once they arrived. He couldn't wait!

CHAPTER 61

JIM HAD NOT BOOKED the trip to Vegas as planned when he returned from the hospital. He had instead sent out a few résumés, and improbably, the prominent architecture firm Swanson and Cross had immediately called him, requesting that he come in for an interview. He had felt a fleeting moment of hope. Could things possibly be looking up?

But now, Jim kicked the door open after unlocking it, not caring that his dress shoe made a black scuff mark on the bright white door. He dropped the briefcase on the floor and immediately began tearing the tie off his neck as if it were choking him. That had gone well, not! This was his first interview since losing his job, and there was no way he would get a callback. He had seen the frowns on his interviewers' faces as he had walked out of the room. It had only been a few months since he had been asked to leave his job. Asked to leave, get real, he was fired. If he ever went back there, he would probably be arrested immediately, since they were all afraid of him. He had time, he guessed. They were paying him for his vacation time, and he had some savings, but he would burn through that quickly without anything else coming in. COBRA would cover his health insurance for a year—18 months? His wife and daughter didn't need to know anything about what had happened. His wife hardly ever called him now, and his daughter—well, she never called him. They didn't even ask him for money, but he still sent them a little each month. It was only fair, and he had always carried the health insurance. The damn COBRA—its cost was exorbitant. No wonder they called it COBRA—it certainly stung like a damn snake bite. So, they didn't need to know jack shit for now. But still, he needed another job to live, to pay the mortgage—he was fond of eating now and then. He hated searching online for employment and knew he would compete with people decades younger than himself. Was it a reasonable risk to hire a fifty-five-year-old architect when they could pay a kid half his salary and train them to do exactly what they wanted? Did they see some old washed-up loser when they read his résumé—or when he walked into the interview this morning? All three interviewers had been younger than him; the woman looked scarcely older than his daughter. He had felt so nervous; he hadn't been on an interview in decades. All three of them had been polite and cordial at first, but when they discovered that he had been one of the architects on the Century City project, they even gave him a modicum of respect.

"That building is iconic," the woman had chirped.

Jim had felt himself start to relax, and that should have been the key right there because when you start to feel better, you always get kicked right in the teeth. They asked Jim some basic questions about architecture, which he answered easily, but then the man with the incongruous lime green tie shook his head and said, "Man, Laney & Broadmoor is one good firm. What made you decide to leave there?"

Jim had his answer preplanned, of course, and while the firm might not give him a recommendation due to all his fuckups, he was almost sure that they wouldn't sabotage him either. But then they hadn't needed to, had they? He was well capable of sabotaging himself. He didn't need one bit of help. Instead of parroting his carefully curated response that he had even practiced in the mirror last night— "I needed a change, was ready for a new challenge, to work with younger partners, and impart my experience"—he broke out in a sweat and looked down, and then, so improbably, he saw Justin's face right in front of his eyes. He had looked up, and the young associate just for an instant looked like Justin. Now he was entirely unnerved!

"Mr. Waggoner?" the young woman questioned, frowning at him.

How could he continue with his canned response? It would look disingenuous. Tell the truth, a voice deep inside him said. He looked up, smiling tightly.

"I've had a little tough go recently. My son, he, well, he passed away."

What was he doing? They weren't going to understand this. He was screwing up royally.

"Oh, I'm so sorry," the young woman said with an intake of breath. "Did he pass away recently?"

"Um, no, two years ago."

He saw the two men exchange a glance. There was silence as if no one knew what to say.

"Well, what have you been working on recently?" the other man asked briskly, determined to move on and past Jim's disclosure.

"I was working on the Tate Building."

"Oh, yes, almost in completion now, isn't it? Were you the lead architect?"

"No, I was only on the project for a few months."

Great, he was floundering again. He had missed so many days that Carl had removed him from the project.

"What was the last project you worked on at Laney?"

"I was, I was…" Jim found himself breaking out in a full sweat. He couldn't remember! He had spent so many days just staring at the wall. He really couldn't remember what he had been working on! Finally, a name, and at this point, he was grasping for a name, any name: "the Manhasset shopping complex," he said, satisfied that something had popped into his head.

Now he watched as all three of them looked at each other with confusion readily apparent on their faces.

"Manhasset?" the woman said. "But that project has been completed, that complex has been open and operational for over a year. You couldn't have been working on it recently unless they are doing a reno that we don't know about."

Jim thought of saying, Yes, that is it. They are doing a top-secret renovation, but that could be easily checked, so what would be the point?

"Oh, yeah, you're right. Guess I lost track of time." Jim looked down, closing his eyes, and guess who popped again in front of his face? None other than Justin!

"Mr. Waggoner, are you all right?" Lime Tie asked.

"Do you need some water?" the woman asked, looking concerned.

"Look, I'm fine. I need a job, ok? I've had some problems, but I know what I'm doing. I'm competent," Jim said. If you're competent, do you say you're competent? Jim wondered, thinking that even to his ears, he sounded bad.

"I understand," the woman said soothingly.

"I'm a good worker," and Jim heard his voice break, and he thought of all his days off, snarling at coworkers, staring at the ceiling, and being pulled off project after project. Was that even true anymore?

"Ok, ok," the other young man muttered.

Jim was blowing this big-time. What if they told other firms about this sad loser who came in? He wouldn't find a job anywhere in the city! He felt tears prick his eyes. He blinked rapidly and stared at the young man with blondish hair that was so much like Justin's.

"Look, Justin, you must know I am more than capable."

The man shook his head.

"Mr. Waggoner, my name's not Justin. I'm Peter."

"Oh, right, yes, sorry, sorry. I…" Jim looked down, staring at the brown swirls on the table. He heard the woman push her chair back first, and he felt before he saw the two men rise. He looked up, then slowly stood.

"Thank you for your time," Peter said, holding out his hand.

The other man shook his hand without saying a word. The woman smiled at him warmly and looked at him somewhat sadly. He nodded and left the room, quickening his steps to exit the building immediately. No one had mentioned getting back to him, now had they? They only wanted to get rid of him as soon as possible. He had blown it. That much was certain.

Now that he was home, he looked around the living room of an empty house that he would be entirely unable to afford in a few months. Each day, it became clearer what he needed to do. He had no choice. They were all giving him no choice. There would be some release in completing the plan he had been contemplating. There had to be.

CHAPTER 62

JIM SHOOK THE BOTTLE OF PILLS. Not too many of the damn things left. Had he almost finished the entire bottle? He had sworn after returning from the hospital that he would not take any of the antianxiety pills, but he had tried one late at night after that disastrous job interview when yet again he couldn't sleep. After about twenty minutes, a pleasant feeling of drowsiness had come over him. He realized he hadn't felt drowsy in months, more like years. He had felt drowsy, and then the next thing he knew, he had fallen asleep and awoken in the morning as light peeked through his bedroom curtains. So, he had finished the pills he had been given at the hospital over a week ago and had made an appointment with his doctor with the express intent of obtaining more of the pills, the benzodiazepines, as he had learned that they were called. His doctor had been somewhat reluctant to prescribe them, had cautioned Jim that they were only to be used short-term, and had needlessly reminded Jim that his son had been gone for over two years and if he were still suffering, maybe some therapy would do him good.

"Tried that," Jim had said, doing all he could to maintain a normal demeanor. "Therapy didn't work for me. Look, I need to get a little sleep, that's all."

His doctor had nodded to Jim.

"I'll write you a prescription, but no refills. I don't want you to take these long term. They do have side effects. If one therapist didn't work for you, it couldn't hurt to try someone else. I can give you a list."

Jim had nodded, but only to placate the damn doctor and only to ensure that he would give him the prescription he wanted.

"How are Jeannine and Jasmine doing these days? I haven't seen any of you in so long."

"Fine, they're fine," Jim muttered.

The doctor was unaware that his wife and daughter had left town.

"They're doing good," he said a little too heartily, hoping that no one else in the office knew that Jeannine and Jazzy were gone.

The doctor held out the prescription.

"Jim, I must warn you, don't mix these pills with liquor. Not safe, not safe at all, even a few drinks."

Jim stared at his knees. How could the doctor possibly know that Jim was drinking again more than ever? Had someone seen him at a bar or the liquor store? No, it was probably something that the doctor said when he handed out the prescriptions. He was getting paranoid.

"Thanks," Jim muttered, taking the scrip and jumping off the edge of the examining table. He was so ready to get out of here. He had what he had come here for.

But now, less than a month later, he had less than five pills left. Would he be able to call and get a refill? As much as he would like to believe that might occur somehow, he didn't think that scenario would play out. Should he even keep taking them? He hadn't stopped drinking, but had drunk less since he had the pills. How would he sleep without them? However, he had to admit they seemed less effective in this area than initially. While with the first few pills he had felt the mellow somnolence of drowsiness almost immediately, now, after only a few weeks, the drowsiness was growing less pronounced. They were not working as well as they did at the very beginning. Also, he was beginning to have a sneaking suspicion that the damn things might be making him feel depressed. He did feel sadder, more glum than ever. Also, he was thinking of and fantasizing about suicide more and more. Could the pills be doing that to him? How could he even take any drug after what had happened to Justin? Drugs were no good. He knew that. He should shit can the rest of them, not contemplate how to get more! Maybe they were making him worse. He moved into the bathroom to return the pill bottle to the medicine cabinet. As he opened the door, he spied his face in the mirror, and instead of looking away, he stared into his own eyes. He saw sadness looking out of his eyes at first, but then he watched his features morph into a scowl, and then a look of pure hatred gazed out at him. He heard a nasty voice snarl, a voice he was hearing more and more lately. "You don't deserve to live," the voice rasped. "Look at how many lives you have ruined, you entire waste of flesh! Serve me," the voice continued. "Do it, take them out. You'll feel better. And when it's done, bang, gone like all the rest."

Jim closed his eyes. Were the pills doing this, or was it him? Was something deeply, deeply wrong with him? Drugs had killed Justin. What the hell was he doing?

"No more, I'm done with that shit," he vowed. Maybe he would stop drinking, too.

CHAPTER 63

OK, MAYBE HAVING THE SHOT of whiskey before he made the call wasn't the best idea, but he had been putting the call off all day. He wanted, no, needed to speak with Jasmine. He just needed a little liquid courage to call the number. His conversations with Jeannine were more brief and ever more stilted as the months went by. He could imagine her rolling her eyes or tapping her foot as she attempted to end the conversation. How often had he seen Jeannine do that with an annoying neighbor or, more likely, her complaining cousin? They would laugh and snicker in the background while the person on the phone was completely unaware. Jeannine and Jasmine were probably making faces and attempting to get away from him as he prattled on endlessly, trying to keep a connection that was dying before his eyes.

Jeannine seemed rushed as she answered the phone breathlessly.

"Jim," she replied tonelessly.

He sighed, feeling a rush of anger coursing through his entire body.

"Not glad to hear from me, huh?" he said sarcastically.

"No, Jim, it's not that. We've just returned from the store. My arms were loaded with bags. I rushed to put them down and get the phone."

"On a shopping spree, huh?" he said, and even to himself, realized that his tone seemed accusatory.

"No, not really," Jeannine said slowly. "We were at the grocery store, Jim. Stocking up on some items."

"Having people over?"

Why did his every question come out sounding like an interrogation? He didn't mean for the conversation to go like this.

"Did you want something, Jim?" Jeannine inquired.

She was growing tired of the conversation—of all the questions, he could tell.

"I wanted to see how my family was doing. I want to talk to my daughter, Jazzy."

"Jim," Jeannine said and paused. Paused so long he thought she might have hung up or the call had been dropped. "Have you been drinking?" he heard instead very clearly in his ear.

"Why would you even ask me that?" he said belligerently.

"Because, Jim, your voice sounds like you have been drinking."

"Yeah, I can't call to see how my family is doing. In case you've forgotten, we're not completely divorced yet, Jeannine. Although I bet you probably wish we were."

"Oh, Jim," and he heard a sigh.

Rage coursed through his body. She was treating him like he was some pathetic piece of shit! He wouldn't have it. He squeezed the phone tightly. "Just let me talk to Jasmine. She's my daughter. I have the right."

"I'm not sure you should talk to her like this, Jim."

"Like what, Jeannine? Are you the morality police? You're so much better than I am, aren't you? Give the phone to my daughter right now."

"Ok," Jeannine said breezily.

There was a long enough silence for Jim to take another large quaff from the whiskey glass he had refilled during the interminable conversation with Jeannine. Finally, he heard a whooshing sound and a voice said, "Dad."

His eyes filled with tears almost immediately. Her voice sounded so much younger than the eighteen years she would soon be. He imagined a much younger girl on the line, and his heart broke at the thought of all he was missing.

"Dad?" the voice repeated.

"Hey Jazzie, hey." He remembered once again, too late, how she hated the nickname now. "How are you doing? I miss you so much, sweetheart."

"I'm ok," she said.

Silence.

He remembered how she used to tell him in excruciating detail about her school day. First, we lined up, then sat at our desks, and the teacher said, and then Brianna told me... she could go on like that almost without a breath for forty-five minutes or an hour? Sometimes he would interrupt her and tell her he had work to do, or he would find himself nodding and only half-listening. Now he found he regretted those reactions with every fiber of his being. What he would give now to listen to her voice going on and on, telling him about her day and week, but now Jim was greeted with only lingering silence.

"What have you been doing? Tell me about your day. About the school?" he inquired.

"Everything's fine," she said.

Silence returned.

He opened his mouth as he searched for another question to ask her.

"Dad, I need to go. Mom needs help putting the groceries away."

He felt the rage return and course through his body again, even as a part of him tried to push the feelings away. He said, realizing his voice was louder than it should be, "And the last thing you want to do is talk to me."

"It's not that, Dad."

"Then what is it, Jasmine? Am I not worth your time? Or did your mother tell you not to talk to me? Is that it? She's trying to keep us apart."

"No, Dad, Mom wouldn't do that, and she's not!"

"Yeah, well, I'm your parent, too, not just her. You need to show me some respect."

"Ok, right."

"What? What was that? Sounded sarcastic to me."

"I'm not. I'm not being sarcastic!"

He thought he heard tears in her voice. What was he doing? He was messing this up so, so badly.

"Jasmine, I just wanted to see how you were doing. Maybe you could come and visit me sometime."

"I don't want to return to that house," she said firmly.

"Why? Is it not good enough for you now? Your place is so much better, huh?"

"Dad, no, it's just that I remember Justin too much when I go back to the house; it makes me sad."

"Oh," he replied.

"Listen, Dad, I do have to go. I'm going out."

"Oh, Jazzy, you have a boyfriend." He meant it as a tease to lighten the conversation. Also, she was so young that she couldn't possibly have a boyfriend.

Silence.

His heart raced.

"You do. You have a boyfriend. Does your mother know? I think you're too young to date."

"Of course Mom knows. I have to go," she repeated.

"Jasmine, you're being rude to me."

"I'm not, Dad, I'm not doing anything."

"Mom," she heard Jasmine stage whisper.

"Oh, is Mommy going to help you get away from me, is that it?"

No answer, more rustling.

"Jim," Jeannine's voice once again.

"You should hang up now before you make it worse than it already is. You talked to her, right? You're welcome to come here if you'd like to see her. I will need you to be sober, however, and please don't call us again if you have been drinking first."

"Who says I have been drinking?" He didn't mean to roar out the words, but he knew he had.

"You can talk to Jasmine better if you are sober, that is all," Jeannine said tightly.

"Now, I am going to hang up, Jim. Get some rest."

He heard the phone click loudly.

"Hang up on me, will you?" he yelled.

"Oh yeah, we'll see about that!"

He punched the numbers again, his fingers flying over the keys with fury. He was up to the very last number when he stopped. He hesitated. He threw the phone down on the couch. At least this time, he had enough control to aim at something soft so as not to cause additional breakage. Well, he had screwed that up royally. There was no hope for him, none at all.

CHAPTER 64

JIM GRABBED THE AMBER BOTTLE of liquor by its neck. He moved to the sink with rapidity and furiously uncapped the bottle. He had to move quickly because if he did not, instead of pouring the Jack down the drain, he would be just as likely to grab a shot glass and knock back several, or swig it straight out of the bottle. No one was here to see or care. Why did it matter that it was barely 10 a.m.? Why did it matter that he had a bumping, thundering headache and a sour stomach, most likely from his overindulgence the night before? What exactly mattered at all anymore? Now Jim knew Jeannine would never return; the initial divorce papers came in the mail yesterday. No longer a legal separation, Jeannine was now requesting an actual divorce. He wasn't even sure he cared anymore. However, he still cared deeply about his daughter, but Jasmine never wanted to talk to him anymore. If she was forced to come to the phone by her mother, the conversation was so awkward and so polite that Jim knew he had had more substantive discussions with telemarketers! Jim still had not followed through on his plans to go to Vegas. Instead, he sat in his dirty house with the closed curtains both night and day. And what exactly did he do each day? The answer, most days, was drink. That was precisely what he had done yesterday. He had headed pell-mell for the whiskey bottle as soon as he had gotten up. And now, no wonder, he felt sick this morning. It was almost empty. He shook his head and poured the remains down the sink. There would be no more drinking today. "So, what will you do today, Jim, if not drink?" The snide voice whispered yet again in his ear. He closed his eyes and hurled the bottle. It passed out of the kitchen and rolled into the dining room, silently resting on the light blue carpeting near the mahogany table. He felt so bad. His entire body ached, and thoughts flashed through his mind one after the other, each more negative than the last. He had stopped the damn pills two weeks ago now. Surely, they weren't still in his system, messing with his mind, were they? The benzos, which had offered sleep and a sweet release at first, had seemed to turn on him, no longer offering relief but seeming to be ineffective and paradoxically increasing the anxiety they were touted to relieve. He had looked this up on the internet, and yes, they were only meant to be taken for a short time, and yes, they did sometimes, and with some people, have a paradoxical effect and increase anxiety. When he had read entry after entry about people trying to quit them after long-term use and struggling, even becoming suicidal, he had said out loud right there, seated in front of the computer, "No more, no more." He hadn't touched one since that night, and though he was back to not sleeping again, he initially thought that he felt better—until he decided to stop by the liquor store one day when he was out on one of his aimless drives. He had nowhere to go, no job, and the interviews had dried up since that last disastrous one. What would it hurt to get one small bottle of his favorite whiskey? He could limit himself to one small snort right before bed to help him sleep, but once in the store, he noticed that his favorite brand was on sale; if you bought the slightly larger bottle, it was a deal. Why not? And while he was here, why not just get two? It had all seemed so plausible, but just like that, the nightly drinking ritual had begun again, and his definition of night had slowly increased until 4 p.m., 3 p.m., until he was drinking most of the day. Who was here to care anyway? No one would ever know. Maybe he could drink himself to death? That wouldn't be a bad way to go, would it? He knew he was becoming more depressed each day; he was fantasizing about various ways to kill himself regularly, yet more disturbing, he sometimes felt murderous impulses toward others. He was staying inside more and more like some pathetic hermit. At least it felt safe indoors. And when he went out, any little thing could set him off: hearing people laughing, seeing fathers with young sons. He would feel especially irate if he saw a parent yelling or seeming exasperated with a child. Just the other day he had been in line after getting gas, standing behind a young woman with a boy of perhaps five or six. The boy had bright golden hair, just like Justin's at that age, he had thought, and he had smiled warmly at the boy. The boy had turned away without smiling and focused on the array of candy on the rack next to the register.

"Mama," the boy had said, pointing at one of the larger candy bars with an almost reverent awe. "Look, can I get that?"

The mother had sighed wearily.

"For goodness' sake, Brian, you don't need all that candy! It's a waste of money."

The boy had stuck out his lower lip. "But I want it," he had said pleadingly.

"I said no," the mother said stridently.

You didn't, Jim thought. *You said he didn't need it, but not no.*

"Don't pout," the mother said sternly, bending down until she was eye level with the boy, who then burst into tears.

For some reason, the crying made Jim step back, and suddenly, improbably, he saw Justin's face superimposed over the young boy's. Jim felt his heart racing and sweat breaking out on his forehead.

"Kids!" the mother said, looking back at Jim and shrugging, fully expecting him to commiserate.

Instead, he glared at her.

"Leave the kid alone," he said in a voice filled with rage.

"Why can't you give him what he wants? Don't you know, don't you have any idea how lucky you are to have him? And you, you are throwing it all away by getting upset over nothing, absolutely nothing, a fucking candy bar, really, a fucking lousy candy bar, and that is enough for you to make your son cry! You, lady, you are a fool," and Jim reached around the lady, plunking his cash on the counter in front of the stunned clerk.

"Keep the change; it's more than enough."

He slammed out of the store and ran to his car, even as his mind thought, *What did you do? What just happened?*

Remembering this incident made Jim wish he had not dumped the whiskey down the sink. He stared at the white, swirled ceiling. He moved to his phone. He picked it up and called the familiar number. He stopped and listened briefly before saying, "Justin, do you remember when I said we would go to Vegas for your twenty-first birthday? Well, let's go. I'll book tickets for next week. It's time, Justin, it's finally time."

CHAPTER 65

THE RESERVATIONS FOR LAS VEGAS were finally made. They were leaving on Monday in just three days. This would be his last chance to talk to Jasmine. He hesitated before making the call since his previous calls had gone disastrously. Still, he had to try. He needed to hear her sweet voice one last time. So now here he was, hanging on the phone wordlessly. He hunched forward in the gray armchair in which he was seated. He began to push the footstool in front of him back and forth, back and forth with his foot as he waited. How long was he going to have to wait?

Now he heard whispering, almost inaudible at first but growing in intensity. His daughter, Jasmine, must be approaching the phone. And then just like that, her voice grew louder and so much clearer.

"Mom, I don't want to talk to him. Why do I have to? I have nothing, absolutely nothing to say to him."

"Jasmine, he's your father. He's trying. Please, you only have to talk to him for a few minutes."

"I. Don't. Want. To." Jasmine said, pausing between each word.

"Jasmine, your father has his problems. You'll hurt him, upset him."

"And this is my problem? He is all messed up. He did it to himself. Is he even sober?"

"Yes, Jasmine, I think he is. He sounds sober."

Did they not realize he was hearing every word they were saying? Or did they not care? Jim thought of just hanging up, but like watching a train wreck, he felt compelled to hang on the line to hear what they would continue to say about him.

"Jasmine, please do it for me. Only a few minutes. He probably won't call again for a long time. You know that."

Jim heard an exasperated sigh, followed by a loud rustling in his ear.

"Jasmine?" Jim questioned.

"Hello, Dad," he heard Jasmine say glumly. He thought she would be more excited if told she needed surgery. His mind flicked through images in his head, and he saw a much younger Jasmine laughing and running as he chased her, pretending to be a monster.

"More, Daddy, more," she would yell, running and jumping on him. The vision brought tears to his eyes immediately.

"Are you going to say anything?" Jasmine questioned.

Jim struggled to keep his voice from cracking and to quell the sadness in his voice.

"I just wanted to call and see how you are doing. I'm sorry I haven't called in a while. I've been… I've been…"

He had been what? He hadn't been working or busy unless staring out the window morosely counted as busy. He let the sentence die away.

As he cleared his throat, he asked, "What have you been doing?"

"Well, we just had midterm exams, so studying a lot."

"Oh, ok, and how did you do?"

"I don't know," she said. "I haven't gotten the tests back yet." She seemed perturbed.

"And for fun, what have you been doing?"

"My friends and I go to the movies. Listen, Dad…"

He could tell he was losing her; she was getting ready to brush him off and escape this inane, meaningless conversation.

"Jasmine," he began to speak rapidly. "I miss you. I want you to know that I always have and always will love you, no matter what. I'm getting ready, I mean, I'm not.."

He was almost going to say I won't see you again. He couldn't say that to her! He stopped speaking mid-sentence.

Jasmine seemed uncomfortable with his show of emotion.

"I have to go, Dad. My friend is coming to pick me up, and I have to get ready."

He wanted to tell her that he had changed, that he wasn't going to drink like he had been, that he was sorry that she had seen him like that.

"But Jasmine," he said, and as he paused, he felt the phone go silent, and he knew she was gone. He hesitated. Ok, so he would talk to Jeannine.

"Jeannine," he said, believing that she was wordlessly hanging on the line, but just as the name left his mouth, the phone made a loud beep, beep, beep, and he knew that the connection was lost, was gone. Jeannine had not even returned to the phone, allowing Jasmine to hang up. Neither one of them wanted anything to do with him. They had moved on without him. He was adrift and alone. He looked down at the footstool in front of him and this time kicked it hard with all his might. It skittered across the room, crashing into the bureau and bouncing off it. The stool turned over with its legs pointed up like a dead bug. Once again, anger coursed through Jim's body. He wanted to damage something. He wanted to hurt something or someone. He needed to. He needed to release all this pain somehow.

CHAPTER 66

JIM COULDN'T BELIEVE he had been sick all weekend, as they were scheduled to leave for Vegas on Monday. He had somehow gotten that nasty virus that was going around this fall, even though he seldom left the house these days. The virus was so prevalent and virulent that it was reported on the news. It sucked to be sick all alone. He had never been one to want to be fawned over or paid undue attention, but to lie in bed each night either nauseous or unable to breathe without anyone else in the house was truly a circle of hell. Just last night, his breathing and choking had gotten so bad that he found himself wondering if he should call 911 or if he was overreacting. He would have given anything to have another human being in the house to consult with. Also, during the day, if he felt a little better and he wanted to try to eat, he had to get to the kitchen and attempt to make food for himself—no one there to bring him so much as a glass of water. Last night, he tried to make soup, but after opening the can, he became so dizzy that he had to grab the counter. In doing so, he sloshed half the can onto the floor. After he had cleaned up the mess, he tossed the rest of the can down the sink. He no longer wanted the damn soup! He closed his eyes while rocking back in the recliner, stroking his stubbly, unshaven face. He thought of Jasmine and Jeannine again. He wished they were here with him, but that was a foolish thought! Neither one cared about him anymore. They no longer loved him. He was such a fool. He stared out the window, taking in the trees and the tops of the houses that he could see in the small cul-de-sac.

Suddenly, a couple taking a walk with a dog entered his vision. They were holding hands as the dog trotted in front of them. The man leaned over and kissed the woman. Who were they, and what were they doing walking in front of his house? He did not recognize either of them. They were not nearby neighbors. He stood and glared at them out the window. How dare they walk by his house! What gave them the right to be here on this street? The dog was probably going to take a shit in his yard, and they wouldn't have the sense to pick it up. *Get out of here, go away!* he thought. His anger was flaring again. It took restraint to stop himself from going to the door, opening it, and yelling at them. He had felt an increasing hatred toward random strangers lately, not just this passing couple, but almost everyone he saw. When he saw and heard people laughing, a sharp physical pain would course through his body. Strangers smiling in his direction at a coffee shop or the gas station would earn a well-deserved glare from him. He knew people were giving him a wider berth, and he liked it that way. He especially disliked seeing people smile and have fun. It reminded him of all that he had lost. He continued to stare after the young couple with the damn dog who were continuing to walk and now had just passed his house. The rage coursed through his body like a flooding river threatening to break its banks. The flood might overtake him, and he could be out of control at any moment. He lifted a finger and pointed it gun-like at the young couple first and then at the dog. He made a shooting sound, whispering at first, but then said it out loud, as if anyone was around to hear him or care. He didn't know how much longer he could control these feelings, or sometimes if he even wanted to control them. He put his hand on the window and pressed his head to the cool glass. He and Justin would make it to Vegas tomorrow, no matter what. Soon, it would be over, all over.

CHAPTER 67

Present Day

"WHAT?" JOHN REPEATED. "Debra, no," he whispered, confused.

"You are planning to kill people," she said quietly, but her voice increased an octave as she said the word *people*, and he saw fear in her eyes.

"Debra, what are you talking about? I don't want to hurt people. Those aren't— you think there are guns in those cases."

She nodded.

"Debra, no, I will show you those cases."

"Are you planning to hurt me?" Debra questioned.

He stepped back from her, stunned.

"No, Debra, definitely not you, never you. Debra. I'm no threat to you, none at all. Please believe me."

John opened the two cases, leaning against the orange chair by the large window looking out onto the strip.

John/Jim, or whoever he was, had shown her that one contained a guitar, and the smaller case contained a pool cue.

"See, Debra, they are not weapons," he said solemnly.

"Can you put it away?" Debra said, gesturing at the handgun that was still lying under the coffee table.

John nodded and moved toward the gun, bending down and picking it up, holding it down and away from his body, almost as if it were a dead rat. He moved quickly past Debra, who moved even further from him as he passed. John moved to the closet, opening it, and she heard the gun make a slight clunk as he placed it in the safe. He moved back into the room.

"It's gone," he affirmed. "Do you want to talk?" John inquired.

Debra looked out at the inky blackness, the dead of the night enveloping the strip even as the bright lights of the casinos still gleamed. Debra nodded, "I do."

"How about you? Do you want to talk? It seems you have things you need to explain as well. Do you have time?"

"I have nothing but time, Debra," John said glumly.

"But what about your son?" Debra inquired. "Will he be coming back to the room soon?"

"Oh!" Debra suddenly stopped herself.

So much was different than what she had thought!

"Do you even have a son?"

"Oh, yes, Debra, I have a son. Those things—the guitar, the pool cue—are not mine but his. They belong to Justin."

"But your son, will he be coming back here soon?"

"No, Debra, he won't be coming back here soon. He won't be coming back here at all."

"He was never here with you?" Debra inquired quietly.

"No, Debra," Jim said, looking up, and such sadness flashed across his face that Debra felt her heart clench.

"I don't even know your real name, do I?" Debra questioned.

"Debra, I'm not lying about my name. My full name is John James Waggoner. It's just that the only person who ever called me John was my mother, and she died when I was ten. I've gone by Jim or Jimmy ever since. My ex-wife and my colleagues always knew me only as Jim. Ask my kids, and they'll tell you my name is Jim. But to call myself John, I guess it's a lie, but it's not a complete fabrication. It is my name on my birth certificate. I wanted to start over, be someone different here, someone different with you, maybe someone better."

Why did you come here?" Debra questioned.

He did not answer. He countered with a question of his own.

"Why do you have a bathroom full of drugs?"

"Why did you have a gun under the coffee table, John?"

Debra stood staring at John as he stared back at her. It was as if they were assessing each other, seeing the other for the first time. Finally, John broke the silence.

"Debra, if you use drugs, if you have an addiction, I can't, I won't see you anymore."

"Do I seem like I take drugs, John? Have I appeared high or stoned any of the times, on any of the days that we have been together?"

"No, not at all," John said frankly, surveying her, "but you can't always tell, you don't always know. People with an addiction are very good at hiding what they do. Believe me, Debra, this is something I know about."

"I don't take drugs recreationally, John, and I haven't taken even one pill since I have been here in Vegas."

"I can't believe you are severely ill and need that many drugs to survive."

"You are right about that," Debra said glumly.

"I can think of only one other reason why you might need that whole pharmacopeia of drugs that I saw."

"Say it," Debra challenged him.

"I think you might be planning on killing yourself."

Debra did not respond but instead gestured toward the closet and the safe.

"John, if you are not planning on killing other people. If you are not going to go to a gun range for target practice, then there is only one other reason for you to have a gun."

John looked down and shook his head negatively.

"Say it," he said, looking back up at Debra.

"Are you planning on killing yourself?" she questioned.

"Well, we both know our plans for the end of the week, right?"

"Oh, John."

"Oh, Debra."

"But your son?" Debra questioned. "Wait. Your son is here, but never around."

She looked quizzical as if she were trying to figure something out.

"Two days ago, I saw you standing beside your son at the blackjack table."

"What?" John questioned, looking puzzled and surprised.

"You're here alone, aren't you?" Debra whispered.

"You know, I have never seen the elusive Kathy either. Are you here alone, Debra?"

"I am. Kathy was never here with me. For all I know, she is at home in Massachusetts or on one of her frequent business trips. Was your son here with you, or did he leave?"

"My son, Debra, is with me every second of every day. You can't see him. No one can see him. When you see me on the phone talking to him, I am talking to an old voicemail system I have had for two years, so I can continue to hear his voice. My son never answers, Debra. My son never answers, but he is always with me because my son is dead, Debra, and has been for almost three years now," John said, his voice cracking at the admission.

CHAPTER 68

DEBRA LOOKED DOWN, picking at the skin on the side of her thumb. Silence permeated the room. John gestured toward the ugly orange chairs near the large windows.

"Please sit down, Debra, so that we can talk."

They moved to the chairs and both sat down heavily.

Debra, with tears in her eyes, told John the truth.

"John, I am not divorced. My husband died of cancer just over a year ago. Ron was fifteen years older than I. We got together when Devon was eleven years old. We did meet at work, like I told you. I loved Ron every day until he died. I love him still."

John remained quiet, as if waiting for her to say more.

"My world became very small after Ron was diagnosed with Stage 4 cancer. I worked with some independent accounting clients, and Ron had semi-retired two years before. We did some traveling. After Ron's diagnosis, he retired completely. I initially tried to keep some of my clients, but as Ron's condition worsened, I had to let them go. It happened slowly, and I didn't even realize it at first, but my world slowly shrank smaller and smaller. I stopped responding to all but my best friend. Who wanted to talk to me anyway? What did I have to discuss with anyone? It was even hard to keep up with the news, and who wants to hear why, yes, Ron threw up five times after the chemo. Last night, he had diarrhea and had to be changed twice. Who wants to listen to that? Plus, people who haven't experienced grief or been touched by loss just do not get it. Grief has an expiration date for them. You are supposed to get over it like a bad flu in two weeks or, at worst, a month."

John nodded, understanding, feeling understood by someone else for the first time in a very long time.

Debra sighed, "I didn't want to tell you my husband had died because I didn't want you to pity me, and I didn't want to talk about death, so instead I said I was divorced."

John nodded and looked at Debra questioningly. He was waiting for her to provide additional details about her husband. Could she do it? Could she tell someone the part of the story that she had shared with no one? She closed her eyes, seeing Ron lying in that hospital bed in their bedroom so clearly. She didn't want to go back there again. Part of her did not want to remember any of it, but the images were flying through her mind, now becoming clearer and more intense. She began to speak without even realizing that she was talking.

"Do you know what death or dying was like for us? My husband died of lung cancer, and he wasn't even a smoker! I find the sympathy you get when you speak of death annoying. People never know how to react; they either look at you weirdly, avoid the topic, or offer meaningless platitudes while attempting to get away from you as soon as possible."

"I get that," John said, nodding.

"You feel that people would be more comfortable if you never mentioned the deceased again."

Debra nodded vehemently.

"Finally, someone who gets it," she said.

"Dying or death for Ron happened very slowly and then all at once, if that makes any sense."

"I think I know what you mean," John replied, "but it wasn't like that for me, for us. Death was a ton of bricks that hit us over the head, bringing me, all of us, really, to our knees."

Debra continued, "Anyway, when Ron was first diagnosed and even when he first started chemotherapy, he could go days, sometimes even weeks, when he felt and seemed normal. He could do things; we would go out. Maybe a little coughing, shortness of breath, but not much more than if he had a cold. It was so easy to pretend that nothing was happening. I would play games with myself that the diagnosis had been a mistake or an awful dream, and that I would wake up tomorrow and it would all have gone away, never happened, and we would be back to normal."

"I understand," John said solemnly.

"Denial can be easy," Debra continued.

"But it didn't go away. I would wake up each day, and Ron would still be sick. He was getting worse every day, but so slowly, ever so slowly each day. It was heartbreaking and sad to watch the life, the vital part of him, slip away. The worst part was that there was no one I could talk to about it. Ron was always my confidante, and I couldn't speak to him about this. Friends, it was so hard. My best friend, Kathy, and I were always very close, but I felt she wanted to offer platitudes and move on to another topic as soon as possible. I know that she tried, and I don't mean to down her because who wants to deal with death? It's better to deny its existence, pretend it isn't happening, except we couldn't. Ron and I couldn't do that because it was constantly in our face each and every day. Ron was adamant about protecting Devon from the worst of it. He didn't want her to see him like that, so he told me repeatedly to have her stay away. I didn't know how to talk about my feelings without sounding like I was complaining or feeling sorry for myself. Who could understand? It didn't take me long to stop talking about anything I felt. Sometimes it seemed that no one even noticed or cared. When I realized no one noticed, that may have been the cruelest loss."

Debra continued speaking, gazing off into the distance, seeming lost and immersed in her story.

"It eventually got to the point where the doctor said that it was time for hospice."

"Debra," the hospice nurse said calmly once they were seated in the living room.

"I think you have a need for our services. We can work to set up a schedule right now if you would like."

Debra shook her head.

"You heard Ron, he doesn't want anyone here. We'll be fine."

The nurse inhaled a large breath and looked at Debra seriously, almost severely.

"Yes, I heard what he said very clearly, but frankly, Debra, it is not his decision alone; you deserve to have a voice and a vote on this decision as well."

"He's the one who is sick, though, so I must respect my husband's wishes. He has repeatedly told me that he only wants me to care for him, and I get that."

"Debra," the nurse said, using her name again, almost as if she were a child.

"Yes, Debra, Ron is the one who is sick, and make no mistake, he is dying, and he has his own process to go through. However, if you feel you need help, you have the right to receive it. Caretaking is an exhausting, never-ending job. You will need breaks, and he will only get worse, not better."

"My daughter will help me if I need a small break."

"Debra, I'm just going to say this," the nurse said, leaning forward and touching her knee. "Your husband is not being completely rational about this. He wants you to do everything, and I'm not sure he knows how much he is asking of you. Right now, Debra, you look exhausted. A little help, even a few days a week, would be good for you. You need to get away from this house, take a break, see the sunlight, and other people."

Debra pushed herself off the couch quickly and walked toward the window, her feet slapping the floor hard as she pressed down with such anger and force with every step. She stared out the window.

"We have windows. I can see the sun from right here inside. Besides, you don't understand, you can't possibly understand. Ron saved me many years ago. My life was a mess. I was a single mother, barely getting by, and everything changed for the better when my daughter and I met Ron. He has taken care of us so well over all these years. I love him and never thought I could love a man again. I owe Ron everything, and it's even more than that. I love him with every fiber, every molecule of my being. I would do anything for him, and I will! If he wants me, and only me, to care for him, I will do that. Case closed."

Debra looked back at the nurse with a severe, uncompromising expression.

The nurse sighed, "You would still be taking care of him; you would be doing almost everything. We set a schedule that works for both you and Ron. Debra, you deserve the break. Please don't take on more than you can handle. We are here to help, not take over."

The nurse opened her mouth to say more, but Debra held up a hand and shook her head.

"No, thank you for your time, but you heard Ron there. He doesn't want help. I shouldn't have called you in the first place."

The nurse shook her head, pulling a card from the puffy black notebook beside her.

"At least take my card. Please call us if you change your mind or have any questions."

Debra nodded, taking the card and moving fluidly toward the door. She suddenly could not wait to be rid of this woman. It took all of her strength not to push her out the door. As Debra closed the door, she saw the woman look back at her and nod sadly.

Debra leaned against the door for support. Before inhaling one more breath, she heard a voice rasp out, "Debra, Debra," then Ron's voice rose slightly in intensity.

"I'm coming," Debra called.

She hurried toward their bedroom, and as she entered, she stopped momentarily. It was still a shock, even after two months, to see the hospital bed in the room sitting adjacent to their bed.

"What, Ron, what do you need? Are you in pain?" Debra inquired.

Ron nodded, closing his eyes.

"Can I have another pill? My back is hurting like a bastard!"

Debra moved to get out the pill, only then realizing that her hands were shaking. She sat with him, rubbing his legs and humming softly to soothe him. After about ten minutes, the tightness in Ron's facial expression seemed to loosen slightly, and he opened his eyes.

"She's gone, right?" he croaked.

"Who? Oh, you mean the hospice nurse. Yes, she's gone."

"Debra, I don't want them here. I can't bear it. I only want you to take care of me. I don't want strangers seeing me like this, and I don't want strangers touching me or seeing my privates."

"I know, Ron, I know," Debra soothed.

"Promise me they won't be back. I can't bear it right now. I only need you."

"I told her that, Ron. I told her to leave and that we don't need help now."

"Good, good," Ron whispered, seeming to relax.

"Maybe if I get better in a few weeks and can do more for myself, they can come back then, but right now, no, out of the question!"

Debra nodded.

"The nurse just said that maybe I needed a little help. I know you don't want strangers here, but maybe if I had Devon or even David stop by, maybe only for a half hour a week or so.." But before Debra could continue, Ron, with great effort, pushed himself halfway up in the bed, wincing all the way.

"No, Debra, NO," he said forcefully.

"Devon is a kid. She shouldn't have to see me like this, nor should David. Please, no."

"Ok, Ron, ok, please lie back down. Relax; you have made yourself clear. No one else, just me."

He collapsed back onto the pillows. He was coughing, but she could tell he was trying so hard not to. He reached out for her hand.

"Thank you, Debra, you can do this, you know. You are strong. You don't need anyone else."

Debra nodded, but something clenched in her belly at the same time. "Don't be selfish," she heard a severe voice say. "He has done so much for you; how dare you complain or ask for help? You are lazy and you are weak!"

Debra held Ron's hand as he fell asleep, remaining perched on the bed long after he was out and unaware of her presence.

CHAPTER 69

THE DAYS AND THE NIGHTS bled into each other more and more now. Sometimes, Debra was unsure where one day ended and another began. She was now awake all hours of the night with Ron. She wasn't sure if he was even aware of the concept of day and night. He was in so much pain, even with the higher milligrams of morphine he was now on. She was constantly monitoring him, caring for his needs. Was his breathing ok? Was he comfortable? The doctor had told her not to chase the pain, not to wait too long to give him the pain medication.

"If you wait until he is in visible pain, he will likely suffer for hours. At this point, do not hesitate to give him more. You can't hurt him at this point," the doctor had said.

So she monitored his breathing, his body twisting and turning, seeming to be in pain. Any conversation between them was negligible at this point. He could converse for a few sentences before becoming fatigued, which had to be either before the medication took effect or as it wore off. And if she let the meds wear off too much, he would become nearly incoherent, seemingly dazed by the pain. He wasn't eating or drinking much anymore. He was wearing an adult diaper, but she rushed to change him almost immediately. She didn't believe he was fully aware that he had a diaper on. She knew that her fastidious husband would be horrified at the thought, so she rushed to keep him clean at all times. She changed him more frequently than she had ever changed Devon when she was small.

Debra sipped the coffee, which was cooling rapidly in the mug. She had poured it forty-five minutes ago but was just now taking the first sip as Ron had called, well, more or less moaned just as she had been about to lift the then steaming cup to her lips.

She had attended to his needs.

Now back in the kitchen, Debra looked at the adjacent calendar to orient herself to what day it was. Her heart quickened, and she was gladdened for just a moment. It was Wednesday. Devon had said she would stop by this morning. Debra couldn't wait. Devon didn't help with Ron's caretaking, but it would be so good to see someone who was vibrant and alive. So good to talk with someone who could comprehend every word she was saying. As she smiled, thinking of her daughter, the phone rang. Debra snatched it off the counter. Ron had finally fallen asleep; she did not want the phone to disturb him.

"Mom," she heard Devon's familiar voice.

"Hi, honey, how are you? I can't wait . . . " but before Debra could continue, Devon cut her off.

"Mom, I am so sorry, but could I cancel coming there today? I know you like to see me, but you don't let me do anything to help with Ron. I really need to do some food shopping, and David is taking a half day from work, and you know we're going away this weekend, and I haven't even packed yet."

Debra felt something sneak into her stomach, like a large boulder. Debra now cut Devon off.

"No, honey, that is fine. If you're too busy, I understand," Debra said, sighing at the same time.

"Mom, if you need me, say so!" Devon demanded, her familiar quick temper flaring.

"No, honey, there is nothing I need. I was looking forward to talking to you, that's all."

"Do you need anything from the store? Does Ron need anything?"

"No, Devon, we are fine."

"You're sure? I'll stop by next week, no excuses," Devon affirmed.

"Ok," Debra said quietly.

"Mom, are you sure you're ok?"

"Yes, of course, I'm just tired."

"Ok, well, get some rest. I'll see you soon."

Debra held onto the phone even after Devon had clicked off and was gone.

It had been a long, hard day for both of them. Ron had, for some reason, seemed to be in more pain than usual. He had been coughing more and had thrown up twice. Deep coughing fits racking his body, making Debra wonder if she needed to call the doctor. He had complained of pain several times, and she had found herself increasing the pain medication dose each time he asked. Debra had a throbbing headache that just would not quit. She realized now that she had needed to see Devon or somebody. She needed a break; the word echoed throughout her mind. She wanted to be somewhere surrounded by life, not enveloped in death.

"Well, aren't you selfish?" the voice inside her head replied once again. "Ron is lying there in that bed. He can't get away! He can't even walk to the kitchen or go outside, yet you are the one who needs the break," the voice sniffed.

Debra sighed and looked at Ron, who finally appeared to be sleeping, but sometimes it was hard to tell.

"Ron," she whispered his name. No reply.

"I'm just going to sit on the deck for a few minutes. Get some fresh air. I'll leave the slider open so I can hear you if you call."

She looked at him, but his eyes remained closed. She did not know whether he had heard her, but she pretended he had. Dusk was quickly approaching. The sun setting in the distance showed a beautiful hue of pink mixed with a light orange. Debra lowered her body into the

Adirondack chair, sighing as she sat and stretched out her legs. It was slightly chilly, but Debra was not cold. It felt good to breathe in fresh air and to feel a gentle breeze skim over her arms and softly blow her hair. Debra closed her eyes. See, this was all she needed. She only needed a little break, just a little quiet. She inhaled again.

"Debra, Debra!" she heard Ron's raspy voice calling out to her.

No, no, she thought. *I need a little more time, not so soon, just a few more moments.* Maybe she hadn't heard him; perhaps it was just the wind.

"Debra, Debra," the raspy voice was louder and more strident this time.

It was not the wind. Some part of Debra knew Ron was calling because he needed her now, but she couldn't answer. She remained rooted to the chair, knowing now that she would tell him that she had fallen asleep and had not heard him. Who could deny such a story? Only Debra would know she had heard him the first time he had called and had chosen not to answer.

"Debra, Debra, help me please!"

Debra opened her eyes. She could not believe her body was seemingly refusing to move even as her brain was telling her to get up, to go. She heard a soft moan, followed by coughing, and then her name was called again. Finally, she rose from the chair, sliding the screen door open and moving to the bedroom. Debra stopped at the doorway. Ron was coughing forcefully now and hanging halfway out of the bed at an extremely uncomfortable angle. She crossed to the bed, and he looked directly at her, fully alert for the first time that day.

"Where were you?" he choked out between coughing jags.

"I fell asleep on the deck," she lied.

Then, immediately, she took over, easing him back into bed, grabbing the pain medication that he had been trying unsuccessfully

to reach for. She began attending to all that he needed over and over
and over again.

CHAPTER 70

DEBRA SHOOK HER HEAD vigorously, reorienting herself to where she sat in John's hotel room for the first time in several minutes. She had been so deep into the memories that it was as if she was back there, back in that bedroom, their bedroom, leaning over that hospital bed once more. Debra looked up at John, who was regarding her from the orange chair adjacent with serious, sad-looking eyes. She looked at him without blinking, and he also held her gaze. Debra turned her head and looked out onto the night sky's blackness before returning her eyes to John and beginning to speak again.

"The worst part is that I did start to resent Ron. I was so exhausted; maybe that is my excuse, but I resented him. I was angry at a dying man for pushing me further than I was able to go. It was too much. I wanted to do it all, to be everything for my husband. I needed help, but I couldn't say so, couldn't tell anyone how sad and angry, how scared, and lonely I felt, so instead I began to wish it were all over. I started to wish that my husband were dead, even though I knew full well that when he was gone, the only thing I would want was to have him back. I began to fantasize about the hospital bed being gone from the bedroom, about going out with Kathy for a drink, going shopping with Devon, and going to a concert again, and the more I wished for these things, the more I hated myself. John, I have never told anyone this, and I thought I never would, but I would fantasize he was gone as I sat right there looking at him, watching him gasp for breath, watching pain furrow his brow. Yet, I did love him. I have to make that so clear. I loved Ron with all my heart. What kind of person thinks those things? What kind of person does what I did? I hated the man I loved!"

Debra stared at the carpet beneath her feet. How could John, how could anyone want her here?

"No, Debra," John replied gently.

Debra could not look up, could not meet his eyes.

"I don't think you hated the man you loved at all. I think you hated the disease that was taking the man you loved."

Debra ran her hands over her face. Hot tears were springing from her eyes. John reached forward and gently touched her on the knee.

"Hey, it's ok," he said gently.

She shook her head.

"It's not ok," she said gently, her voice muffled behind her hands.

"What?" John inquired gently.

Ok, so she had gone this far. She might as well tell him the rest; all of it needed to come out, and then he would hate her and tell her to go. She placed her hands back in her lap. She drew her breath in and began to speak.

CHAPTER 71

"SO, MRS. MYERS, here is what you can do," the young nurse said chirpily.

"Your doctor said Mr. Myers is in increasingly more pain, so there is an override on his pain med pump. We don't tell patients this because we don't want anyone to overdose, but well, Mr. Myers is no longer able to regulate his doses, so you will have to do it for him. We don't even tell all our patients this, but Dr. Ryan trusts you and says you are intelligent enough to know what you are doing."

She motioned for Debra to move closer to the medication pump.

"See this button here. If you give two quick pumps in succession after you have turned the key at the bottom, you can get a double dose."

Debra nodded.

"Also, if you do that, please don't give him the liquid pain meds at the same time. It might be too much."

Debra nodded again without speaking.

"Also, Dr. Ryan said to tell you that you are still eligible for hospice nursing, and he thinks some help might serve you right now, this close to, you know..." For the first time, the young nurse faltered before gulping and saying, "the end."

Debra gave a tight smile and shook her head.

"No, no, we are fine," she asserted.

The nurse shook her head.

"Dr. Ryan said you would probably say that."

"Ok," she said, picking up her black bag from the floor.

"Mrs. Myers and Mr. Myers, it was very nice to meet both of you."

She touched Debra's hand and smiled at Ron, whose eyes were firmly closed. He had not acknowledged the nurse's presence even once while she was in the room. Debra no longer knew if Ron was asleep or awake, or how much of the conversation he had heard or understood. But just when she thought he knew or had heard nothing, he would perk up and suddenly say, "Where did Devon say she was going or what did the doctor say again?"

It was creepy and weird. Debra showed the nurse out and returned to the room where Ron's eyes remained resolutely closed.

♦ ♦ ♦

The days and nights bled into each other now. There were more bad days than good days. Today had been a horrible day. Debra wasn't even sure how to describe, using words, how bad the day had been, and now, at 11 p.m., it seemed to be more, much more of the same. Ron had spent the day writhing in pain, moaning, and when he had been coherent enough to engage with Debra, he had been short with her. When she put an extra pillow behind his head in an attempt to help his neck, he had snarled, "No, Debra, damn it, get that thing out of there. It's damn uncomfortable."

She had removed the pillow at once, but still he writhed, seemingly unable to find comfort in any position. She turned the key on the medication pump and pressed the button quickly. She watched and waited. Usually, after a few minutes, she would see his face—his forehead—relax. How many doses had she given him today? She looked at the notebook where she carefully charted his intake. Her face blanched. Had she not made even one notation for today! What was wrong with her? Now, Ron began to cough and wheeze. She squeezed his shoulder in an attempt to provide comfort; he jerked away from her

Vegas Goodbye | 253

with a cry that sounded to her like irritation. After what seemed like hours but was probably minutes, the coughing, wheezing jag stopped, but he still moved his body left and right as if seeking a comfort that his body could not find. Her finger hovered above the medication pump's button. She couldn't give him more, could she? She had just given him a double dose. Her eyes moved around the room, finally coming to light on the liquid pain medication with the syringe for the mouth lying next to it. She had not used this medication today, but the nurse advised against using both. Debra stopped but then crossed rapidly to the dresser where the med bottle lay. She drew the syringe into the bottle, removing the stopper to allow the medicine to flow into the syringe. She filled the syringe with twice as much medicine as usual. Ron continued to moan, writhe, and make agonizing noises behind her. She closed her eyes, removed the syringe from the bottle, and crossed toward him on the bed.

CHAPTER 72

DEBRA STOPPED IN HER RETELLING. She knew all too well what she needed to tell John next. The thing she had never told anyone—not Devon, David, or even Kathy. No one knew what had happened in that bedroom the last night of Ron's life. Debra had been silent for so long that, eventually, John said, just above a whisper, "What happened, Debra? Finish telling me."

Debra could feel her heart beating so fast that she thought John must be able to hear it from where he sat. She closed her eyes, her hands shaking as she recalled that night. John sat completely still, so quiet that it was as if he wasn't breathing. Debra did not, and she could not open her eyes. The images of that night—so strong, that awful, awful night.

"Debra," John whispered, "did you..." and he hesitated, "did you help; did you help your husband pass?" He said it so gently when she had expected that he would regard her with disgust.

She opened her eyes to see that he was regarding her not with disdain but with kindness and with tears in his eyes.

"Did you?" he repeated, oh so quietly.

"No, no, John, I couldn't. I thought I could, but as I crossed to the bed and looked at Ron, I knew I couldn't give him more than I should. I squirted the medicine into a Dixie cup on the tray beside the bed. Then I took the cup and ran into the bathroom, throwing the medicine down the toilet and flushing. I was crying and gasping. I had come that close to overdosing him, and it wouldn't have been accidental. I knew what I was doing. By the time I returned to the bedroom, he wasn't gasping or uncomfortable anymore; the medication from the pump must have taken effect. I apologized to him over and over. I stroked his face. He never responded to me. I don't know if he knew what I was doing, what I almost did. I just wanted the suffering to stop, but I will feel guilty for what I almost did for the rest of my life. One day later, that was it. He was gone. So, now you know what kind of person I am," Debra said in a hushed tone.

John shook his head. "Oh, Debra, you didn't do anything. You didn't do it. We all have evil thoughts that shouldn't see the light of day. Thinking is not doing."

"But I came close and almost acted on my thoughts," Debra said.

"Yes, but you stopped yourself. You didn't kill Ron. He was suffering a lot, and you, you were suffering, too."

CHAPTER 73

SUDDENLY, JOHN LOOKED VERY UPSET. Then he said in a hushed voice, "I killed my son!"

Debra looked stricken.

"You killed your son, John? Why? How?"

Debra felt her chest constrict. Was she in a hotel room with a psychopath? What had he done?

John sighed deeply and ran his hand over his face.

"My son started using drugs when he was around thirteen years old. He was a popular kid, had many friends, and was very athletic. We began to smell weed on his clothes. Jeannine was immediately worried. We did talk to him. He admitted that he had tried marijuana and didn't particularly like it. Things went downhill fast from there. He used more and more, tried the harder drugs, and we eventually found out. At eighteen, he collapsed in the hallway right in front of his younger sister, Jasmine. He had overdosed. We got him into rehab. Jeannine was relieved and all for it. I wasn't so sure. I thought he was just a little wild, a kid sowing some wild oats. I drank a lot when I was in high school, smoked my share of pot. I had some issues, but all that is a story for another time. Anyway, Justin went to rehab and even opted for an extended stay. I was ecstatic when he got out. We did all the family meetings, etc. I just knew his troubles were all behind us. Debra, I know now that he started using again almost immediately when he came home from rehab. Jeannine sensed that something was wrong right away. Me? I was in total denial. When Jeannine mentioned that Justin might still have problems, I fought her with all I had. I denied what I could see with my own eyes. He would come home impaired, say he was fine, and I would agree with him. Jeannine was so frustrated. Even Jazzy, my daughter, knew what was going on. I denied it repeatedly. Jeannine wanted him to return to rehab, and I fought against that so hard. All the time, he was getting worse and worse, and then…"

John stopped speaking and brought his fist to his mouth, trying to hold in a sob.

"John," Debra said quietly, leaning toward him in her chair. John closed his eyes.

"I found him dead in his car in the driveway. He overdosed right there, right at his own home."

"I…" John broke down, his body racked with heart-wrenching sobs.

"My baby boy, my boy," he choked out.

Debra stood and leaned down, putting her arms around John. She held him for several minutes, letting him sob. Finally, he took a deep breath and patted Debra's shoulder. She returned to her chair across from John.

"Sorry about that," he whispered.

"No, John, no, don't be sorry. That was an awful thing to have to endure."

"Oh, Debra, I should have insisted he return to rehab! I should have forced him to. I knew it was what Jeannine thought should happen, but I repeatedly dismissed her concerns and denied her reality. I told both my wife and my daughter that they were wrong over and over again. I am not a good person, not a good father."

John put his head in his hands, trying hard not to sob again.

"I believed every word that Justin told me because I wanted to. I should have been able to see with my own eyes that he wasn't right and struggling, but I missed or actively ignored every single one of the signs. If I had done the right things, said the right things, Justin might be alive; he could be sitting right here with me today if I had fulfilled my role as a parent instead of listening to a person with an addiction. He was just a kid. It was my job to help him, and instead, I killed him with my neglect and my blindness."

"But, John," Debra said quietly.

"I think his disease, his addiction, killed him, just like you said to me with Ron. I had no power to keep Ron alive, and you didn't have the power to keep your son alive. He made those choices, not you. He chose to use, to lie to you, all of it. You didn't put a needle in his arm, John; he did that."

In the past, the minister and the therapist he saw ever so briefly had told John something like this. Their words had enraged him, and he always thought bitterly, *You don't understand, you couldn't possibly understand.*

But now, here with Debra, it was different. She understood loss. She understood the callous cruelty of people who didn't know how deep the wound of loss could be. He stopped to consider her words, to feel maybe a slight lessening of guilt for the first time.

"Enough about me," John said suddenly.

"Tell me more about Ron. Tell me about your first husband, your daughter's father."

Debra knew he was deflecting and needed a break from discussing such a charged topic.

"It is hard for me to convey how much Ron meant to me," Debra said, smiling at the thought of him. It was so good to go back in time and almost relive happy memories. Debra opened her eyes, only then realizing that she had shut them as the memories played out in front of her eyes like a movie. John was gently smiling at her, waiting for her to continue.

Debra remained silent, and John said gently, "Debra, I understand, I understand all too well how much it hurts to love someone, but you have a daughter; why don't you want to stay alive for her?"

"Oh, John," Debra said gently.

"You have a daughter, too. You do realize I could say the same thing to you!"

John nodded but closed his own eyes and looked down.

"My daughter hates talking to me. She hates me. I think it might be easier for her if I were gone. She has no use for me anymore, not that I can blame her, all the drinking I did, the anger. I was of no use to her. I think she believed I loved Justin more than her. It wasn't true, but how much must a thought like that hurt? When she confronted me, I was in too much of a stupor to deny it and explain how I felt, so I sat silently, and she took it all so very wrong. I have hurt her badly. I hurt my ex-wife. I have a life insurance policy; if they could get that, the money would be more useful to them than I ever was or will ever be."

John shook his head, wanting to speak of this no further.

"Your daughter, you seem to get along with her, Debra. Am I wrong?"

Debra shook her head.

"Devon and I are close, well, we were close. I think I understand Devon better than most people. Some people find her harsh and abrupt. Unlike me, she tends to anger easily and has never been afraid to speak her mind. Her husband, David, gets her as well. Much of her anger is merely a façade to conceal her true feelings and sensitivity. John, sometimes you remind me of Devon. She isn't like me at all, you know. She has always had anger issues since she was a young child. I think you are hiding an anger as well, John?"

Debra ended the sentence with a question.

John nodded.

"Oh, Debra, I have much to hide and regret. I can't see you ever wanting to be with me after you hear my entire story."

"Oh, John, I can't see you wanting to be with me after you know my whole story," she countered.

"You know, sometimes I wish I were more like Devon. She is always forthright and unafraid to tell anyone exactly what she wants. Devon knows her mind, and I have never seen her give away her power, even as a child. She has always held onto her power as if it were sacred, which it is. Your reaction, John, to the man on the bridge with the selfie stick? It was justified, and your response was exactly what Devon would have done and said. Your anger seems to me, John, to be fiercely protective of those you love, which is not necessarily bad. Devon also reminds me very much of my ex-husband, Gary. She acts like him; she looks like him. It is all so weird because she didn't grow up around him. Makes you wonder how strong genetics are. Devon is now forming a relationship with her father."

Debra shuddered without meaning to, and John frowned and looked at her thoughtfully.

"I take it he was a bad guy."

"Oh, John, a very troubled man, and Devon knows none of it. I didn't tell her about her father, only that he had left us. He drank and used drugs; he was violent toward me, and I am certain that he would have been violent with Devon if we had not left. In fact, I know he would have been. By the time Devon was old enough to truly understand and maybe know a little more, we were happy and with Ron. Devon didn't bring her birth father up very often, so why would I bring up the past? It would only hurt her. Ron was a father to her in every way. I didn't tell either of them, but I used to pretend that Ron was her father, that Gary had never existed. After Ron's death, Devon searched for Gary and found him. That is why I want to leave this world. Devon wants her father to be more and more involved in her life, and she wants me to be involved too. I even reluctantly went to Gary and his second wife's house for the 4th of July. It was awful."

How did you meet Gary? John questioned.

"Gary had just graduated from college, and I had two more years when we met. He made me feel safe at first. He was so large—he had played football all four years. He was back on campus for homecoming. They were honoring all the former football stars during the game. My friend and I were at a small bar called The Hill, just off campus, the night before the game. This older guy was in the bar quite drunk, and he would not stop harassing my friend and me. We changed seats and ignored him; still, he wouldn't leave us alone. At some point, I went to the bathroom, and he followed me down this dark corridor where the bathrooms were. The older man stood close to me when I came out of the ladies' room. I turned to go back to the restroom, but he grabbed my wrist so that I couldn't go.

"Let me go!" I yelled, and then just like that, someone picked him up by the collar of his shirt and lifted him right off the ground. I stepped back. My rescuer, of course, was Gary.

Gary said, "I've watched you, old man, bother these ladies all night. It's over now, get the hell out."

"Gary released him, giving him a shove, and the man held up his hands and slunk away. I was so grateful. Gary politely asked my friend and me to sit with him at the game the next day. We did, and that's how it all started. Gary was so large, yet he was gentle with me then, and I felt safe and protected. He was so handsome, with a full head of thick, black hair. Women always looked at him when he walked by. We started dating right after that football game. I guess there were signs of who he was. He would always encourage me to cut class to be with him. If I said no, he wouldn't get mad, but would be very sad, almost crying, and say, 'I need you, I need to be with you.' He didn't care that he was affecting my grades. He only wanted what he wanted. He would get angry sometimes when we were out—rude servers, drunks in bars, if anyone was rude to me. He wasn't afraid to yell or roughly handle anyone. All the incidents seemed justified, though, so I thought it was okay. He was my hero. So wrong about that," Debra snorted.

"Gary wanted to get married immediately, but my parents were against it. Gary was so persistent. He said he couldn't live without me. I eventually gave in, dropped out of school, and caused a rift between my parents and me. A rift that never actually healed. Anyway, we got married. I got a job as an accounting clerk, telling my mom repeatedly that I would go back to school just as soon as Gary got situated, but even though he had a college degree, he was drifting. He would have a job for just a few months, then tell me that all the people there were against him and he had no choice but to leave. Everyone there was incompetent. It took me a while to realize there was a pattern and that the pattern was Gary. He couldn't fit in anywhere, and his temper was causing him to lose job after job. I supported us, and we didn't have much money, but it all seemed okay. I would often come home to find Gary stretched out on the couch with an open beer on the coffee table, instead of job-hunting, but I still thought it would all be fine. We never fought. Even though he was having all this trouble getting along at work, we got along great. He was romantic, bringing me flowers almost weekly and writing poems that he would leave on my pillow. We always did what Gary wanted; I see that now, but then I was anxious to please him, so I always acquiesced. One time, when I chose the movie—do you remember that very popular one that won many awards with Robin Rottmann? I wanted to see it so badly. Gary wanted to see some action thing. I lobbied hard for my choice, but after we arrived at the theater, Gary pouted, and once we were inside, he kept commenting about how lame the movie was. People were beginning to turn around and glare at him, so we got up and left. We ended up in the adventure movie that he had wanted to see all along. Still, I thought I was in love, and I was happy. I was even happier when I found out I was pregnant. It hadn't been planned, and God knows we didn't have much money to support a child, but we loved each other, so I knew it would all work out. Gary wasn't happy when I first told him. He asked me how I could have been so stupid to let it happen, like I had done it all by myself. I started working more hours to save as much money as possible, but Gary changed as suddenly as a light switch turning off. Maybe this was when he began drinking and using seriously; I honestly don't know. I do know that from then on, I couldn't do anything right. If I worked a lot, I was ruining our relationship by spending no time with him; if I worked less, well, how were we supposed to provide for a baby if I was going to be this lazy? It never ended. The dinners I made were wrong, the way I looked was wrong, and the apartment was dirty, even though he was home more often than I was. He didn't hit me until I was six months pregnant, and I couldn't believe it when it happened. He apologized afterward, saying he was very stressed, but also said it was my fault. I was unreasonable and hard to deal with.

"If people knew what you were really like, Debra," he would say, "I deserve a medal for what I have to deal with daily!"

"I didn't think I was unreasonable, but I was becoming uncomfortable and irritable, so maybe it was me, I thought. I promised him I would try harder and do better. We would be fine for several weeks, then he would erupt over something or nothing, and the whole process would start again. He was beginning to drink more; I had started to notice it. I was afraid to call him on it. He said he needed to find the right job, and it would all be fine. The few times when I tried to broach the drinking—whether it was interfering with his job search, shouldn't he cut down for the baby's sake —he would get mad. He would usually head to the refrigerator and pop open another beer or pour another shot of whiskey."

He said repeatedly, "I drink, Debra, because how else could anyone deal with you?"

"I thought once he saw his daughter, it would get better, but he got worse, so much worse. I had to get away, save my baby, John, and I did, that I did!"

John nodded.

CHAPTER 74

"DEBRA, YOU SHOULD KNOW I developed a drinking problem after Justin died. I was…" He hesitated, "I am an awful person."

"John, John," Debra said so very gently.

"You are a good person. The man I see in front of me, whom I have spent time with over the last few days, is kind and funny."

"Kind and funny?" John repeated with a sardonic smile on his face.

"Those are not words anyone would use to describe me for the last two years."

"It is what I see," Debra repeated, tears coming to her eyes. She could tell, she could feel how much pain this man was in, and a deep ache resonated through her abdomen. John might know pain, but oh, could she understand because she felt so much pain deep in her body, too.

John continued, "So, at first, I was silent and glum, offering no support to my wife or daughter, just sitting and staring night after night. It was a sad house. A house shrouded in grief and regret. And believe me, I had so much regret. I was the one who dismissed both Jasmine's and Jeannine's concerns over and over again. I scoffed at them and insulted them with my dismissive attitude. They wanted Justin to get help, and I refused time and time again. I convinced myself that I was supporting my son, but I was just being conned by a young man who had an addiction and had lost his way. It was all my fault, and I felt so much regret, and there was no way to fix this, to erase my mistakes and start over, because he was gone. We were all locked into our bubbles of grief for the first few months, but about six months in, Jeannine, thank God, took some action. Jasmine was hurting. It was possible we could have lost her as well. Jasmine needed a way to ease her pain. Anyway, Jeannine started reaching out. She would try anything, go anywhere—therapy group, trauma support, counseling, and Reiki. She dragged Jasmine with her unwillingly at first, but then Jasmine started to like some of it. I saw them changing right before my eyes, and the more they healed, the more I dug my heels in and refused it all. Of course, they invited me, urged me to come with them. Jeannine even demanded that I come, but the more she pushed, the more I turned away. It felt like they were moving on and forgetting all about Justin. They were building a new life that he couldn't be a part of, which made me mad. It was then that I started drinking in earnest. It got to the point where I couldn't wait until they left, so I could run to open the bottle. The funny thing was that I barely drank before Justin died—maybe a beer here or there, a glass of wine with dinner—but now I made sure the house was stocked with beer and wine. Then I started buying the harder stuff, too. I was hiding bottles all over the house. It was so important to me that I never run out, and the more I drank, the more I pushed them both away. I would see the looks of disgust on their faces when I came home drunk or when they came home and I had drunk as much as possible while they had been gone. The looks on their faces gutted me, but still I couldn't stop. Each time before that first sip, I would feel such relief, as if, ahh, this will help, I'll feel better soon, and you know what, for probably the first two sips, I did feel better, I did feel a sense of relief, a release of all that pain. But it turned on me quickly. By the bottom of the first glass, bottle, shot, whatever, I was already chasing the feeling and having more to make the relief come back, but it never did. By the time I had had way too much and was thoroughly drunk, or when I was hungover the next morning, I would swear that I wouldn't do it again. I had enough clarity to realize that it wasn't helping, but wait a few hours, and the pressure and anxiety would build and build as if I would explode. I was scared and sad and angry, and I just needed the pain to go away, just for a little while, and there I would go again, grabbing for the bottle, hoping to pour out relief that never came. The more I drank, the more delusional I became. I began to pretend that Justin was alive. 'Pretend' probably isn't the right word, but I did fantasize that he was still here. When I was drunk, it was easy to think that he was alive. I started to scare Jasmine and Jeannine, so I learned to shut up about what I saw and felt. I couldn't let them know that I was scaring myself as well. Don't look at me like that!" John said as he looked at Debra.

She shook her head. "I'm not judging you; I'm listening."

"So, they thought I was delusional, cracked up, and I will admit I acted like I was, especially when I was fueled with liquor, but…"

Debra watched as John tightly closed his eyes and balled his hands into fists.

"I always, always knew that he was gone, not just gone but dead. I wouldn't admit this, though, especially not to myself."

Debra touched his knee again, resting her hand lightly as John opened up his fists and gently placed one hand over Debra's.

He sighed deeply and said, "Debra, guess what, the worst is yet to come. The more they looked at me, either with disgust or with wariness—'Let's see if Dad is drunk today or maybe he's just crazy today'—the angrier I became. The booze wasn't working; my pretend game of Justin is still here wasn't working, and my girls were gone more often than at home because who would want to share living space with me? So I became angry, mad at the world, everything, and everyone. I was quite likely to yell out the window at passing dogs and people to 'stay off the lawn' or 'pick up that dog shit' like some deranged old man. I glowered at people because they dared to look happy. Work was a nightmare. I hated everyone there. I would often yell at coworkers. I made so many mistakes. It would be over a year before I knew they were covering for me at work. I wish I could say that I was drunk while engaged in all this irrational yelling, but I wasn't, so I can't even use that as an excuse. I was just an angry, unpleasant guy. Around this time, Jeannine started planning to leave, to save herself, but most of all, to save Jasmine from the dysfunction. She made the right move. Of course, I didn't see it that way at the time. After they left, I got even angrier. Loneliness, alcohol, and anger are not a good combination, but that was what I was left with. Jeannine would call to check on me. Most of the time, I ignored her calls, so I understand, Debra, how you said your world just got smaller and smaller, because that happened to me too. Smaller and smaller until I felt that I was trapped in a box, a tiny box of my own making.

"After Jeannine and Jasmine were gone, my anger got much worse. It morphed into something else, something much more dangerous. I fantasized about hurting others. I truly did. Feel free to run from the room now. I wouldn't blame you," he said bitterly.

Instead, she reached out her hand, lightly touching his knee. "I'm not running. Do you want to hurt people still?" she inquired gently.

John shook his head.

"I don't think I have it in me to hurt anyone else, but would I like to hurt myself? Oh, yes, the only person who doesn't deserve to live is me!"

Debra nodded. "But John, I feel the same way. Ever since Ron died, I have woken up every day, knowing deep in my heart that he is gone, but I am the one who deserves to be gone, yet each morning, over and over again, I am still here."

John nodded, stunned by how similar their troubling thoughts were.

"I wish I were strong like Devon, John, I do. I know she didn't get her strength from me."

"Are you sure, Debra? What if you are stronger than you know?"

"What if you are, John? What if you are stronger than you think?"

"I don't know if strong defines me in any way," John said, shrugging.

"I guess I tried to block out my pain with the anger. I have tried to hide the anger away. I have even pretended that that angry, sad man is an entirely different person, but I have never been entirely successful at doing so, as hard as I might have tried. I haven't been successful at all. I do know that the angry man—I don't want to be him anymore. I want no part of him. I don't think that I ever did."

"It sounds as if it has been awful for you, and I get it, I truly do. People have all their suggestions for ways to heal and feel better. I get what you said about therapy. It didn't work for me either."

John nodded.

"You know, as time passed, I think I became jealous of Jeannine on top of our other issues. I knew she was hurting as much as I was, but she wasn't afraid to try anything to heal. She did it all; she would at least try almost every therapy technique suggested to her. And I guess it worked for her because she began to heal. She would come home and be so high about this therapy or that grief technique, and the more she was into something, the more I was against it, whatever it might be. It was like she was soaring, and I was stuck in a mud pit, sinking deeper and deeper and getting dirtier and dirtier. You can do acupuncture for trauma; did you know that?"

Debra shook her head.

"Well, I guess it's a thing. Jeannine raved about it. She insisted that I try it. Jasmine had gone, and she liked it, too. It was the last thing I wanted to do, but I let them talk me into it. It was weird. You walk in, and everyone is either silent or whispering. People sitting around in chairs with needles stuck in them."

"I don't like needles," Debra whispered.

"Me, either!" John said stridently. "And the needles just reminded me of Justin and how he had stuck a needle in his arm over and over. I was so tense, and the acupuncturist, wow, what a flake! She approached me and bowed, saying she could help me feel better. All I wanted to do was run, but I let her lead me to this recliner. She told me to take off my socks and shoes. Some big dude is snoring in the corner. I was so uncomfortable. There were flags everywhere, and these weird bells were tinkling. This lady is closing her eyes, then opening them and sticking needles in me, saying she knows I will find my path. Yeah, I'll find my path, lady, and it leads to the door so I can get out of here. She said that I was very troubled and was causing pain to be attracted to my body. That I had been troubled since childhood, and it wasn't my fault. She said I must stop the pain, or I would hurt others around me. Thanks, lady, that makes me feel so much better. I never went back."

"It sounds awful," Debra agreed.

"Did anything help you?" Debra inquired. "My friend, Kathy, kept giving me grief strategies that she would find online. I know she was trying to help."

"What strategy did I use, Debra?"

John snorted.

"Is drinking a strategy? Because that was what I did. It is why my daughter hates me to this day. How about rage? Feeling rage has been my go-to for a while," John said, looking away.

"But John, you have been calm and kind to me. You are also funny. You make me laugh."

John looked down, smiling.

"I think I used to be like that, but before I came here, I lost my job of over 30 years, mostly just for being angry."

"I'm so sorry," Debra said.

"Maybe those things you say, calm, kind, funny—perhaps I used to be like that, but that part of me is now buried deep inside."

"But it is there, John," Debra replied, "because those things are part of the man I see before me."

"There are no easy answers, are there, Debra?" John said seriously.

She nodded. They had been talking for hours, but Debra didn't feel tired. There was so much to say, and surprisingly enough, John's understanding of the world mirrored her own in many ways. She knew that he felt pain deep in his bones just as she did. She also knew he was deeply frustrated at not being understood by the world around them.

"It's too easy to pick a side and remain there," Debra replied.

John nodded rapidly.

"Yes, choose a belief and adhere to it through thick and thin, disregarding all evidence that it is wrong. If you do that, you don't even have to try to think. Just follow your side, your philosophy, your political party, your creed, and believe all they believe without deliberating, thinking about each idea on your own."

"So true," Debra nodded. "If we turn other people, other humans, into some kind of 'other'"—she made air quotes in front of her face—"then we no longer have to worry about them. They are not like us and not worth our time. It is indeed so much easier to put people into tidy little boxes and expect them to behave in a certain way, and as far as grief goes, for a limited time. John, if others are not like us—those who grieve, those who hate, those who look different, those who take drugs, I could go on—then we can discount them, put them away. And if we put them away and deny their existence, then that grief, that fear, those bad choices will be unable to come to us. We will be safe, so they shut us out so they don't have to deal with their feelings. But make no mistake, the grief, the fear, the bad choices, the death—it will come whether we pretend it won't or not."

"And that, Debra, is why people run from us screaming—because if they see our pain, if they see death, drug addiction, depression, anger, hell, even suicidal thoughts, if they acknowledge they exist in us, then those thoughts, actions must exist in their lives as well."

"Exactly," Debra said, truly grasping how alone she had felt for the first time. And also realizing for the first time that maybe it wasn't all about her. It wasn't that she was all wrong, couldn't cope. It was all too possible that others—Devon, Kathy—made mistakes, too. Maybe they did not know what to do or what to say. It wasn't that Debra was fatally flawed. She was doing the best she could, just as they all were.

"They can't watch us suffer because it means they are not immune to suffering, and it could happen to them, too. They don't want to feel that, any of it. Seeing us suffer means they have to suffer, too. So they walk—no, they run—away from the inevitable, for grief, pain, hatred, fear—it is out there and it comes for all of us. I wish others could understand what others feel without waiting until they are directly affected. It would make for a better world, wouldn't it, Debra? A kinder, understanding, empathetic world. I kept all the hurt and pain inside, and I think you did too, Debra."

Debra nodded almost imperceptibly.

"It is almost easier, more socially acceptable to talk about sex in gory detail than it is to talk about death, grief, and loss, and that lack of ability to speak, to share, hobbles us all. John, do you think there might be a way out for us?"

Debra said this so quietly that her words were little more than a whisper.

John did not reply immediately, but when he did, he whispered, "I don't know. I wish I knew, but I don't. But for the first time in a very long time, I think I might be willing to try."

CHAPTER 75

"JOHN, I WOULDN'T THINK that you had a problem with alcohol at all, watching you this week."

"I know," John acknowledged, "and I haven't felt the need to drink that much since I have been here with you. We conceal so much of who we truly are, don't we, Debra?"

"I would never know the person I had dinner with and had coffee with and who took those walks with was in such pain," Debra replied.

"Am I an alcoholic, Debra? I honestly don't know. I drank when I was young, socially and for fun, probably more than I needed, more than I should have. After Jeannine and I married, I drank less. Jeannine was never much of a drinker, and then after the kids came, I just stopped. We were both busy—maybe a glass of wine here and there, a nightcap after a Saturday night out—but that was it for years and years. I thought drinking made me feel better after Justin's death, but it didn't. Jasmine hated being around me when I was drunk, and who can blame her for that? What kind of role model was I? Here, kid, here's how to cope with grief, loss: drown yourself in a bottle and act like a fool. Jasmine could have copied my behavior, but it is only because of her strength and Jeannine's guidance that she didn't. I have been a fool, a miserable, deluded fool for so long now. But I have felt happy here with you for the first time in years."

Debra nodded. "I have felt the same with you."

"You truly can't tell what someone is going through by looking at them, can you, Debra? You can't see the wounds, the open sores. Maybe if our wounds were visible, we wouldn't continue to destroy each other with casual, hurtful words. If we could lift each other and validate what someone else feels instead of being mired in our thoughts and perspective."

Debra nodded again and said quietly, "We are so quick to judge, to think we know the whole story of another when we know so very little."

Debra pulled at a loose thread hanging from the orange chair. "It is too easy to tell another that they are wrong, to snap out of it, so easy to believe that our wants are their wants."

Debra was thinking of both Kathy and Devon. While neither one had meant to hurt her, they had hurt her as they had touted their agenda. Devon so wanting to get closer to the father she never had, and pushing Debra to socialize with a man who had only caused her pain and hurt. Kathy, who was busy with her own life, wanted Debra to move on and no longer be sad, so she wouldn't have to worry about her and could continue with her own life.

John nodded, looking at Debra with a piercing gaze. It felt so good to be understood. After being thirsty for so long, it felt like being offered a quenching glass of water.

"We have all made mistakes. It's like we can't get out of our own way and instead leave a path of destruction in our wake. Debra, I couldn't reach out and ask for help or admit that I needed any assistance. Yes, many people practice callous disregard, which is hurtful and wrong, but I refused to reach out to tell anyone the truth of what was going on with me. I pushed others away until all that was left was pain, hurt, and anger, and there was no way back. I had gone so far down the path that I couldn't turn around, and I damn sure had no interest in moving forward until, until…" and John stopped speaking, choking up.

Tears sprang to Debra's eyes, and she reached for his hand.

John looked at the carpet at his feet and smiled.

"Debra, I think that the man who was so angry at the world wasn't the real me. I mean, he was me, a part of me at least. I wasn't angry like that at all when I was young, except for once when I had too much to drink. The anger only bubbled and festered after Justin's death. I felt such guilt. It was all my fault that he was gone. I said that to myself repeatedly. Jeannine wanted me to get help. Even Jazzy knew I needed help, but I could only deny reality. The longer I was alone, the angrier I got. I convinced myself that I hated everyone and alienated those I met, but there was only one person I hated the most, and that person was me. The anger caused me to be fired from my job, and I loved my job, but the anger dissipates when I am here with you. I feel relaxed, and it starts to fade away."

He looked up at Debra, now standing near the curtains adjacent to the chairs. He saw pain and sadness emanating from her face. He reached out ever so gently for her hand. She allowed him to envelop her hand with his.

"Debra," he all but whispered. "You can't go. You can't kill yourself. I see so much good, so much potential in you. You are kind and loving. You have helped me. You can't go yet. You have more to do in your life."

Debra smiled at him warmly.

"Oh, John, I could say the same thing to you. You are warm and kind. You are so much fun to be around. You have more to do in this life, too."

"Debra, could there be good inside us that we can't see?"

Debra looked at him, holding eye contact for a very long time. She sat back down in the chair as a strange comfort washed over her.

"John, you don't believe we both have a reason to go on, do you? Could it even be possible for us, both of us, to choose hope over despair?"

John didn't say anything.

Debra stood again, crossing over to the plate-glass windows abutting their chairs; she pushed the heavy drapes back further than they already were.

"Look, look outside, John. The sun is just starting to come up."

John rose from his chair, standing behind Debra and looking over her shoulder.

He sighed.

"Yes, I see," he remarked. "The darkness is receding ever so slowly."

She turned to look at him.

He smiled and touched her cheek as they turned back to look out the window again, continuing to watch the sun rise.

Debra whispered, "What if there is joy out there again, even without them, and even for us with all the mistakes that we have made?"

"I think there might be," John whispered.

CHAPTER 76

"AREN'T YOU GOING TO ANSWER THAT?" John inquired.

Debra's phone had rung once when they had been heavy in the midst of talking in the night, and now it had been ringing and pinging with texts for the last twenty minutes. She sighed and pawed the phone out of her pocket. At least, she could switch it to silent, she thought. Five missed calls, three voice messages, and three texts flashed onto the screen. Debra thumbed to the first voice message, which had been left hours ago. They were all from Devon.

"Mother," Devon said, and though she sounded angry, Debra also heard fear in her voice. It was this fear that tore at her heart.

"Mother," Devon said as Debra listened to the first voice message.

"Dave and I are on our way to the airport right now. We are taking a red-eye to Las Vegas. I hope you are still at the hotel you checked into. You are not with Kathy. We ran into her at a coffee shop this afternoon. She has never been with you. What are you doing there? Why are you there all alone? Are you ok? We should be there soon. Please hang on, Mom, if something is wrong."

Her voice caught, "Mom, I love you, we love you. See you soon," and Debra heard a sob followed by a click.

My daughter and her husband are on a plane. They are coming here to Vegas to find me. They found out that I am not here with Kathy.

"Ok, that's a good thing, isn't it?" John questioned.

Debra shrugged, "I guess, but I will have much explaining to do."

John nodded, "I get that."

Debra opened her phone case in response to the new text she was receiving. She nodded and looked at John.

"It's Devon," she affirmed.

"They just got here. They're waiting for me downstairs by the check-in desk at my hotel."

John nodded, "You'd better go. Your daughter and son-in-law must be so anxious. I am sure they need to see you to ensure you are all right physically."

Debra nodded but felt so reluctant to leave. She did not want to leave John/Jim when it seemed that they had just found each other. He crossed over to where she was standing, still holding the phone. He reached out and enveloped her in a hug.

"I'll see you later. I'll be right here waiting for you."

Debra nodded into his shoulder. She stepped out of his embrace and began to cross the room toward the door, but then she stopped abruptly. John was standing half-turned to gaze out the window at the sun shining brightly now, and standing halfway turned toward her.

"Come with me," Debra said, holding her hand toward John.

"What?" John questioned.

"Debra, do you think that's a good idea? Your daughter and son-in-law will think you picked up some random guy, some stranger in Vegas."

"Maybe," Debra acknowledged, thinking of Devon's quick temper, especially when she was scared or upset.

Debra inhaled deeply.

"John, I have spent my entire life twisting myself into a pretzel, trying to ensure everyone else is happy and has all their needs met."

"No, no more," Debra said, shaking her head back and forth vehemently. "I have always tried to please everyone, to do what is right, what I should," she said as she made air quotes to emphasize the word should.

"I have been unhappy and so sad for a long time. I have ensured that everyone around me always had exactly what they wanted, whether it was what I wanted or not. It is time, it is finally time to have what I want. It is time to be who I want to be, to do and say what I mean, and not what I think others want me to say. And right now, John, I want you to be with me more than anything."

Debra held out her hand once again.

John looked down, then he looked up at Debra.

He quickly crossed the room, grabbing her hand.

They walked out the door together.

CHAPTER 77

Two months later

DEVON SIGHED LOUDLY and looked at her mother challengingly.

"It's your life, Mother, but don't you think it's too soon for him to move in full-time? I understand him visiting, but you haven't been together that long. It just seems too soon to me."

"No, Devon, I don't think it is too soon. In Vegas, we became very close, very fast."

Devon let out a sigh again to express her disapproval.

Debra straightened her shoulders, sitting up taller in her chair. She no longer felt the need to explain and defend what she wanted. She no longer felt intimidated by the need to please others. She deserved to have what she wanted, to do what she wanted, no matter what anyone else thought, even someone she loved as deeply as she loved Devon. Debra had a newfound strength to speak her truth now, and while she knew that John and his companionship and love gave her strength, it was more than that. She now found that she felt comfortable in her own body. She was more aware of what she wanted, not what others wanted of her, for her—not what was best for them, but what was best for her. Debra thought the therapy sessions she and John attended seemed to be paying off, and she smiled to herself. She smiled kindly at Devon, but still sitting up straight and tall, she said without any equivocation, any justification, "No, Devon, it is not too soon. It is what we both want. It is what I want. John is moving in here at the end of the month. You are welcome here whenever you want to visit, but from now on, he is a part of my life."

Devon stared back at her mother without speaking. Debra wondered whether Devon was formulating what she wanted to say in protest or was stunned by Debra's new forthrightness. Debra could not tell. Debra also knew now more than ever that it was time to tell Devon the rest of what she needed her daughter to know.

"And, Devon, while we are discussing the future you should know I will not go to your father's house with you. Let me be clear, I will never go with you to your father's house ever again. I am extremely uncomfortable in that situation."

Devon opened her mouth to respond, but before she could, Debra held up a hand to stop her words and continued speaking.

"You have every right to have a relationship with your father. You are an adult. As for me, I don't wish to relive or rehash the past. Gary was cruel to me in the past. I will no longer deny what happened or how it made me feel. I will tell you more if you want to know or not. It's your choice, but know without a doubt that I will have nothing further to do with your father. I have very good reasons for feeling the way I do."

Debra stopped speaking and waited for Devon's onslaught of words, for the entreaties, for the coercion she was so used to. Debra knew that she would not back down, no matter what Devon said. At first, Debra had thought that John was giving her this strength just as Ron had given her strength when he was alive. She had depended on Ron so much, but this strength was different. This strength was hers alone. It was not coming from another, but coming from inside herself. She was expressing her truth and her real feelings, and doing so made her feel so free. Doing so was making her strong.

Devon continued to stare at her, and when she finally spoke, she did not protest but said quietly, "Ok, Mother, I understand if that is how you feel."

CHAPTER 78

JOHN FOUND HIMSELF SMILING as the conversation with Jeannine progressed. And yes, he did think of himself as John now. John was no longer a persona but who he had become. All the negativity of Jim gone now, all the regret, remorse, and unreasonable anger, too. He had morphed into a different person, closer to the man he wanted to be. Who knew you could leave the past behind if you tried and were determined to change? He had a long way to go, and many feelings he had were unresolved. Problems are never solved overnight, but he was working toward a new life and a new way of being in the world. And he had no doubts that he would achieve or at least progress toward who and what he wanted to be. He was going to make it. He knew he would because he had Debra by his side and she was making her own progress. They attended therapy weekly now, sometimes separately, sometimes together. Improbably enough, he had found an alternative treatment that he truly related to, Qi Gong. He and Debra attended twice a week. They had also started attending a local church. It was a small church that was very accepting of a diverse population. John's house in Connecticut had finally sold, and John was packing the last of his belongings. He was anxious to move in with Debra full-time, although he had spent significantly more time at her house in Massachusetts over the past month than in Connecticut. He still needed to connect with Jasmine, but his therapist had encouraged him to write his thoughts to her instead of engaging in more disastrous phone calls, which he had been doing. She had written back twice. He considered this a great success. And now, as this conversation with Jeannine progressed, he could feel a connection he had not felt in so long. She was not rushing to get away from him this time. He realized she knew so little of what had transpired in his life, and he knew not all at once, but over time, she and Jasmine needed to understand what he had gone through and how he was finding his way out.

"I will move in with my friend, Debra, as soon as the closing ends. I told Jasmine that. I assume she told you."

"She did, Jim," Jeannine said. "I am happy that you found someone."

She hesitated. "You know, Craig, the man I have been seeing? Maybe Jasmine told you, maybe not. He asked me to marry him, and I said yes, but we are not rushing into anything."

"I'm happy for you," John affirmed.

"Jasmine likes him, and he seems to understand her."

"What does he do?" John inquired.

"He's a pediatrician."

"Oh, Jeannine?" John said teasingly. "Moving up, huh?"

"Stop," she said, but she giggled, and he was glad to hear lightness in her voice.

"What about your job, Jim? Do they have another office in Massachusetts? Surely, you can't commute. It would be way too far."

John was silent. There was so much he had kept from them, for months, for years. Well, the silence was over now—no more lies or deceit.

"Jeannine, I lost that job over eight months ago now."

"Oh, Jim!" Jeannine said, and he could tell she was startled at this information. "I am so sorry."

"You know, it's ok. None of these changes I'm making would have happened if I hadn't lost that job. If I hadn't lost that job, I would never have met Debra and probably wouldn't have stopped drinking. Good can come out of bad, Jeannine. Maybe I believe that for the first time, for the very first time."

THE END